THE SIGN OF THE GUARDIAN

JOHN ARTHUR LONG

**A TOM DOHERTY
ASSOCIATES BOOK**

**PINNACLE BOOKS
NEW YORK**

SIGN OF THE GUARDIAN

Copyright © 1981 John Arthur Long, E.G.I. Productions, and R.K.R. Productions.

A Tom Doherty Associates Book.

First printing, July 1981

ISBN: O-523-48005-9

Cover illustration by: Paul Stinson

Printed in the United States of America

Distributed by Pinnacle Books, 1430 Broadway, New York, New York, 10018.

THE SIGN
OF THE GUARDIAN

PROLOGUE

It was an act of rage. The stifling midday heat had passed, and the sprawling African savanna once more seethed with life. Feeding time was approaching. A slender waterbuck lifted its head from grazing and stared, motionless, into the distance. A bat-eared fox peeked through the tall grass and then was gone. A female rhinoceros snorted heavily, suddenly thundered away, her young one struggling to keep up. A reed-thin, tall Masai leaned on his spear, scanning the distance, as his herd of cattle grazed nearby. A small group of chimpanzees, grooming each other within the protection of a grove of acacia trees, suddenly scattered, chattering loudly. The sudden call of a bird, the quick skittering hooves of a frightened gazelle, were signs to be heeded. For the time of the hunt became the hour of death to the unwary.

Deep within the trees, it was a low, muffled, breathing from behind that caused the victim to stiffen, a startled twist to its body. And, for a brief moment, as the victim turned, the act paused, caught on that last guarded edge of reason which separates living compassion from deathly evil. This would not simply be an act of survival. The sound of the stalker's breathing, the rage-filled hissing rasp of air had an evil quality to it. Heavy sibilance among the wild, chattering calls of alarm that rang through the thick tangle of undergrowth. And then, the victim's fear, its jerking gasp of panic, pulled the surging rage forward.

The stalker caught the victim's body by the neck, the hands filling with vise-like strength as they choked off the death gasp. The victim's mouth widened in a choked scream that became a vent of inner horror in the aftershock of pain. The fingers, curled clawlike, thrust inward and then tore downward, ripping open the neck in jagged strips that gleamed as the ruddy seeping fluid burst into rivers of flowing red.

The larynx made a sharp, cracking sound as one curled finger hooked and twisted into the curved hollow, and jerked the cartilage outward. And the victim fell, screaming silently as the weight of death's determination descended.

The victim became a mass of involuntary grasps and clutchings, the final cries dying with the nerve endings of consciousness. All movement was in vain. The rage had transformed itself into something else. Somehow, the emotional force of the act had released a darker form. A form that fed on the victim's deaththroes. A form that tore and gouged, mutilating with a snarling, mounting lust for the thrill of destroying life.

Then, after the last dark rites, the act was finished. And, in a hazed afterglow, the stalker sank back into the regions of the unknown. Under the sway of the vengeful guardian.

Softly, a warm rain began to fall. It was a quiet, steady rain that tapped against the thick foliage, and then fell gently on the victim. Water, however, could not cleanse away the act's remains.

An evil had been aroused. An evil that sought to satisfy its lust through an act which only served to awaken its thirst, to arouse its awareness.

And the evil would be driven again—to vent its rage, to satisfy its desire for the unquenchable thrill of death. To reduce a life once again to nothing. Once again to escape all control.

ONE

Before the first mutilations occurred, Dune Beach was virtually free of hard crimes. About the worst thing that ever happened in the small Fire Island village was a break-in at a deserted cottage. Certainly there had never been any psychopath stalking the dunes. People came to the isolated stretch of sandy beach and summer houses to escape those tensions that are ever present in our normal lives. And so, of course, they were ripe. Ripe for the kind of evil that creeps up unnoticed and lashes out at the unguarded.

Although the strip of land making up the village of Dune Beach was narrow, a great number of vacation homes were clustered in that section of the island. The houses were situated among rustic but carefully landscaped flowers and shrubs that lined the streets—or, rather, the sidewalk paths. Except for one along the north bay side where the ferry from Long Island landed, and one called Midway which ran down the middle of the island, all the cement walkways were short connectors between the Great South Bay on the north shore and the Atlantic Ocean on the south. It took less than five minutes to walk from the bay to the ocean side of the village.

David Paddock stood on the platform above the beach at the end of the path called Holly Lane, and watched the orange sun creep higher above the misty horizon, breathing life into the ocean. The greenish sea sparkled, and the summer sky took on a brilliant blue glow. It was going to be a perfect day for early August. David pulled his attention from the ocean and glanced at his watch. Then he turned and headed back toward his house.

The Paddock house was modest compared to some of the modernistic Dune Beach dwellings, which were furnished with everything from Bloomingdale's finest to priceless antiques. However, its location was superb.

Across the front, serving as an entrance to both the living room and the master bedroom, sliding glass doors opened off a rambling redwood deck. Beyond the deck and across the dunes was an unobstructed view of the ocean. A screened-in porch which faced the sidewalk served as the main entrance to the house. Then, through the inner door of the porch was a dining-living-room combination, and, beyond it, a hallway that led past other bedrooms and opened unto a flagstone patio in the back.

Although one side of David resented the fact that the house had been a wedding present from his wife Pamela's wealthy parents, another side loved the escape the house offered. Here he could forget for two months that he was no longer twenty and entering what he considered a humanitarian profession, but rather a tired, uninspired Sociology teacher quickly approaching forty.

And, he mused, the summer months at the Fire Island house were also perfect for Missy, his eight-year-old daughter, and his joy. There was nothing David loved more than his daughter. No matter how he felt she could make him smile. And, although there was no open competition, it was also apparent that Missy chose David over her mother. Pam was Missy's disciplinarian, while her father was her pal. Over the years, the Dune Beach summers had settled into a routine. While Pam partied with her rich and, in David's opinion, somewhat obnoxious childhood friends, he and Missy had become a part of the less pretentious neighborhood life.

As David reached the front porch, Missy came barreling out the screen door. She was jamming a last bite of toast into her mouth.

"Is it time, Daddy? Can we go now?" she said, running up to him.

"Pretty soon," said David. "Did you finish your breakfast?" Missy nodded and tugged at David's hand. "All right, take it easy. The ferry isn't due for a while yet. Is Mommy ready?"

Missy shook her head. "No, she's in the kitchen. Daddy, do you think the chimpanzee will like me? What if he doesn't? What'll I do?"

David smiled. "I wouldn't worry about it. Marty says that Jinks likes everyone." He opened the front screen door and gave his daughter a pat on her bottom. "Now, let's go. Inside and clean up. And make sure your room looks nice, bed included." Missy returned her father's smile and trotted off toward the bathroom as David crossed the living room and glanced into the kitchen.

Pam, dressed in her short blue bathrobe, was sitting on a stool at the counter with a cup of coffee and the morning newspaper. Her slender back was to him; even from behind, there was an attractive sensuality about his wife that excited him. It had been there when he had first met her; now, nearly ten years later, it had not diminished. It was also, of course, he remembered with a twinge of guilt, the main thing that had drawn him away from Marty when she had needed him the most. He stuck his head through the kitchen doorway.

"Hey, come on, Pam. It's only half an hour 'till the ferry. Shouldn't you get moving?"

"Why don't you go ahead with Missy, David?" Pam said, without looking up. "I'll straighten things up here. There's really no need for all of us to go."

David frowned. "Of course we all have to go. What are you talking about?"

Pam sighed and slowly turned to face her husband. The front of her robe was tied with a casualness that revealed just enough of her tanned breasts to be disturbing. In some women it would have been a studied casualness, but David had come to learn that, in his wife, it was an unconscious expression of her personality. When she spoke, Pam's voice had a slight edge to it.

"David, please don't make a big deal out of this. I just don't feel that well, and I'd rather not have to walk all the way to the dock and back. All right?"

"No, it's not all right," David said, coming into the room. "What kind of chicken-out bullshit is this? I thought we had agreed that it was time to deal with this thing. Both of us. Now come on, Pam, get dressed. We're going to face this together, remember?"

Pam took her coffee cup to the sink, rinsed it slowly under the faucet, and then turned back to David. "I don't want to go, David. I'm sorry."

"Pam—"

"I know. I know we talked it out, and I know I agreed it was the best thing. It's just that now that the whole thing is going to happen, I—I really don't want to face her. I keep thinking about how much we must have hurt her, David. And I know I'll see the pain in her eyes when I look at her. I know it."

"Well, I've got news for you. Five minutes after she steps off the ferry, she's going to come through the front door. What the hell difference does it make whether you see her there or here?"

"I don't know. When she gets here, I'll have to deal with it, that's all. But I just don't think I can do the happy greeting scene at the ferry. In fact, the more I think about this visit, the more I think it was not a good idea."

12

"Pam, I'm not trying to be unsympathetic, but she's on the ferry, for crying out loud. It's a little late for a reversal."

"I know she is. I'm just telling how I feel."

"You're making too big a deal out of the whole thing. It's been a long time. Marty has obviously resolved everything in her own mind. Why else would she have agreed to this visit?"

"I don't know," Pam said, "maybe she thinks it's resolved. But I know Marty, David. She's always had a strong sensitivity to things. You know that. And I don't care how long it's been, she can't have changed that much. I think being here will only eat away at her. I mean, let's face it. We have a home, a daughter, this vacation house. What has Marty really got except a smelly monkey?"

"Not quite just a smelly monkey."

"You know what I mean."

David ran his hand through his hair in frustration. "Well, why the hell didn't you just say no when we first discussed her coming to visit? We could have left it at the superficial letter-writing it's always been."

"Because I thought at the time it was a good idea. The fact that her last lecture on the tour was at Columbia made this the perfect opportunity. I guess I really saw it as a way to get rid of the guilt I've been carrying around all these years."

"Well, so did I. And it is. So what's the problem? Sure, it might have some rough moments. But it won't kill me. And we'll all feel a lot better for having faced it."

Pam came to her husband and touched his arm. "David, that's just it. I don't think this visit is going to do that. I think it's going to make things worse."

David took his wife's hand reassuringly. "I think you're suffering from last-minute panic."

"Maybe." Pam said, finally meeting his eyes, "but

don't tell me you have this all neatly worked out. You've been twitting around here like a kid all week since you found out she was coming.''

''I didn't say I had it all worked out,'' David said, pulling away slightly, as he flushed with anger. ''Believe me, Pam, I am blatantly aware and certainly not proud of the fact that while my supposed fiancée was recovering from an accident that might have left her permanently damaged for the rest of her life, I was balling my brains out with her best friend. And, yes, I am completely panicked about seeing her again after all these years. And I certainly don't relish meeting her alone. Where am I going to tell her that her old best friend is? Overwhelmed with guilt and hiding in the kitchen?''

Pam did not answer, and David turned, suddenly aware that his daughter was standing in the kitchen doorway.

''I'm ready, Daddy,'' Missy said quietly, looking from her father to her mother. ''Aren't you coming, Mommy?''

Pam hesitated a moment, and then smiled at her daughter. ''No, you go along with Daddy. Mommy's going to clean up the kitchen so that everything looks nice when Marty and Jinks get here. Okay?''

''Okay,'' Missy said. ''Can we go now? Please, Daddy! We're going to be late.''

David gave Pam a final look, and then took Missy's hand.

''Sure,'' he said cheerfully, as his daughter pulled toward the front door. ''Let's go see what that chimpanzee of Marty's looks like. Don't forget the wagon.''

Marty collected the child's wagon that they used to transport goods from town, and they set off down the path.

The Dune Beach ferry terminal was at one end of the business district, on the bay side of the island. This main

14

section of the village was laid out in a rectangular promenade, with stores and shops along the sides and landscaped lawns and flower gardens at the center. In between O'Dwyer's Restaurant at one end and a disco called The Cherry Thicket at the other, were clothing and hardware stores, real-estate offices, pizza parlors, and a town hall that doubled as a movie theater in the evening.

As David and Missy came into the crowd of people milling around in the weatherbeaten open-air docking terminal, two men engaged in a heated argument were holding nearly everyone's attention. Sam Kline, Dune Beach's resident physician, waved and strolled over to the Paddocks.

"Hello, David, Missy," Sam said, folding his newspaper and tucking it under his arm.

David pointed toward the argument. "What's going on?"

Sam Kline made a clicking sound in his cheek. "Oh, Clyde's at it again. Apparently the Felding girl dropped a piece of paper, I guess it was a candy wrapper, on the dock. Anyway, Clyde told her to pick it up, and she said something smart back to him, and you know Clyde. He grabbed her arm, and told her she wasn't going anywhere until she picked up the paper. That's when Mayor Nilscoff stepped in."

David shifted his attention to the two men. Clyde Bartley was a plumber and all-purpose handyman who lived a few houses from the Paddocks on Holly Lane. He was a native Fire Islander; of all the locals, David liked Clyde the best. His crusty personality had an unconscious openness that was refreshing. And David was not alone. Most people who knew Clyde liked him for his earthy humor and blunt opinions. Lately, however, Clyde had mounted a crusade to keep Fire Island beautiful and to stop the "elements" that were slowly, in Clyde's opinion, destroying the island. And the "elements," mainly what Clyde called the "summer spoilers," had begun to be irritated. In fact, several, including both summer renters and Dune Beach businessmen, had registered harassment complaints with Ernest Nilscoff. Now, from the sound of Nilscoff's voice, it seemed that Dune Beach's loquacious Mayor had just about had it with Clyde's behavior.

". . . And I'm telling you, Bartley," the mayor was nearly shouting, "this is going to stop. I will not tolerate you harassing the people of this town. Do you understand?"

Clyde's leathery neck was beet red, a sure sign that he was fuming. He gave his head a characteristic jerk.

"Sure, I gotcha," he snorted, "it's sidle up to the richies and to hell with everything and everyone else."

"That's unfair, Bartley, and you know it. I have always been equally fair to all segments of this community."

The mayor was getting his voice under more control now, and it was apparent that he was speaking not only to Clyde, but for the benefit of those who were standing around.

"But you are telling me," Clyde said, pointing an accusing finger "that this spoiled little girl here can throw trash wherever she feels like it." Plump, eight-year-old Brenda Felding, stood slightly behind the mayor's protective presence.

"No," Nilscoff said, his voice rising again, "I'm telling you that you cannot force her or anyone else to do anything. It's not your responsibility and you don't have the authority. And if you don't stop, you're going to force me to take action against you."

Clyde stared at the mayor for several seconds, and then, without another word, stooped down, picked up the paper, threw it in the trash container and strode heavily out of the docking area and down the sidewalk. Nilscoff, turning friendly in the manner that is part of every politician's personality, quickly apologized to the people around him for the disturbance, and then headed out in the same direction Clyde had taken.

David exhaled and looked at Sam. "I'm surprised Nilscoff would allow himself to get involved in a public scene like that. Clyde's crusade must be getting to him."

Sam's eyes narrowed. "Don't kid yourself, Dave. Nilscoff never does anything that isn't to his advantage. I'm sure to these people he just came off as the conscientious town mayor taking charge and rebuking a local crazy."

Missy, who had stood quietly beside her father during the argument, frowned up at the doctor. "Clyde isn't crazy, Dr. Sam."

"Of course he isn't, Missy," Sam said. "I just meant that some people might think his actions are a little strange."

"And don't worry," David said, "he isn't mad at Brenda either. He just wants to make sure the island stays nice for all of us. Do you understand?"

"Sure. Clyde tells me all the time how people are ruining things around here," Missy said. She waved to Brenda Felding, who came running over to them. "Hi, Brenda, don't worry. Clyde's not mad at you."

The Felding girl made a face. "Well, you heard Mr. Nilscoff. He can't tell me what to do. And he better not touch me again either, or I'll tell my parents. Then he'll be in trouble."

David and Sam exchanged a quick glance. It was well known that Brenda's father never came to Fire Island, and that her alcoholic mother made it a practice to attach herself to and sleep with as many young, slick, New York City types as she could squeeze into her summer stay. All of which explained, of course, why Brenda constantly vied for everyone's attention, and was out at all hours "running wild" as Clyde would say.

"Well, Clyde was right, you know, Brenda," David

said, unconsciously slipping into the corrective teacher mold, "the paper does belong in the trash can. Maybe it would be better just to forget the whole thing and be more careful next time."

"What are you two doing here at the dock so early, anyway, Dave?" said Sam, changing the subject before Brenda could respond. "Meeting someone coming over on the ferry?"

Missy smiled and answered instantly. "Someone and something. Guess what the thing is, Dr. Sam?"

The doctor pulled at his chin and frowned. "Well, I don't kow, Missy. I'm not much good at guessing games. Maybe you better tell me."

"A chimpanzee!" Missy said gleefully.

"Really?" said Brenda, her face brightening with interest.

"A chimpanzee. . . . Well," said Sam, "that is something."

"Un-huh . . . and it talks, too."

"What do you mean, it talks?" Brenda said quickly. "How can a chimpanzee talk? That's stupid!"

"No, it isn't. It does too talk, doesn't it, Daddy?"

"Sure does, honey," David said, smiling at Brenda.

"And, Dr. Sam," Missy continued, "Daddy's friend is going to teach me how to talk to it, and they're going to stay with us for a while right here. . . . Can you believe it?"

Sam smiled at David and shook his head. "No, I'm not sure I can. I don't believe I've ever met a talking chimpanzeee before. I have to go to the mainland this morning, but will you introduce me to this chimp when I get back, Missy?"

"Sure," Missy said.

"Me too," Brenda said anxiously, "I'll meet the chimp too, won't I, Missy?"

"Well, I don't know. . . ." Missy spoke lingeringly, enjoying her power.

"Sure you can, Brenda," David said reassuringly. "Don't worry, there'll be plenty of time for everyone to meet Jinks."

"Oh, I hope he likes me," Missy said, her eyes wide with self-doubt. "Do you think he'll like me, Dr. Sam?"

Sam Kline placed his hand warmly on Missy's shoulder. "Missy, I can't imagine anyone or anything not liking you."

"I'll bet he'll like all of us, Missy," Brenda said, pulling on Missy's hand. "Come on, let's go to the end of the dock and watch for the ferry."

"Missy turned to her father. "Can we, Daddy?"

"Sure," David said, "go ahead. Only don't get too excited when you see it and fall in."

The two girls let out little shouts of laughter and disappeared into the crowd. Sam Kline looked at David doubtfully. "A talking chimpanzee, Dave?"

"Would my daughter lie to you, Sam?"

"No. . . . So what's the catch?"

"The talking isn't vocal. It's sign language. Something called Ameslan."

Sam nodded. "Ummm. The sign language of the deaf."

"Well, a friend of ours specializes in animal behavior. She's bringing a chimpanzee with her that apparently can communicate in this language."

"I remember reading something about these experiments a few months ago," Sam said. "Looked like it was probably just rote training to me. You think it's on the level?"

David shrugged. "I don't know. I've never seen the chimp. I met Marty Goodman years ago when I was doing graduate work at Columbia, but I haven't seen her for quite a while. Anyway, she just ended a lecture tour this month at Columbia, so we invited her to come out and relax for a while."

Sam frowned. "Kind of strange, her bringing the chimp, though, isn't it? I mean, you'd think he'd be too valuable to just bring on vacation."

"No, that's the whole point," David said, checking his watch. The ferry was going to be late. "This chimp has been with Marty constantly since its early infancy. And, by treating it as you would a child, Marty has been able to really teach it a language. In fact, according to her, the breakthrough came during the chimp's toilet training. One day, instead of unloading in his pants as usual, Jinks—"

"That his name? Jinks?" Sam interrupted.

David nodded. "Anyway, Jinks signed to Marty that he had to 'make dirty' and he was immediately led to the toilet. There, after much ceremony, Jinks excreted in the bowl, Marty applauded, and Jinks flushed and washed his hands. Then Jinks turned to Marty, gave her a hug, and signed that he loved her. He never soiled his pants again . . . and, I guess, from that point on, his learning progressed rapidly."

Sam Kline laughed aloud. "And now he can talk and wipe his ass just like you and me?"

"Apparently so," David said. "Marty says Jinks wears clothes, eats with the proper utensils, brushes his teeth after meals, and can sign over three hundred words in infinitely flexible combinations."

"Well, I'll have to see it to believe it," Sam said, shaking his head. "How did your friend happen to get involved with the signing chimps? Sort of off the normal path, isn't it?"

David's hesitation lasted only a moment before he continued. "By accident, really . . . and literally too, I guess. We used to have these long discussions of her subject—physical anthropology—and Marty was always fascinated with the 'big leap' and how it all came about. You know . . . ape to intelligent being. And, of course, Marty was also fascinated by Jane Goodall's work with the chimpanzees in Africa. I guess actually I was the one who suggested she apply for field work at Goodall's reserve. Then, because of her record was outstanding, she was accepted. She loved it there, too. Apparently Tanzania is breathtaking. Unfortunately, a freak accident cut her field work short. One morning a jeep loaded with caged chimpanzees ready to be shipped out suddenly burst into flames. Marty ran to pull the cages from the fire just as the vehicle exploded. The blast sent a jagged metal fragment into the side of her skull.''

Sam Kline's eyes narrowed with interest, and David nodded to what was obviously a medical response. ''I'm sure you can appreciate even better than I could, Sam, how serious her situation was. In critical condition, she had to be flown to Nairobi, and from there to London, and, finally, on to New York. She underwent a series of operations that, by a very narrow thread, were able to save her life. She needed a long recuperation period before she could start functioning normally again, so Africa was out. When she heard about the signing experiments they were doing with chimps at a primate reserve in Oklahoma, she applied for a position. They accepted her, gave her Jinks to raise as she recuperated, and she's been totally devoted to the project ever since. In fact, I think this is probably her first vacation, except for a trip or two back to Africa, in years.''

Sam smiled. ''Sounds fascinating. Missy's sure going to enjoy the two of them, that's for sure. How about Pam? What's she think of all this?''

Again, David's hesitation was hardly noticeable. ''Oh, she's looking forward to seeing Marty. As a matter of fact, they were roommates in college.''

''Really,'' Sam said. ''Well, no wonder you know this Marty so well.''

''She's not too crazy about the chimp, of course.''

''That's what I figured,'' Sam said, ''somehow I

didn't think Pam would like having a monkey in the house, even if it does use the toilet."

David gave a quick smile and looked out toward the water. "Where is the ferry, anyway? Shouldn't it be here by now?"

"Probably went to Bayview first. They do that sometimes in the morning. Don't worry, it'll get here. Always does."

The urge to kill . . . to experience the surge that came from taking life. As yet the desire was vague. But the signs were there . . . the beast-signs. Anxiety. Tension began to grow and to grow on the superficial veneer of normality . . . smoldering within, feeding on emotions. The need to lash out gathered increasing force.

So long. It had been so long. Extreme forces hovered at the very edge of control. Soon the control would snap; soon the inner hollowness that blossomed from the vacuum of need would overwhelm. All that was needed was the right circumstance to light the fuse, to ignite the rage. Soon the thrill of killing would come again.

TWO

Marty Goodman glanced briefly at the chimpanzee; she held his leash loosely in her hand. Jinks was sitting quietly on the seat beside her, staring out of the window of the ferry as it moved slowly across the Great South Bay toward Fire Island. There was a morning haze hanging over the water, but the chimp seemed to love the small rippling waves created by the boat as it cut through the water.

The lumbering wooden ferry had two passenger compartments, and Marty had purposely chosen the lower, interior area in order to avoid the commotion bringing Jinks into the open-air seating space above them would have caused. As it had turned out, it was a wise decision. The few people who had chosen to sit below, after some initial comments on Jinks, began reading and left Marty and her companion to themselves.

Marty took a deep breath, grateful for the momentary solitude, and closed her eyes, allowing her body to relax with the gentle rocking motion of the boat. However, her mind refused to cooperate, and a far from peaceful scene filled her thoughts. She saw herself at the edge of the woodpaneled stage in a small auditorium at Columbia University. The evening lecture was merely a prelude to the next day's major demonstration, and most of the audience were sceptics or students who were fulfilling course requirements. She was tired from her strenuous tour, and, sensing the lack of enthusiasm in her listeners, Marty hurried through her introductory remarks. Next to her, Jinks sat on a folding chair. The four-year-old chimp was dressed in a blue suit, and was happily and somewhat comically peeling a tangerine.

Briefly, Marty filled in the audience on her project of training Jinks from infancy to communicate with the sign language of the deaf. The casually-dressed audience fidgeted restlessly in the lumpy seats of the ill-maintained lecture hall. One student in particular, who was seated near the front, made no attempt to conceal his boredom. He murmured continually to those next to him as Marty spoke. When Marty demonstrated the sign for "eating," the student said a little too loudly that as far as he was concerned, the entire lecture could "eat it." The comment set of a wave of muffled laughter in the surrounding rows, and, irritated, Marty moved to the side of the stage, glaring down at the heckler.

"I'm sorry," she said, her voice even. "I didn't hear you. Was there a question?"

The student looked around him in fake surprise, and then, grinning shyly, he stood amid scattered laughter. "Ah, yes. I do have a question. I was wondering if, considering the fact that your monkey is so smart—well, I was wondering if he understood this sign?" The student raised his middle finger high in the air, smiled broadly, and sat down.

Angered and embarrassed, Marty spoke above the laughter in the hall. "No. Jinks understands good manners."

Not wanting to be bettered, the heckler "ooohhhhed" loudly in answer to Marty's authoritarian remark. Other members of the audience picked up on the sound, oohing and aahing in turn. Disgusted, Marty turned to collect Jinks and leave the stage. As she did so, Jinks became agitated, his eyes shifting nervously from Marty to the audience and back again.

The heckler stood on his seat, loving the attention of the crowd, and began screeching and jumping up and down in imitation of a monkey. Jinks' face stretched into the taut chimpanzee grin of fear. Marty shouted for the student to stop, but her pleas were drowned out. More and more students began screeching and howling. Jinks jumped up and down violently, hurling the tangerine into the unruly crowd. Laughing, the heckler jumped from the seats, and came loping monkey-like toward the stage, hooting back at Jinks.

"No! Don't!" Marty shouted, her hand out against the oncoming student, but already Jinks' demeanor had changed. Enraged, he rose to his full height—over four feet—and the long hair covering him rose until it was on end all over his body. Then, his yellowish fangs bared, the ape emitted a piercing howl and lunged toward the edge of the stage and the advancing heckler. Suddenly frightened, the student stopped; he stumbled backwards and fell into the front row of seats. Marty frantically grabbed Jinks' arm and, in a commanding voice, shouted to divert the animal's attention.

At the very edge of the stage, the chimpanzee stopped. Several of the students ran from their seats, screaming. The atmosphere of the lecture hall dissolved into chaos. Jinks continued to strain at Marty's grasp, snarling and screeching down into the auditorium. His dullish, yellow-white-rimmed eyes bulged, and white flecks of saliva dripped from his curled open lips. No longer was Jinks a refined, friendly chimpanzee, but rather a savage, primitive beast. . . .

Marty opened her eyes to erase the upsetting image from her mind, and gazed at the now passive chimpanzee beside her. Although she knew there were certainly good reasons for Jinks' outburst, the severity and the bestial wildness of the reaction had been deeply unsettling to her.

His personality was normally obedient and lovingly playful. The only other time she had ever seen evidence of another side to him had occurred when the chimp was suddenly started by a loud thunderclap during one of their visits at the Tanzania chimpanzee reserve. To everyone's surprise, Jinks had begun an aggressive chimpanzee display, screeching raging cries at the darkened sky and racing into the savanna. When he returned hours later, he had splotches of dried blood on him. No amount of signing could coax information out of him. Where had he been, and why? Marty assumed some animal had attacked him, and he had come loping back to the safety of his friends. In any case, there was no evidence that he had been destructively violent. And he had stopped his outburst at the lecture hall when she commanded him to.

Marty reached over and scratched the chimp behind his ears, amused that Jinks refused to look at her. The chimp had been sulking the entire ferry trip because she had forced him to wear a leash despite his signing "no" and other overt objections. Marty had insisted on the leash. She agreed with David that it was the best way to introduce Jinks to the summer community. Marty smiled and rubbed Jinks' head affectionately, pushing her anxiety from her mind. Her chimp wasn't dangerous. He was just adolescent.

As land came into view beyond the window, people began to gather their belongings together. Marty realized that she had been avoiding all thoughts of meeting Pam and David. It struck her that maybe she had been concentrating on Jinks so that she wouldn't have to think about them. One of the teenage boys who were running the ferry service passed her, and Marty motioned for his attention.

"Is this Dune Beach?"

"No, ma'am," the boy said, lifting a large carton of groceries, "Bayview. Dune Beach is the next stop."

Marty nodded and glanced back out the window at the smiling, waving people in the Bayview terminal. Although she tried, this time she was unable to stop the thoughts of Pam and David that tumbled through her mind.

David saw the ferry at just about the same time as the two girls came running toward him.

"Daddy!" Missy shouted. "It's coming! Look, here it comes!"

David smiled and hoisted his daughter into his arms so that she could see the arriving ferry slice through the greenish water. The boat passed through the jetty mouth, and then turned ponderously at the pilings on the side of the dock. And, even as the ferry made its turn, Missy shouted: "Look! There they are!"

There in the doorway, flanked by a businessman and several vacationers, stood Marty Goodman, and at the end of a leash the chimpanzee, two suitcases at their feet.

Marty saw David and waved. The people waiting to board the ferry gaped at the chimpanzee beside her. Sam Kline gestured toward the ferry door with his newspaper.

"Good God, David," he said, "that's not a chimpanzee, it's an ape. Look at the size of that animal!"

"Does look kind of big, doesn't he?" said David, smiling and returning Marty's wave. Missy and Brenda squealed with excitement.

"Does Nilscoff know about this?" Sam asked. David shook his head and lowered Missy to the ground. "Well, I would say you'd better get ready. When our

28

friendly mayor finds out about your animal houseguest, you're going to hear from him."

"I know, I know," David said as they followed the girls toward the ferry doorway. "Actually, I'm kind of grateful to Clyde. He inadvertently got the mayor out of the way so I won't have to deal with the whole thing right now. Anyway, don't worry, I can handle Nilscoff."

"Sure you can," the doctor said. "Good luck. Tell the chimp I'll talk to him when I get back from the mainland." Sam tapped Missy on the head affectionately and then disappeared into the ferry, nodding to Marty Goodman as he passed.

David took the small bag Marty was carrying and gave her a clumsy hello kiss. He leaned in to kiss her cheek, but she moved her face the wrong direction, and he ended up kissing part of her upper lip and the corner of her nose. Feeling like a stupid adolescent, David stepped back awkwardly, and Marty smiled warmly, the familiar dimples forming in the cheeks of her slightly roundish face. There was a perky sort of energy to Marty, so that she looked much younger than a woman in her late twenties had any right to. As he had expected, Marty's casual, straightforward appearance was the same. Her hair was cut short, and her body, dressed in jeans and a blue work shirt, was still athletic and healthy. In fact, even after ten years she continued to look like the carefree undergraduate she had once been.

"So how did the last lecture go?" David said, unconsciously running his hand over the gray hair at his temple.

Marty shook her head. "Well, it could have gone better, David. It amazes me how many people in the scientific community are still skeptical about our work, even when I show them the proof. I know one thing for sure, I'm dead tired."

"Don't worry," David said, "you're in the perfect place to recuperate. Just forget everything and relax."

Marty gave a weary sigh. "Thank you. That's exactly what I intend to do." She turned to the two girls who were staring wide-eyed at the chimp, studied them for a minute, and then chose the one standing closest to David. "And I bet this is Melissa, isn't it?"

"Yes, it is," David said, putting an arm around his daughter's shoulder. "Missy, this is Marty Goodman."

"Hello," Missy said. It was so abrupt it bordered on being rude. David apologized as his daughter returned her attention to Jinks.

"I'm used to it, David. Jinks always rates over me as far as children are concerned."

David nodded and looked at his daughter. "Don't you think you should introduce your friend to Marty, Missy?"

"This is Brenda, Marty," Missy said quickly, her eyes still on the chimp. "Does Jinks answer to his name? What do I say to him?"

"I guess you can say anything you want, Missy," Marty answered.

"He's so big," Brenda said. "Is he an ape?"

"All chimpanzees are apes, Brenda," Marty said, moving closer to the girls, "Jinks is just a big chimpanzee."

Brenda raised her hand tentatively. "Can I touch him? He doesn't bite, does he?"

The chimpanzee turned his head to look at Brenda, causing the leash to tighten slightly.

"No, of course he doesn't bite," Marty said lightly, "but I think it would be better if you just looked at him for right now."

"But I want to touch him. Look at his hair. It's all wiry-looking."

"You heard Marty," David said, placing Marty's bag

30

in the wooden wagon. "Don't worry, Brenda, there'll be plenty of time to play with Jinks."

"Oh, all right," Brenda said sulkily, lowering her hand as Jinks looked away, "but make him talk. I want to hear him talk."

"I don't make him talk," Marty said patiently. "He only talks when he feels like it."

"I'll tell you what, Brenda," David said. "Why don't you run along now? Let Jinks and Marty have time to get settled. Then you can come over and visit Missy."

"But I want to hear him talk. You said he could talk."

"Brenda. . . ."

The child made a face. Then she brightened. "I know, I'll go tell everyone he's here. Can I?"

"Yes, that's fine. You go right ahead."

"Okay," Brenda said excitedly. "See you later, Missy."

"Somehow," David said as Brenda ran past a couple who had stopped to point and stare, "I don't think it's going to be necessary for Brenda to announce Jinks' arrival."

"Word does tend to spread quickly when we arrive somewhere," Marty agreed. "Where is Pam, anyway, David? She isn't ill or anything, is she?"

"Oh, no," David said, sounding very casual. "She just wanted to clean some things up. You know Pam. Obsessive as usual. The house is only a short walk from here." David glanced around for the large suitcases; the chimpanzee was holding them. "Why don't we put the suitcases in the wagon? Then Jinks won't have to carry them."

The chimpanzee was wearing denim cut-offs, a Mickey Mouse T-shirt, and a small checkered ivy-league cap. The hat's tiny bill was pulled down tightly over his forehead. He had been staring at the sidewalk, but when

David spoke he looked up. Then he returned his gaze to the walk, his hands tightly gripping the handles of the luggage. David looked at Marty, and when she spoke, her voice sounded slightly annoyed.

"Yes, David, he understands you. I'm afraid Jinks is having a small temper tantrum." She pointed to the leash that ran from her left hand to the collar around the chimp's neck. "He doesn't like being treated like an animal. Thinks it's degrading."

David grinned. "You're kidding!"

"No, I'm perfectly serious. Jinks refuses to admit he is on the simian side and not the human side of the primate order."

"I'm sorry, Jinks," David said, approaching the chimp. "I just thought the leash would be a good idea until people got used to you. See, there's a law that dogs have to be kept leashed in Dune Beach."

The chimp's head snapped up. He dropped the suit-cases, and made signs in David's direction. Then he again grasped the suitcases and returned his head to its original gaze. Marty smiled at David's confusion.

"He's just being smart now, David. Ignore him."

"Why? What did he say?"

"He said he's not a dog."

David was amazed. In spite of what Marty had written to them, it shocked him that the chimpanzee actually comprehended what he said. "You mean he can really understand and answer in conversational English?"

"Well, not exactly. He knows the meaning of the word 'dog' and probably assumed you were comparing him to one. What he specifically said was, 'Jinks not dog.' We're not certain how much English he really understands, but he does respond relatively well to ordinary conversation."

David turned back to the chimp. "I know you're not

a dog, Jinks," he said, squatting down so that he could look at Jinks' face. "I just don't know how other people will react. I want you to be able to stay with us."

As the chimp's gaze met his, an almost human expression of irritation on his face, an eerie feeling passed through David. He realized that actual reason could be pulsating through Jinks' brain. Slowly, in a gesture of friendship, David reached up and unsnapped the leash from the chimp's collar. Jinks' only reaction was to turn his head away. David stood and handed the leash to Marty.

"Forget it, David," she said. "If he wants to be stubborn and carry the suitcases, let him. It'll serve him right after the way he's been acting lately."

"Why? Has he been a problem on the tour?"

"Not a problem. He just hasn't been responding with his usual predictability. I don't know what's the matter." Marty shrugged her shoulders. "Maybe it's puberty."

Missy, who had been watching and listening to everything in a sort of joyous stupor, looked from the chimp to Marty. "What's puberty?" she asked.

Marty hesitated, and then, after a glance at David, answered. "It means that Jinks will soon be an adult. Maybe the bodily changes that are occurring as he grows up are upsetting him."

Missy accepted the answer, and apparently decided it was her turn to speak to Jinks. She walked up very close to him and then pivoted her head around sideways so that she could look up into his downcast face.

"Hello, Jinks," she said with a child's seriousness. "My name is Missy. Don't be upset about your puberty. We can be friends. I know some games we could play. Would you like that?"

Jinks tilted his head and studied Missy for a moment. Then he set the luggage down and placed his hand over his eyes, a gesture which he followed with a series of signs.

"I think you said the magic words, Missy," Marty said. "He wants to know if you can play hide and seek."

Missy nodded. "Oh, yes, I can play that and lots of other games. Would you like to play?"

Jinks answered by giving Missy a hug, and then he gestured to her in large, clear signs. Marty interpreted.

"He's telling you his name is Jinks, Missy. He says you and Jinks are friends, and he wants to know when the two of you can play hide and seek."

"As soon as we get home, Jinks," Missy said. David didn't think he'd ever seen his daughter happier. The two turned to leave as Marty spoke.

"Uh . . . Jinks. What about the suitcases?"

The chimp looked at Marty, and at Missy, then placed the two bags on the wagon. Then he walked to David and signed as he had to Missy, ending with his hand over his eyes.

Marty laughed. "He wants to know—"

"I know," David said. "I'm catching on to this pretty fast." He nodded down to him. "Yes, Jinks, I'll play hide and seek with you. Now let's go."

Wanting to avoid the stares going through town with Jinks would cause, David took the long way home. If the people on the ferry dock were any indication, the commotion would start soon enough.

They walked in silence as Marty took in the island around her. And, as they turned on to Midway and headed toward Holly Lane, it suddenly came to David why he had felt so strange when he had looked into Jinks' face. In every chimpanzee he had ever seen, the part of the eye around the iris was always heavily pigmented with brown. However, Jinks' eyes were different. Each iris was a rich brown, and the part around the iris was white. Exactly like a human eye.

THREE

Missy and Jinks ran ahead of them down Holly Lane. David was just beginning to feel the weight of the growing silence when Marty finally spoke.

"It's beautiful here, David. The air, the foliage, everything is different. It's as though I've taken the ferry to another world. I can't believe a place like this exists so close to New York City."

"I know," David said. "Even the beaches on Long Island don't match this. Partly it's so nice because there are no cars, and nothing to do except enjoy the sun and relax. We've been coming here every summer, and each January I start thinking about how nice it is to escape to this place."

"Sounds ideal, as far as summer is concerned. How about the rest? Have they been good years for you, David? Since Columbia?"

"Depends on what you mean by good, I guess," David said. "They've been fairly easy. I'm not killing myself; teaching allows for plenty of time to do what I want. Of course, I'm not moving the world, but I do spend a lot of time with Missy. I like to think that's worth something."

"She's a wonderful girl, too, David. I could see that immediately. And Pam? Is she happy?"

David shrugged. "To tell you the truth, I don't think

we ever discuss whether we're happy or not. I assume she's not miserable.''

Marty stopped and turned to David. "She's dying about my coming here today, isn't she?''

David pursed his lips and nodded. "I would say that is a fairly accurate assessment.''

Marty smiled sadly. "Poor Pam. I've never known her to face any crsis or problem head-on if she could possibly avoid it. Her two classic symptoms were always acute diarrhea and obsessive cleaning in between trips to the bathroom.''

"Well, actually," David admitted, "we fought each other to get to the john over this one. I'm not exactly calm underneath this elegant exterior, you know.''

"Don't worry. It's unanimous, David. My stomach knotted the minute I saw you standing on the dock. But it will pass. I know that. It is time to stop all the silly avoiding and superficial communications, David. We all meant too much to each other.''

"I agree, Marty," David said, feeling less uncomfortable. "I can't tell you how glad I am you decided to come. And Pam will be fine once the panic passes, believe me.''

Marty started to respond, but movement ahead caught her attention. Jinks stopped short and rose to a standing position to look at a dog being walked in the distance. The dog started to bark annoyingly.

"Neighbors' dog, Marty. Don't worry, it always barks like that. Size complex. It barks at everyone and everything constantly to prove to itself that it isn't an insignificant little rat. Which is exactly what it looks like. Its name is Wubbles.''

Marty frowned in amusement. "Wubbles?''

"Or Wubbie. Cute, huh? According to Winnie Dukirk, my neighbor, when her husband Leonard first got the puppy for her, it wobbled when it tried to stand,

and its saliva made little bubbles in the corner of its mouth. Hence the name. See, Wubbles is a combination of—"

Marty laughed. "I get the derivation, thank you."

"Anyway, I don't think much of the name, or the dog either. It never shuts up."

"Well, I hope having Jinks around doesn't make it worse."

"Nothing could make it worse, believe me," David said. "By the way, speaking of Jinks, isn't he awfully big? I always thought chimpanzees were smaller."

Marty nodded. "That's because the ones you see in movies and circuses are baby chimps. They use them because they're easier to work with. Even though Jinks is a pretty big boy now, he's still easy to control. It's because we can really communicate."

"Is he strong?"

"Well," Marty said, "right now he's probably five times stronger than you are. But don't worry, David. He doesn't know it. He still acts like a baby, and he'll obey any human's command without question."

David frowned and began to speak, but a high-pitched, squeaky voice cut in from behind the path-side shrubbery: "Missy, is that you?" David's expression changed and he chuckled. Missy had stopped and answered, and a conversation had begun.

"I think you're about to meet our town recluse," David said to Marty as they moved forward. "The voice belongs to Jerry Dile. People think Jerry's strange. For one thing, he's a very private person. In fact, his entire past is shrouded in secrecy. About the only thing anyone knows about him . . . and you'll find this interesting . . . is that apparently he's originally from South Africa. Rumor has it, of course, that he left because of trouble with the police. People probably came up with that because, judging from the lot he owns here, he's obviously got plenty of money. Anyway, he's also an eccentric; it amuses him to yell at people in a squeaky voice as they pass by."

Marty smiled. "Your neighborhood sounds more and more fascinating."

"Oh, I haven't even mentioned Clyde," David laughed, pointing to their right. "Clyde Bartley lives across from Jerry. He's another local you'll find interesting. Anyway, what a lot of people don't know about Jerry is that behind that high shrubbery blossoms an incredible garden. Probably it's a carryover from his Africa days. And Jerry usually yells at people because he thinks they're disturbing his plants. He may be weird with the squeaky voice and all, but you should see his plants. It's stunning—both local and exotic flowers and vegetables. Actually, you would probably recognize some of them. The only reason I've seen his private Eden is because Jerry likes Missy. I guess he figures he has to be nice to me."

"But I don't understand why he uses a squeaky voice."

"Oh, sorry," David said, lowering his own voice. They were nearing the spot where Missy and Jinks were standing. "I should have explained that. He has no choice. No voice box. Uses one of those portable amplifiers that you hold against your neck. I have no idea what happened. Throat cancer, probably."

Jerry's high voice spoke through the bushes. "Is that you, David?"

"Yeah, Jerry, it's me."

The voice sounded irritated. "Is that the Dukirk dog barking?"

"Yes," David said, "I guess Wubbles doesn't like our house guest."

"You mean the chimp?"

"Yes. Did Missy introduce you?"

Missy nodded, and the voice cackled. "Sure she did. I told her to bring it in some time, and I'll give it some bananas. But just her. Not the lady staying with you. Can't have strangers in here. Disturbs the plants. You understand, don't you?"

"Whatever you say. But Marty's a very nice person, Jerry. You'd like her. She's spent quite a bit of time in Africa."

The voice beyond the shrubs hesitated before answering. "We'll see. . . . We'll see. Don't worry, I'll watch her and decide. Does she like plants?"

"Yes, I do," Marty answered, her voice warm and friendly, "I like them very much."

"Well, we'll see. I'll talk to Missy. I want you to do something for me, David. Will you?"

"If I can," David said.

"I want you to talk to the Dukirks. Tell them to keep that dog quiet. It's upsetting my plants, and I won't have it. You tell them, David. Will you tell them?"

"Yeah, I'll tell them. I'm not sure it'll do any good, but I'll tell them."

"Thank you, David. Tell them plants are sensitive."

"What's all the racket out here?" a voice shouted behind them. They turned to see Clyde Bartley come out his front door and down the steps.

"Clyde," David whispered quickly to Marty as the handyman approached them.

"It's Dukirk's dog, Clyde," Jerry's voice answered, "Can you hear it?"

"How the hell can I help but hear it?"

"David's going to tell them to keep it quiet, aren't you, David?"

"Well, I—"

"Good," Clyde grinned, "you can tell them for me too, Davy."

" 'Bye, Missy."

39

" 'Bye, Jerry," Missy said. The shrubbery shook slightly as Jerry Dile's body could be heard moving away from it.

Clyde Bartley took his sodden-tipped unfiltered cigarette from his toothless gums. He looked from Missy to the chimp that sat beside her, and his face cracked into a smile.

"Who's your friend, Missy?" he said.

Missy returned Clyde's smile. "This is Jinks. He and Marty are going to stay with us for a while, Clyde. Isn't that great? And Jinks can talk! And he and Marty have been to Africa, just like Jerry. Jerry said maybe Marty and Jinks could see his garden."

"Is that right?" Clyde eyed Marty warily. "I was in Africa during the war. Course there's a big difference between playing with monkeys and sneakin' up on some kraut in the middle of the jungle. The war was no safari, that's for sure. You Marty?"

"Yes. Marty Goodman," Marty said, smiling.

Clyde nodded. "Clyde Bartley. What's Missy mean, this here monkey can talk?"

"Actually, Jinks is a chimpanzee, not a monkey, Mr. Bartley."

Clyde squinted suspiciously. "Looks like a monkey to me. What's the difference?"

"Monkeys have tails, Clyde," David said. "Turn around and show him, Jinks." David wasn't sure Jinks would, but the chimp did an abrupt about-face and presented his backside for inspection, after which he again faced forward. "See there, Clyde. No tail."

Clyde snorted. "Well, now I'm glad you cleared that up for me, Davy," he said. "I guess I haven't spent much time looking at monkey rumps." Missy giggled. "Excuse me, Missy . . . Miss Goodman."

"Don't worry, Mr. Bartley," Marty said, her voice light with humor, "I've heard the word before. And

40

I've looked at quite a few, too."

"Me too," Missy said brightly, "it means rear end, right, Clyde?"

"That's right, Missy," Clyde said, nodding jerkily, ". . . among other things." He turned to David. "Which reminds me, Davy, you do know there's a mob of kids waiting for you at your house, don't you?"

"What?"

Clyde shrugged. "I saw that Felding kid come by with a mess of them just a little while ago."

"Great," David said, giving Marty a concerned look, "Pam's going to love that. Missy, go see what's going on."

"Can I take Jinks with me?"

"No, Marty will bring Jinks. You just go find Brenda and help keep everyone under control so Mommy doesn't get upset. We'll be right there."

"Sorry about the crack . . . really, Davy," Clyde said, as Missy ran down the sidewalk toward the Paddock house. "I shouldn't have said that with Missy here."

"Forget it, Clyde, I'm not worried about a few words corrupting my daughter."

"No, words won't, but you know what will. Hanging around with that Felding brat isn't going to do her any good."

David nodded. "I know . . . but I'm not going to tell my daughter who she can play with. I don't think that's the way to handle it. I saw your encounter with the mayor earlier, by the way. Looked to me like he meant what he said."

Clyde's neck reddened, and his head jerked. "You know what Nilscoff can do, too, don't you? He's just as bad as the rest of the spoilers."

"Clyde really likes the summer folks," David said ironically to Marty, "he can't wait until they start arriving in the spring."

"Sure," Clyde said, "the way some of these richies act and behave when they come out here. They've already ruined most of this island. Oh, some of them are alright, like Davy here. But a lot of them. . . . You'll see. Garbage everywhere. And they all got dogs like that Dukirk mutt yapping away down the street. Poodle dog-shit on the beaches and all over the paths. And if dogs weren't enough, now one of them's runnin' his horses on the beach. You watch them. Women flaunting their bodies on and off the beach. Men too. In those string suits. All hopped up and switchin' and what not. No Bartleys though, I can tell you that. The Bartleys were among the first to settle this island, and I'll tell you something. Some of them have been on Fire Island all their lives. Still only leave it in emergencies. And they may hit the booze to get through the winter, but they're still a hell of a lot more civilized than some that come here. The groupers and all." Clyde pumped his thumb toward the row of expensive beach houses that lined the dunes far in front of them. "I could tell you a few things about these houses. I know what I'm talking about. Davy can tell you. I'll tell you one thing, though. The wife keeps her titties in her suit . . . always has too."

Marty's expression hovered between amusement and disbelief. "I'm sure there are all kinds of people here just like everywhere else, Mr. Bartley. However, I'm not so sure nudity is a sign of being uncivilized. Perhaps it's just a way in which some people feel more open and honest."

Clyde looked at Marty for a moment. "All I know is they're slowly destroying this island, and it's got to stop. I don't care what the mayor says."

"Look, Clyde," David said, "we better get to the house. Marty's going to be here a while. Don't worry, you'll have plenty of time to fill her in on your crusade."

"I'll look forward to seeing you again, Mr. Bartley," Marty said, extending her hand, "and when I do, please call me Marty."

"Fine . . . and I'm Clyde," the handyman said, shaking Marty's hand. "And you can also fill me in on this monkey of yours. Take care, Davy."

"See you later, Clyde," David said; Marty and Jinks moved with him down the sidewalk.

"Well," Marty said softly, when Clyde was no longer close by. "It may be relaxing around here, but it doesn't seem to be very boring."

"It has its moments," David answered, stopping. Clyde had been right. A crowd of children was gathered on the Paddock front walk. They were clustered around Missy and Brenda, they stared and chattered as they saw the approaching chimpanzee. Across the walk, Winnie Dukirk struggled with Wubbles' leash; the tiny dog barked wildly and strained toward Jinks.

"I got everyone, Mr. Paddock," Brenda shouted.

David pushed down rising irritation. "I can see that, Brenda. Nice job." He looked from the children to Marty and shook his head. "What do you think we should do?"

Marty shrugged. "Why don't Jinks and I put on a little show for them?"

"Hell of a way to start relaxing."

"I know," Marty said, smiling wearily, "but maybe if we get it over with, everyone will just accept Jinks as a part of Dune Beach for the rest of the time we're here."

"You may be right," David said. "Okay . . . I'll go tell Pam."

"No, I think it would be better if you stay out here and kept things organized. Send Missy in with a few of the kids, and I'll take Jinks inside, say hello to Pam, and tell her what's going on. Actually, this isn't so bad.

The diversion should make it easier for Pam to handle my arrival."

David sighed, pulled the wagon across the walk as a sort of gate, and raised his voice. "All right, kids, listen. You're all going to have a chance to meet Jinks, but we're going to take just a few of you in at a time. That way you can really have a chance to talk to him. Okay? Missy, you and Brenda take the first ten closest to the front door there inside. The rest of you line up here behind the wagon and wait your turn."

As Missy led the first group inside, the rest ran screaming and yelling to line up behind the wagon. As David attempted to bring order to the line, Marty started to lead Jinks to the front door. The chimp held his ground, however, his attention riveted on the dog barking at him from across the path. Marty tugged at Jinks' hand, and gave him a strong command. It broke the chimp's stare. But David noticed that as the chimp followed Marty through the front screen door, he kept looking back at the noisy dog.

Now the urge was clawing for release in frantic need. No longer could it be suppressed. It was a drive hammering for release . . . battering at the senses for satisfaction. But intelligence was there, and care would be taken. This was not the savanna, where death was a commonplace event. Here death would draw attention.

It was necessary to wait. Wait for the cover of darkness. And there could be no struggle. It would have to be someone weak, defenseless. Wait, just a little longer, for the cover of night. And then . . . the time for death would come again.

FOUR

When Marty entered the living room with Jinks, the excited children did overwhelm her greeting to Pam.

"Marty," Pam said through a forced smile. A child bumped into her as she stepped back from the obligatory hello hug. "What's going on? You didn't bring all these *and* Jinks, did you?"

"No, your daughter's friend did," Marty said, indicating Brenda. "Jinks and I are going to give them a little demonstration."

"What?"

"Sorry, Pam, I know you probably just got through making this entire house immaculate, but it seems to be the only way out. I like the house very much, by the way."

"Where is David?"

"Outside with the rest of them."

"The *rest*?"

"It's all right, really. I don't mind," Marty said, leading Pam over to the kitchen doorway. "You might as well stay over here, out of the chaos, and enjoy the show." Pam stood somewhat dumbfounded, but watched tolerantly while Marty attempted to get everyone seated. Then, in what had to be the finest hour of her eight years, Missy served as hostess and introduced the children to Marty and Jinks.

The children were enthralled. And as Marty explained the chimp's actions, it was obvious that Jinks enjoyed performing. He tied his shoe and told time; he pointed at objects in the room that the children named. Everything the chimp did had an exaggerated, clownish quality that drew laughter and applause from the children.

Only two people were not totally enthralled with the show. One was Pam. Watching unnoticed from the kitchen doorway, she did not appear to be at all pleased with the antics in her living room. After glaring silently, she turned and disappeared into the kitchen. The other unhappy individual was Brenda Felding. Brenda seemed more concerned with the attention Missy was receiving than with what the chimp could do. Finally she was unable to cope with her jealousy. "What Jinks does is just a trick! There is nothing so great about watching a stupid monkey point to things!" And she stood up suddenly.

Startled, Jinks brushed against an antique vase on an end table, and the vase shattered on the floor. The sound brought Pam rushing into the room. Seeing the broken vase, she shook her head angrily.

"I knew it!" she said. "I knew something would happen." She looked first at her daughter and then at the now silent children. "All right. Who's responsible for this?"

Missy and the children looked toward Jinks. The chimp immediately jumped up and down and pointed at Brenda. The children laughed, Jinks chattered and clapped his hands, and Brenda, both angry and embarrassed, burst into tears and ran out the front door.

"I'm sorry, Pam," Marty said, and bent to pick up the pieces of porcelain. "It was an accident."

"Don't worry about it," Pam said, sighing deeply

and bending down to help. "Let me get this. You just keep these kids entertained before something else gets broken."

Outside, as Brenda ran past him and down the sidewalk, David was trying to keep the remaining children orderly while he talked to Winnie Dukirk.

"I can't make him stop barking," Winnie said, shaking her head in frustration. In her left hand, Winnie held a small plastic shovel and a baggie; she had been taking Wubbles out for his daily walk. The shovel was for scooping up "his business" as Winnie called it. "It's your friend's pet. Wubbie just keeps barking and barking at it. He won't listen to me, and Leonard isn't home. I don't know what to do, David."

"Well, you better do something. A voice from the bushes up the street sent me with a message that Wubbles is disturbing the plants."

Winnie sniffed. "Oh, that crazy man! As if he had room to talk with his yelling at people and scaring children."

"I'm only delivering the message, Winnie. Maybe you should go down and talk to him."

"Not on your life. I have never spoken to Mr. Dile and I intend to keep it that way. He's an escaped criminal, you know."

"Are you sure about that?"

"Well, it's what everyone says." Winnie pulled at the leash. "Oh, I know the barking is annoying, David. I wish Leonard were here. Wubbie listens to him."

"Jinks is quite friendly," David said, smiling politely. "I'm sure Wubbles will get used to him."

"I hope so," Winnie said. "Come on, Wubbie." She moved away, pulling at the leash, and Wubbie's feet skidded across the sidewalk, his bark continuing without interruption.

The sound of the front screen door slamming drew David's attention. Pam, wearing a bikini and carrying a beach blanket, brushed passed him. She looked gorgeous and furious.

"Wait a minute," David said, grabbing his wife's arm, "where are you going?"

Pam pulled her arm from his grasp and spoke a little too loudly. "To the beach. I prefer not to watch that sideshow in my living room."

"Oh, come on, Pam."

"No, David, I'm sorry. Frankly, I don't think this could have started off any worse. They haven't even been here an hour, and already that smelly monkey has smashed the vase on the end table, which I'm sure I don't have to remind you was one of my mother's antiques. Furthermore, you did not ask me if you could bring in the entire neighborhood. You just did it. I think that's pretty unfeeling on your part when you knew how upset I was about this whole thing to begin with. And, if you don't feel I need to be consulted about what goes on in this house, I don't think I have to stay here and be a part of it."

"Well, I'm sorry," David said, "I just tried to come up with the fastest solution that would keep both the children and our guest happy."

"Fine," Pam said coolly. "While I'm at the beach, I would appreciate it if you would also make sure that our guest's hairy companion doesn't wreck my house."

"Pam, damn it, cut it out! Considering the panic you've been in, do you think anything that I might have done would have made you happy?"

"I think we'd better discuss this some other time," Pam said, gesturing toward the children who were staring at the two of them with avid curiosity.

David nodded angrily. "All right. You just go have a good time. And thank you for all your cooperation!" he yelled after her.

David turned to the children who stood gawking at him. "Okay, that's it," he said irritably. "No more today. The rest of you will have to come back some other time."

Cries of protest arose around him, but David ignored them. He kicked the wagon off the front sidewalk, and stomped into the house, where he closed the show with the promise of more in the days ahead. As he plopped down on the couch, and the children filed out, laughing and shouting goodbye to Jinks, Marty looked with concern toward David.

"The vase was an accident, David. But maybe we shouldn't have brought the children in on Pam like that."

David shook his head. "No big deal, believe me. I just think you've had enough for today. We've done our duty. The rest can wait. It won't kill them."

As David spoke, he noticed that one lone little boy still remained standing just outside the screen door. Tears streamed down the boy's cheeks, and he held one arm behind his back. Marty smiled sympathetically, looked at David helplessly, and opened the door. She knelt down to the boy, and the child, sniffing back his tears, brought his arm around, displaying a banana. Marty's smile widened. Wiping the tears from the boy's cheeks, she called Jinks over to them. To the boy's delight, when he gave Jinks the present, the chimp chattered in appreciation, and gave him a hug. Missy gave a happy giggle as the boy left and glanced at her father. He grinned back, and Missy ran over and proudly showed him the sign language she had been learning.

"How's she doing, Marty?" David said as he watched Missy shape her hands in an attempt to mirror the signs she observed. "Is Missy a good student?"

"Yes, she really is," Marty said. The banana had not

gone down neatly; she opened her bag and started to dress Jinks in a fresh set of clothes. "In fact, she's catching on surprisingly fast."

Missy smiled at Marty's praise and turned back to her father. "Watch, Daddy. Want to see what I can do? Guess what this means." She held her hand in the air with two fingers raised and then brought her hand over her heart. David thought for a moment.

"How's your heart?"

Missy frowned. "No, it means I'm sorry." She repeated the action, ending with her hand against her heart. "See . . . I'm sorry."

David nodded. "Yup. Makes sense. That's pretty good."

Specifically it's 'I . . . sorry'," Marty said. "Ameslan omits the copula in its language, but we usually add the necessary forms of 'to be' in translation because it sounds better."

"Copula, schmopula . . . but these signs are more than just spelling, aren't they?" David asked.

"Oh, yes. Ameslan is much more than the finger spelling of English. It is a complete language that the deaf use for communication."

David smiled at his daughter affectionately. "I'll tell you what, Missy. You work hard and learn as much as you can, and then you can teach me. It might be kind of a nice reversal to have you telling your Dad what to do. What do you say?"

"But I have to learn first, Daddy."

"I know. I mean after you've learned. You wait until you really know how, and then when you feel comfortable with it, you can teach me. Okay?"

"Okay," Missy nodded, "if Marty will help me. Will you, Marty?"

"Of course I will," Marty said. "It will be nice for Jinks to have someone besides me to talk to for a change.''

"Marty?" Missy said. She was watching Jinks squirm into the blue T-shirt that Marty was pulling over his head.

"Yes?"

"Does Jinks think you're his mother?"

Marty laughed. "No. Jinks knows I sort of adopted him. I told him that his real mother became sick and died when he was just a baby. Actually, the word I taught him for me was 'guardian' . . . someone who protects and watches over you."

"You mean like Jerry Dile," Missy said, slowly. "He keeps people out of his garden and watches over his plants to protect them."

"Yes, it's something like that, I guess."

"And Clyde could be one too, right? 'Cause he's trying to stop people from wrecking Fire Island."

"Mmhmm, he could be one also. It's really any person who assumes responsibility for someone or something, the way a parent does."

David stood up. "Well, this particular parent is taking responsibility for food. All who are interested, into the kitchen. We'll eat and then go to the beach for a while, if that's all right with you, Marty."

"Fine. What's the menu?"

David ushered them ceremoniously through the kitchen doorway. "Oh, a gourmet's delight."

After their tuna sandwiches and potato chips, they headed down to the beach. Pam was still out of sorts, David saw irritably. Jinks became the main attraction as he showed off his skills. He tried everything from flipping a frisbee to playing volleyball, each time drawing an applauding and appreciative crowd. Missy was absolutely overjoyed with the chimp and his antics, and the two romped and played together for hours in the afternoon sun.

After Marty was sure the people on the beach had accepted Jinks' presence, she left the chimp "helping" David and Missy to construct an intricate sand castle, and walked over to Pam, stretched out on a blanket in the sand.

"Do you mind if I join you?" Marty asked, sitting on the vacant half of the beach blanket.

"Of course not," Pam said, rising to lean on one elbow. She shaded her eyes with her hand, and glanced over at Missy and Jinks. They were dribbling wet sand onto the castle. "I have to admit one thing, Marty. Having Jinks here is keeping Missy busy. I'm amazed at how well they play together. It's as though she's found a new friend."

"I know. They do seem to have hit it off," Marty said, leaning forward with her hands around her knees, and staring out at the expanse of blue ocean and cloudless sky. "And I can't get over this place. I'm just beginning to realize how much I needed this. I'm very happy you invited me out, Pam, and I'm terribly sorry about this morning. Jinks just got excited. . . ."

Pam sat up beside Marty, fixing her gaze on the clumps of white foam at the edge of the surf. "Don't be ridiculous, Marty. The only problem was my own over-reaction, and we both know it. I was just scared of seeing you, and couldn't deal with it. It's as simple as that."

"It was a long time ago, Pam. You needn't worry . . . not anymore."

Pam turned her face toward her old room mate. "It just happened, Marty. I'd give anything if it hadn't, but it did. I even tried to stop seeing David when I realized how close we were becoming."

Marty put her hand gently on Pam's arm. "Pam, you don't have to do this. That's not why I came here. I came here because I wanted to see you. You don't have to explain anything to me."

"Yes, I do . . . because I want you to understand. At first, David just came over to talk . . . about you. He was so low, so lost, really, when they brought you back to New York and you had all the operations. He kept blaming himself for suggesting you study in Africa. Actually, I guess we kind of consoled each other during those first long days. And then we went out to dinner to celebrate when they took you off the critical list. It seemed like a natural thing to do . . . and . . . and we'd talk about you and your progress and then one night . . . one night he just didn't go home."

"Pam—"

"And I tried to stop it there," Pam said, her eyes clouding with water, "but I couldn't. I just couldn't, that's all. And then we couldn't tell you because of your weak condition, or maybe that was just an excuse we found, but anyway . . . after a while there just was no way to tell you gracefully because it had been too long. And so I wrote you the confesson letter."

"Pam, I know it wasn't intentional."

"But you must have hated us! God, how you must have hated us."

Marty nodded. "Yes. I went through the emotions. Dreaming of the two of you together . . . wanting to strike out at you . . . wishing I had been killed instead of just wounded. But I worked it out, Pam. It had happened. There was no changing that, and I really had no choice if I were going to go on but to deal with it. And I have."

Pam shook her head. "I think that's one of the reasons I was afraid to face you. I know I would never have been able to resolve such a thing if it had been me. I'm just not that strong a person."

"Don't give me too much credit, Pam," Marty said, "In a strange, bizarre way, what the two of you did

54

helped me, because it pushed me when I might otherwise not have been able to go on. It gave me something aside from my shattered self to concentrate on."

Pam watched David as he stood, inspected the completed sand castle, and headed toward them. "And it doesn't bother you, seeing David again after all this time?"

"Oh, I won't kid you," Marty said. Missy and Jinks were signing at them from the middle of the castle. She waved back. "It hit me pretty hard when I saw David this morning. I'm still fond of him." She looked directly at Pam and smiled warmly. "I'm fond of both of you, Pam."

"Oh, Marty, I am glad to see you," Pam said, giving her guest a quick hug. "I should have known you'd make this whole thing easy for me."

"I can't believe those two," David said, flopping down on the blanket next to the two women. "Have you been watching them? Really, Pam, I think having Jinks here is going to work out fine."

Pam took her husband's hand and squeezed it affectionately. "Thanks for the effort, but you don't have to try so hard to convince me. I'm fine now. And I'm sorry I was so nasty this morning. I'll try to make it up to both of you. I'm going to a Sixish later this afternoon. I'd like you to come along if you want to, Marty."

"A Sixish is Fire Island's name for a six-in-the evening drinking party, Marty," David said with a grimace. "Personally, I hate them, but I do think you should experience one."

Marty shook her head. "I think I better pass tonight, Pam. I need one evening just to catch my breath. You go ahead, though. I'll be very happy spending the rest of the day doing absolutely nothing."

"Well, if you're sure. . . . I really should go. The people are old friends of mine."

"I'm positive," Marty said, motioning toward the sand castle. "Looks like your daughter is making up with that little girl who was embarrassed this morning."

"Yeah," David said, as he watched the two girls chatting by the water's edge. "What was that all about with Brenda, anyway?"

"Oh, Brenda just made one of her scenes, that's all," Pam answered. "She and Missy will work it out."

David was only half listening. His attention was diverted by a figure waving to him from the landing above the beach. "Uh oh, it looks like we still have one problem. Excuse me."

Swearing softly to himself, David hurried across the sand toward the landing. The man beckoning to him was a real-estate agent named Charlie Bende who sometimes delivered the mayor's messages. David stopped at the top step.

"Charlie, you want me?"

"From what I hear, your house guests are the hit of the beach this afternoon, David," Charlie Bende said pleasantly.

"Yeah, everyone seems to be enjoying the chimpanzee. What's up?"

"Why, Nils was wondering if you wouldn't join him for the sunset at the marina this evening, David. Judging from the look of the sky, it should be a nice one."

David gave Charlie a look. "I'm sure you're right, Charlie," he said. ". . . Tell the mayor I'll be there."

FIVE

A Fire Island sunset—the way the dipping sun spread its rays across the Great South Bay—was a sight. David wasn't the only one who loved it. The bayside population always increased at early evening.

Benches along the walk that lined the bay marina. Every evening, Charlie Bende would come to sit there and watch the myriad color changes in the sky and the bay. Charlie told David once that it was an addiction to him; missing a sunset left him with a hollow feeling. The mayor used the sunsets in a more practical way; he did a lot of politicking on those benches.

As it happened, David was late getting to the marina and almost missed the sun's evening plunge. Pam had left early to attend the Sixish, and by the time David had cleaned up after dinner, showed Marty the essentials for bedding down Missy, and walked to the marina, the sun was just disappearing behind the Long Island horizon.

Charlie Bende was there, of course. His short-cropped hair slicked down and neatly parted, he was sitting as always in his freshly pressed slacks and short-sleeved shirt on the third bench from the right. Ernest Nilscoff was sitting beside him.

Nilscoff had been Dune Beach's mayor for as long as David could remember. It was well known that about the only thing Ernest Nilscoff ever got moving were his own two lips, but there was a certain charm to him and he won elections.

Behind the benches which lined the wooden walk in front of the marina was a sand-floored children's playground filled with swings, jungle gyms, and teeter-totters, all of which were occupied. David waved to some friends of Missy's, and then turned and seated himself beside Charlie.

"You're late, Paddock," said the mayor. "Almost missed it."

One of the things about the mayor that irritated David was the way he referred to people by their last names. It seemed to inflate his position somehow. David leaned forward and spoke past Charlie.

"I've been pretty busy today."

"So I understand," said Nilscoff.

Charlie Bende, his face radiating contentment, nodded out toward the water. "Pretty, isn't it, David?" he said without removing his gaze from the bay.

As usual, the view was spectacular. The sun was gone, but the colors that remained were incredible. Brilliant rainbows of pink and lavender flared across the cloud-laced sky. And the calm bay seemed to breathe with life as the afterglow spread its panorama across the water, creating millions of vibrant pulsations of pinkish blue.

"Yes, it is beautiful," David said.

"So. Tell me about the chimpanzee, Paddock," Nilscoff said. "I understand he's pretty big."

"Yes. Marty Goodman, his trainer, says he weighs about ninety-five pounds."

"That's pretty heavy for a chimpanzee, isn't it?"

"Not really," David said. "He's fairly mature, and I understand that his weight is about right." David leaned forward so that he could see Nilscoff and folded his hands together as he rested his arms on his thighs. The mayor unconsciously copied David's actions before he asked his next question.

"How strong is he?"

David tried to sound casual. "Oh, not too strong. About normal, I guess."

"Hm. Very unusual the way the chimp uses his hands to communicate, I understand."

"Yes," David said. "He certainly entertained a lot of children this morning, at any rate."

Nilscoff straightened up again. "So I hear. And that's my point, Paddock. I've had a few calls today. People are a little concerned. You know, about the size. One mother said she thought it was a baby gorilla. Now I know this Goodman is your houseguest and I'm sure she can control—whatsitsname."

"Jinks."

"Right. Jinks. But she's not going to be with the animal all the time. Are you sure he's not dangerous? As a lawyer, I can tell you that if anything happens, the responsibility is yours."

David stood up. "Listen. I spent the entire morning playing Mr. Greenjeans with the childhood population of Dune Beach so I wouldn't have to put up with this. Jinks looks large because he's almost full grown. Most of the chimps people see are babies in either circus acts or in the movies. But, damn it, Jinks is not a circus clown! He's a recognized, scientifically trained chimpanzee who is so tame he becomes indignant when you treat him like an animal. Now, I've tried to introduce Jinks to this community in the right way. Furthermore, Jinks is toilet trained, so you can tell your fine citizens they don't have to worry about stepping in chimp turds on their way to the beach. Which, I might add, is a lot more than I can say for their dogs. If what I've done isn't enough for the people of this town, then, by God—"

Charlie Bende raised his hand and patted the bench.

"Sit down, David," Charlie said. The mayor nodded. David sat down. "Nils here has an idea."

Nilscoff leaned forward again. "Look, Paddock, I know you've taken precautions, and I appreciate your efforts. But I still have to listen to the complaints. I'm the mayor, you know."

"I know." David said.

"And, frankly, I've had about all the complaints I care for because of all Clyde's craziness."

"Well, Clyde's got a point, and you know it. A lot of the people around here don't give a damn what happens to this place as long as they have a good time and get their rays."

Nilscoff gave Charlie Bende a look. Charlie's relaxed smile had widened. "Look, Paddock, you don't have to defend Clyde to me. Charlie has been doing nothing else. My point is, I have to keep everyone happy. I'll tell you what. I have a friend who's having his big party of the summer tomorrow night for a lot of the regulars here in town. Why don't you, your wife, and this Goodman come as my guests, with the chimpanzee? Then I can introduce you around, people can see the chimp is harmless, and it'll solve both our problems."

"Sounds reasonable," David said, well aware that it would also make the mayor the center of attention.

Nilscoff stood up. "Good. I'll meet you in front of Eaton's Stationery tomorrow night around seven-thirty and we'll walk over to the party. That all right with you?"

David rose and shook the mayor's extended hand. "We'll be there."

"Fine," Nilscoff said. "See you then. Good night, Charlie."

David sat back down. After Nilscoff had disappeared around the corner, Charlie Bende looked at David with amusement on his broad face.

"Sounds like a good party," he said.

David snorted. "Yeah. Right. Who's his friend?"

"Man named Silverman. Bernard Silverman. Pretty well off. Invested his family's funds into a company that made bubble gum."

"Bubble gum, huh? How well off is he now?"

"Millionaire."

"That's a lot of bubble gum. You going?"

"No. I'm not much for those social affairs," Charlie said, rising to his feet. "Want a drink?"

David got up slowly. "No, I better get back. Pam's out, and I left Missy with my houseguest. Say hello to Sam and Clyde, and have one for me."

Charlie grinned. "We'll probably have several for you."

"Be my guest," David called back as he started down the sidewalk in the fading light.

Even before he got to the house, David heard Wubbles barking from the Dukirks' porch. Obviously, the ratty dog sensed Jinks' presence. The chimp was with Marty on the platform above the beach at the end of Holly Lane. They were standing on the first step leading to the beach; Marty, a coffee cup in her hand, was leaning against the wooden railing. She was wearing a long, white, flowing beach robe, its hood lying in soft folds on her shoulders, the fine material billowed slightly in the evening breeze. The afternoon sun had given Marty's face a rosy color, and David noted that she looked not only refreshed, but very pretty.

"Pam back?" David asked, leaning against the railing opposite Marty.

"Not yet."

"Well, don't wait up for her. Those things have a habit of stretching on and on." David smiled. "I'll tell you one thing. You look a hell of a lot more relaxed now than you did this morning."

Marty returned his smile. "Thank you. I am. How was your view of the sunset? It looked pretty nice from here."

"Yeah, it was nice, wasn't it? Maybe tomorrow you can see it on the bay. But I was right. It was better that you didn't go with me. The mayor wanted to see me about Jinks. We've been invited to a party tomorrow night so that Jinks can pass inspection. If that's all right with you."

"Fine."

"Any problems with Missy?"

"No. She's a darling . . . went right to bed. She did make me promise to come with the two of you at dawn to see the horses, though." Marty gave David a questioning look.

"A guy named Evan Robbins owns them—race horses. He runs them on the beach early in the morning. I guess the sand builds their stamina. That's what Clyde was talking about this morning when he mentioned the horses. He seems to think it's just one more intrusion on the island, and has been trying to get Evan to stop. Personally, I don't see what harm it does. Anyway, Evan lets Missy feed the horses sometimes. They're out pretty early. You don't have to go if you don't want to."

"No, I'd love to," Marty said. "Besides, I'd never break my promise to someone like Missy. Your daughter is a pretty special little girl, you know. I can't believe how fast she's learning sign language."

Wubbie's barking was louder; David looked around. Winnie was leading the dog out onto the sidewalk.

"Well, she loves having you here. I can tell you that," David said, raising his voice to drown out the yaps.

"I'm afraid your neighbor's dog doesn't agree with Missy," Marty said.

"So I notice. Winnie says he won't listen to her, and Leonard isn't home."

"Is Leonard the husband?"

"Yeah."

"Where's Leonard?"

"New York. Only comes out on weekends. Mostly Sundays. Leonard Dukirk owns a contracting company he inherited from his Daddy, who was what they call your basic slumlord. Actually, Leonard is doing quite well. According to my friend Charlie Bende, Leonard buys up old rent-controlled buildings full of elderly people who want nothing more than to be left alone in their cozy roach-filled apartments until they die. Leonard then proceeds to harass the old folks under the guise of renovation until they either leave in fright when their ceilings collapse, die from inhaling construction dust, or balk at the renovations. Then he triples the rent, and fills his freshly painted roach-infested apartments with young transient singles. Daddy would be proud. Of course, it never occurs to him that he's destroying the only thing these senior citizens have left."

"Nice person," Marty said.

"Well, I guess you can't blame him," David said. "He's only doing what Daddy taught him to. Besides, how would you like to come home to a whimpering Winnie and a little dog named Wubbles that barks constantly and looks like a rat? At least it keeps him out of the house."

Marty laughed aloud. "You could always make me laugh, David. Even when I didn't want to."

David started to answer, but a mosquito bite distracted him and he smashed the insect against his arm. A spot of blood blossomed there. At the noise Jinks turned his head.

"Don't worry, Jinks," David said, "just a

mosquito."

Marty leaned forward. "Oh, David. Look at the blood."

"Yeah," David said. "He must have been sucking on me for a while. We better go in before reinforcements arrive."

Marty's face clouded. "I . . . was just wondering how the water looked."

"Oh, you want to go down?" Marty nodded. "All right, come on. I'll go down with you."

"Let me put Jinks in first," Marty said, taking the chimp's hand. "I don't want him to get all wet and sandy now that he's cleaned up."

David gestured for Marty to lead the way, and followed her back to the house. There Marty found the morning newspaper, and using its pages made a make-shift nest in the corner of the front screened-in porch. She bedded Jinks down, instructing him to stay put and go to sleep. Then Marty hurried David back to the plat-form and down the steps to the beach.

They left their shoes at the bottom and walked across the sand toward the surf. Full night had fallen. There was no moon; the stars arched down and met the black ocean far on the horizon. The sand was soft at first, but crusty to David's feet as they walked out beyond the high-tide mark. David gazed out over the water and the white foam of the swollen, breaking waves. And, as they stopped at the foam's edge, David winced slightly as the cold water ran over their feet. He turned toward Marty. Light from the oceanfront houses beyond the dunes filtered through the darkness, there was a smile on Marty's face as she spun in a circle, her arms extended.

"Oh, David . . . it's beautiful," she said, coming to a halt. She pointed to the wide belt of whiteness over-head. "Look at the Milky Way . . . it's so clear. It reminds me of an African sky. Even the nights are incredible there, David. You feel dwarfed by the clear immenseness of the heavens when you're on the savanna." Marty suddenly grabbed David's hand. "Let's go for a swim."

David frowned and pointed to the robe that the wind was molding aginst her body. "In that?"

"Of course not," Marty said. The fingers of her left hand started to undo the to snap of her robe.

"Hey, wait a minute," David said. "I think swimming at night is against the law . . . besides, this water is freezing."

"Oh, come on, David, get your clothes off. Just a quick swim. You won't believe how good it feels. I used to swim in the lake at night when I was in Africa. It's amazingly invigorating."

"Yeah, but in the nude? The water's like ice."

"Of course, that's the whole point . . . the freedom." The robe fell from Marty's body, and, except for her brief bikini panties, she was suddenly standing before David naked.

She inhaled deeply and rubbed her arms. There was no fat on her body, yet she wasn't all skin and bone, either. Her shadowed body looked healthy, muscled. And although her body lacked the instant sensual appeal that was so much a part of Pam, it was still very feminine. It was also a body that David remembered. His eyes lingered over the erect nipples of Marty's small, firm round breasts; he was surprised at the feeling of desire that memory awakened.

"Will you get your pants off and come on, before I freeze to death?" Marty hollered.

"Marty, they patrol this beach at night, you know," David said. "That's all we need . . . to get arrested for skinny dipping."

"I don't recognize this streak of conservatism, David.

You're getting old." Marty pulled her panties down her legs. David gave Marty a look, and shed his cut-offs and shirt as Marty jumped up and down, staring at him. "I take it back. You look like you're still in pretty good shape."

"Thanks," David said, throwing his clothes onto Marty's robe. "I run a lot when I'm here."

Marty laughed. "Well, let's see how well you can swim."

With that, she turned and plunged into the water. David followed after her, inching his way forward slowly.

"My God, Marty, it's cold! I'm freezing my ass off—literally!"

Her laughter floated back to him through the dark. Then a wave crashed over him, and the initial shiver of water covering flesh passed through him.

David pushed his way out beyond the breakers. He could just barely make out Marty's arms cutting swiftly through the water. He was amazed at her agility. David had always found ocean swimming difficult, but Marty moved horizontally across the back of the waves as if she were in a swimming pool. When she stopped, bobbing in the water, David fought his way to her.

"Where did you learn to swim like that?" he shouted.

Marty moved toward him. "You forget. I'm a nature girl. The Tanzania Reserve didn't exactly have hot and cold running water to shower in. Lake swimming was the standard way to clean up. And you learn to swim fast when there are crocodiles."

David laughed and, out of his depth, treaded water, shaking the hair out of his eyes and back over his head. Marty dog-paddled close to him.

"Now, admit it. Doesn't it feel good?"

"Absolutely not," David grinned. "I'm freezing."

"Don't move for a second," Marty said. "There's

something I've always been curious about, and I want to find out."

"What?" David said. Marty placed her right hand on David's shoulder for support. Suddenly, her other hand closed cup-shaped over his crotch, her fingers feeling at the underside of his scrotum. David pulled back open-mouthed in stunned surprise, went under, and came up sputtering. Laughter bubbled from Marty as she back-pedaled around him. David coughed for a second, and then found his breath. "What the hell are you doing?"

"Just scientific inquiry, David," she said. "I read somewhere that to avoid the cold, a man's testicles recede as far up into his body as possible. I always wondered about it, but I've never had a chance to check it before."

"What a liar," David laughed. The inside of his nose burned slightly from the intake of water and he forced air through it to ease the pain. "I can't believe I fell for that. How could I forget? Goodman, the ball-grabber. How could I fall for that? You always got me, remember? And it was always in some public place too."

Marty splashed toward David, laughing even harder. "And you always doubled over just like that too. I'm sorry, David. I just couldn't resist. It was so perfect. I hope you're not offended."

"I'm not offended. I just damn near drowned from the unexpected shock, that's all. I'd forgotten how crazy you can be, but it's all coming back to me very quickly."

"What do you mean?"

"You know what I mean. You were always doing some nutty thing while I tried to keep you in line."

"You loved it, and you know it," Marty answered.

David smiled. "Yeah . . . I guess I did. I really kind of miss all the silliness of those days at Columbia, to tell you the truth."

The moment David finished speaking, he felt astonished at his own words. It was true. He did miss his graduate-school days with Marty—more than he had ever admitted consciously to himself. And he was suddenly aware of how being with Marty again and talking to her had caused his suppressed feelings to surface. He had said the wrong thing. Marty had paddled off to the left while they were talking, and even though she said nothing for several seconds, David could feel her looking at him through the darkness.

"I can no longer feel the lower half of my body, you know," David said, attempting to keep his voice light. "Are you ready to get out yet?"

"I'll tell you what. I'll race you to shore," Marty said, coming back to him. "See if you can beat the weaker sex." Her challenge delivered, Marty dove into a wave and David splashed after her. The water pounded against him, but David strained forward, determined to get to shore first. They both reached the shallows at the same time, but Marty scrambled faster than David, and he realized that she was going to beat him. In a final effort, he surged ahead and dove, catching Marty's ankle, both of them to crashing forward into the sand with David landing heavily on Marty's back. He pushed his hands into the sand and raised himself slightly.

"Are you all right?" he said, gulping to catch his breath. Marty turned under him, and then she was lying on her back looking up at him.

"Fine. . . ," she said.

In the back of his mind, somewhere beyond his emotions, David knew it was dangerously wrong to allow his arms to relax so that his body covered Marty. Yet, somehow, it was all so natural, and the past became the present, enveloping and dominating him completely as his confused thoughts melted into the familiar. The husky quality in Marty's voice. The message in her eyes. The hungry quality of her lips as her tongue darted across his mouth. And the feel of her against him—the soft mounds of her breasts pressing into his chest, the shifting of her thighs so that she met his body in just the right way, her left arm around his neck, her right hand automatically caressing the small of his back.

Marty moaned with a soft urgency. Her body began to move under him, and David knew he must stop immediately.

"Marty," he muttered, searching for words as he pushed his hands into the sand. The moment he spoke, Marty's body stiffened slightly, and she pulled her arm from around his neck.

"I know," she said in a hoarse whisper, rolling out from under him and pulling herself up to a kneeling position. "Oh, Christ. . . . I know . . . I know."

David pushed himself to his feet and waded further into the water. He began splashing the sand off of himself. Marty followed his example, and then walked to where she had dropped her robe, picked up her panties and stepped into them. David slowly followed her as she grasped her robe from under his clothes, pulled it up over her body, and put her arms into the sleeves. David stopped in front of her and exhaled slowly.

"Marty," he said, "I. . . ." She was fastening the front of her robe. She stopped and placed her hand lightly on his mouth.

"Don't say any more, David. Please." Marty shivered, and pulled the hood up over her head. Her face disappeared in its shadows. "David, I honestly did not mean for this to happen. I was in such a good mood. It felt so nice seeing you again. Just in terms of the wonderful friendship we once shared, I mean. The same with Pam. I was just having fun and, I don't know, wanted to swim . . . and have a few laughs. But when we fell. . . ."

"I know, Marty. I felt it too," David said quietly.

"I know you did. I could see it in your face. That's the problem, David. In all the time I spent deciding I wanted to see you and Pam again, for some reason I didn't anticipate the look that came into your face. I never expected to see that kind of look from you again, David. And now that I have. . . ." Marty's voice broke, and she turned her head down and away from David. "It hurts. . . ."

Marty started to sob. David, not knowing what to say, stood there shivering, feeling awkward. Finally, she wiped at her face with the sleeve of her robe, and stuffed her hands into her side pockets. David pulled on his clothes, and tried to sort out his thoughts.

"Marty, the last thing I want to do is hurt you any more than I already have. It took me completely by surprise. I just responded to being next to you, and I'm sorry. . . . I guess I'm not quite as good at handling seeing you again as I thought I would be."

Marty's hands came from her pockets and she lifted her hood back, shaking her damp hair. She looked in David's direction, but he could not see her eyes. They were in night's shadow.

"Maybe we both were kidding ourselves, David. It looks like Pam was the only one who was really honest with herself. She admitted she was afraid."

"Well," David said, "I would like to think that it was just the night that got to us, but I'm afraid I can't make myself believe that."

Marty sighed heavily. "So. What now? Do you think I should leave?"

David frowned and shook his head. "Don't be ridiculous. Marty, it's just that we had something very special, and it still has an effect on us. And we'll have to come to terms with that fact. I'm not about to let you go running out of here. That's not going to solve anything."

"All right, David," Marty said, moving closer to him and meeting his gaze, "but I have to say this. I know you're confused about your feelings right now. We haven't seen each other for a long time. And you're right—what we had was special. Maybe that's what tonight's urgency was. An attempt to recapture the past. But if you think it was more than that, David, don't tell me until you're sure. I still care a great deal for you, David. But I can deal with that. I've had a lot of years to come to terms with it. And I can be friends with you too. I know that. I wouldn't have come here if it weren't true. But if anything like tonight happens again, it has to be real. That's all I ask, David. Be sure. Because I don't think I could stand to be hurt again."

"Marty, I swear to you, I wouldn't—"

"I know," Marty interrupted. She gestured toward the Paddock house beyond the dunes. "Come on, we better go in. I expect Pam is home by now."

David stared in the direction of the house. "Think we look guilty? Shivering and soaking wet?"

"Not at all. We went for a swim, that's all," Marty said, a smile coming to her face. "And it was very refreshing."

David grinned, but shook his head. "Sorry. It was not refreshing. I will not admit swimming in ice water and freezing my ass off is refreshing."

"Well, getting up at dawn isn't any fun either, and we're going to do that in the morning, so we're even."

"That's right," David said, as they headed across the sand toward the platform steps. "I forgot about that. You don't have to, Marty. Really. We'll do it another day. Why don't you sleep in tomorrow and get some of the rest you came here for."

"Don't worry, David," Marty said, taking another look at the vast, dark sky above them. "I'll survive. I'm a pretty tough girl, you know."

. . . Not an internal debate, not a decision, it was an action that must be taken . . . a path that had been chosen on the African savanna when, just for an instant, the emotions had escaped the bounds of all control, pushing the act over every edge of decency, setting free an unholy thing, a fiend that fed on mutilation and destruction. Now it had come again. There was no choice, only the action. . . .

SIX

It was two o'clock in the morning. Although Missy was tiptoeing, Jinks' eyes opened before she got halfway across the porch. Missy jerked to a stop, bringing her finger to her lips in a plea for Jinks to remain quiet. Then she scurried over to the chimpanzee's nest of newspaper and began whispering as quickly and quietly as she could.

"Please be quiet, Jinks, *please*. I know I shouldn't be doing this, but I'll be right back. And Brenda was so upset—you know, because when you pointed at her, everyone laughed—and I promised I'd make it up to her, and this is what she said she wanted more than anything else in the world. I'm only going to show her Jerry's garden for a second. I promise. Right in and right back out again. I know he probably wouldn't like it, but he won't even know, and she wants to see the inside so bad. Okay? Don't worry, I'll be right back. So you stay here and don't make any noise. You can just go back to sleep if you want to. I'll be careful not to wake you when I come back in. Okay?"

Jinks tilted his head slightly and looked at Missy curiously. Missy took his silence to mean he wasn't going to react, and gave the chimp a hug, followed by a series of signs.

"Oh, thank you, Jinks," Missy whispered,

". . . anyway, I think this is the sign for thank you. . . . I knew you wouldn't give me away. We're friends now, right? You just go to sleep, and I'll be right back."

The chimpanzee still did not respond, but followed Missy with his eyes as she crept to the screen door. Missy inched the door open, gave Jinks a last look, and then slipped outside and down the sidewalk.

Brenda was waiting for Missy beside Jerry Dile's shrubbery just as they had arranged. However, once they had lifted the latch of the gate, and entered the garden, things began to go wrong.

"I don't care what I promised," Brenda said in a loud whisper as the girls crouched beside a row of huge beet tops. "I've always wondered about this place, and I'm not going to leave without exploring a little. Didn't you say there was a greenhouse? Let's go see that! Where is it?"

"It's in the center. But I think we should go. . . . Really, Brenda. What if Jerry finds out we're here? He'll kill us!"

"How's he going to find out? It's the middle of the night. Where's his house?"

Missy pointed off to their left at a long row of tall bamboo stacks. "Over there . . . the other side of the bamboo."

"So, what are you worried about? We're not even going near there. Come on."

Brenda started to crawl down the beet-row, and Missy, whispering Brenda' name loudly in protest, hurried after her when suddenly a loud cracking noise sounded from within the bamboo. Both girls froze.

"What was that?" Brenda whispered, scuttling back to Missy.

Missy shook her head. "I don't know. . . . Come on, the gate is this way."

The moonlight filtering through the thick overhead

foliage briefly illuminated the two girls as they scrambled rapidly on hands and knees down the row, but again they were stopped—from within the bamboo something cracked again. This time it was closer to them. Tentatively the girls stood up, shivering in silence. A slight breeze rustled the surrounding leaves, and long shadows shifted and moved through the greenery. Then, loud rustling broke the silence. Something or someone was moving quickly toward them. Now heavy, hissing breathing came from the darkness in front of them.

Brenda gave a tight little scream, and the girls broke into a run, smashing headlong through the garden, thick leaves and stems slapping at their faces and bodies. There was the open gate. Then Brenda fell. Missy, panting, pulled her up. They tumbled through the gate, slamming it shut behind them. They stopped for a moment, listening. The surf crashed against the beach in the distance. There was no other sound.

There was movement beside them. Missy gasped and spun around. Clyde Bartley came up to them out of the darkness.

"Hello, there, Missy," Clyde said, looking from Missy to Brenda. "Anything wrong?"

"No, Clyde," Missy said quickly, her voice full of relief. "We were just taking a walk."

Clyde eyed the two girls for a moment, then cleared his throat. "Seems to me it's very late for walking . . . at your age. I think maybe you had better get on home, Missy. What do you think?"

"Well, we're not going home," Brenda said, sounding mulish. "We're going to the playground. Aren't we, Missy?"

"No, I think I better get home," Missy said, "I'll see you later, Brenda."

"Oh, come on, Missy, don't be a scaredy-cat," Brenda said, "I go there lots of times at night."

"You heard Missy," Clyde said, stepping forward and glaring down at the plump girl in front of him. "She's going home. And you better do the same before you get into trouble, young lady."

"You can't tell me what to do! And you better not touch me, either. . . . You heard what the mayor said."

"I'll give you the lickin' of your life if you keep it up, mayor or no mayor, you little brat! And you better believe it. Now get out of here! I don't care where you go. You can go jump in the ocean for all I care." He turned back to Missy. "Now come on, Missy, I'll walk you home."

"Okay, Clyde," Missy said. "Sorry, Brenda, I'm going home." ·

Missy and Clyde started a short distance down the path.

"Okay, scaredy-cat," Brenda yelled. ". . . See you later, scaredy-cat." And she started off in the direction of the playground.

"Whose idea was this late walk, anyway?" Clyde said. "Brenda's?" Missy nodded. "Well, I don't think it's such a good thing to hang out with Brenda so much, Missy. And this running around at night is just why I think that."

"You won't say anything, will you, Clyde?" Missy pleaded, lowering her voice as they turned up the Paddock front walk. "Please. Daddy and Mommy will kill me if they find out."

Clyde pulled the front door open and lowered his own voice to a hoarse whisper. "You just think about what I said. Now, go on, inside with you."

"Thanks, Clyde. . . . Good night," Missy said, stepping through the doorway. She stopped suddenly. "Clyde?"

"What's the matter?" Clyde whispered.

"Jinks," Missy said. "He's gone. And he was right

there in the corner when I left." The starlight showed the nest. It was empty.

"Forget the monkey. He doesn't need any beauty sleep anyway. He's too ugly. It's little girls who need beauty sleep. Now get to bed. You're too pretty to get dark circles under your eyes."

"Okay," Missy said, a tentative smile curving her lips. She closed the door and whispered through the screen. "He probably went in with Marty, anyway. Good night. I'll see you tomorrow."

"Sure thing," Clyde answered.

As the handyman turned onto Holly Lane, he glanced up at the bright stars, and then continued up the narrow path toward his house. The high shrubbery of Jerry Dile's garden looked strangely threatening.

"Who's out there?" A rasping voice screeched. Clyde jumped. "Somebody's out there!" It was Jerry Dile, sounding cross . . . or frightened.

"It's me, Jerry," Clyde said softly.

"Somebody was in my garden, Clyde. I heard them. Did you see anyone out there? Did you?"

Clyde glanced back down toward the Paddock house, and then moved closer to the shrubbery. "Yeah . . . that Felding girl was hanging around. I told her to get out of here."

"Did she go? Did she? She better not come in here again. I mean it."

"Yeah, she's gone," Clyde said, his expression hardening. "She said something about going to the playground by the marina. Child that age ought to be home in bed."

The deserted playground was eerie in the starlight. Brenda Felding shook herself and crossed the area, passing the push merry-go-round and the gleaming jungle gym. Now she was at the swings. What if her mother were drunk again, with that creepy man "cousin Joe," locked up in her big bedroom? She would have fun anyway! There was nothing wrong with swinging, no matter what that old Clyde said. She pumped her legs. The swing squeaked discordantly. The mooring buoys chimed softly as they bounced on the dark waters of the marina. Brenda pushed the swing higher, and threw her head back in glee. Then, out of the corner of her eye, she thought she saw a piece of the darkness move behind her.

She dug her heels into the sand and brought her body bolt upright, stopping the swing. And, as she turned toward the movement, a snarling shadow lunged at her from the darkness.

Brenda pushed the swing wildly at the oncoming figure, and began running blindly through the playground. She brushed past the merry-go-round; the metallic cylinder moved with a loud, scraping creak. The shadow's heavy, hissing breathing was close behind her.

Ahead of her was the jungle gym. She scrambled desperately onto it. Its metal was cold to her clutching fingers. Higher and higher she climbed. Suddenly, as her small fingers closed on the top bar, her body jerked to a halt. Something had grabbed her by the ankle. Brenda stared down in whimpering horror. The shadow pulled, savagely. Her clinging hands lost their grip. Brenda plummeted downward, her hands clawing at the air. Then her head smashed brutally against the lower gym bars.

Brenda was no longer aware when her body was dragged through the sand until it was beside the teeter-totter. She did not feel her body being lifted swiftly, then hurled down with a sickening thud. Bone splintered against wood. Heavy, sibilant breathing rose and fell.

The empty swing moved gently in the light breeze.

SEVEN

The early morning was cool as David, Marty, Missy, and Jinks walked to the high platform at the end of Holly Lane. There they stopped, waiting for the sun to rise. Pam had stayed in bed, saying she had no intention of getting up in the middle of the night to go look at a horse.

Right on schedule, as the sun nudged its color above the ocean's horizon, Evan Robbins galloped bareback toward them down the beach, his Arab stallion splashing through the early morning foam. Evan thundered by, waving, and Missy shouted as she jumped and waved back in glee. Then, as the sun became a firm, red ball far in the distance, Clyde strode out across the sand toward the stallion. Evan pulled his horse to a halt as the man came up next to him.

"Looks like Clyde's not taking the mayor's advice," David said, pointing toward the men talking at the tide's edge. He looked at Marty and grinned. "I'd love to hear the conversation. Evan is not the most agreeable person you'd want to meet . . . especially when it comes to telling him what he can and cannot do with his horses. That would not deter Clyde, of course."

As David finished speaking, Evan appeared to bring the conversation to a halt. He made a sweeping upward gesture with his hand at Clyde, turned the horse sharply by the reins, and headed back toward Holly Lane. Clyde returned the gesture, yelled something at the departing rider, and started walking back toward the dunes.

Evan slowed the horse as they approached and Missy, carrots and sugar in hand, ran down the steps to meet them.

"Wait a second, Missy," Evan said, as Missy reached the beach. "Don't give Butler those carrots if they're from Jerry's garden. I think he's been adding chemicals to make his plants grow, and I don't want to take any chances."

"Did he tell you he was using additives?" David called. He came down the steps and retrieved the vegetables from his daughter.

Evan shook his head. "No, but look at the stuff. It's just not real. With that size he's got to be using something. I just told him I couldn't use any more vegetables. Besides, Jerry and Clyde are pretty good friends and I don't like the way Bartley's been on me lately. With Jerry's reputation, I'm not sure what my horse might be eating."

"Oh, come on, Evan," David said.

"Well, you never know, David. I'd rather be sure. Butler's only getting what I know's okay."

"Can I still give him the sugar?" Missy asked.

"Sure," Evan nodded. Missy moved happily to the horse and as she held out her hand, Evan said, as he usually did, "Just hold your hand flat so he won't nip you, Missy."

Missy did as she was told, and as the horse dispatched the lump of sugar, half turned to the stairs.

"Daddy, can Jinks feed Butler?"

David shrugged. "I don't see why not."

Missy waved excitedly to the chimp. "Come on, Jinks."

"Now wait a minute, Missy," Evan said, as Jinks

came bounding to the bottom of the steps, Marty following behind. However, Evan's protest came too late. The horse whinnied loudly and suddenly reared.

"Missy, look out!" David shouted. He ran forward as Evan loosened the horse's reins.

"Whoa, Butler! Easy, boy," Evan urged. His legs hugged the horse's flanks as Butler's legs pranced in a nervous staccato on the sand. Missy had jumped back in fright, dropping her sugar when the horse's legs went up, and she was crying as David reached her and pulled her back onto the steps. However, Marty was behind them, and before she could get there, Jinks reached down for the sugar. This time the horse bucked. The hooves skimmed Jinks' head, and the chimpanzee swiped back defensively with his arm.

Evan fought for control and yelled: "Will you get that Goddamn ape out of here?"

"Jinks," Marty commanded as she ran, "get over here." The chimpanzee scooped up sand and sugar lumps together, and bounded past Marty to a safe position beside Missy and David on the steps, cramming the sugar lumps into his mouth as quickly as possible. By the time Butler was quieted to a nervous prance, Evan was flushed with anger.

"What the hell's the matter with you people? Bringing a Goddamn monkey down here without asking me. This stallion's Arabian, temperamental and skittish as hell." The horse snorted heavily and jerked his head. "Go on, get that Goddamn ape out of here."

"Jinks is not a Goddamn ape, Mr. Robbins," Marty said. "He is a valuable, scientifically trained chimpanzee."

"I don't give a shit if he's an orangutan, lady, get him out of here! Do you know what this horse is worth? Bucking like that might cause him to snap a leg or tear a ligament."

"Whatever the price, I can assure you that Jinks is worth far more than any horse, sir, and he was in equal danger of being hurt."

"Any time some hairy ape is worth more than Butler will be the day, lady," Evan bellowed.

David noticed that Marty was signing with her left hand as she spoke. When she took a deep breath and pulled her hand back to her side, he broke in on the exchange.

"Missy, take Jinks back to the house, okay?"

Missy had stopped crying and frowned up at him. "No, Daddy . . . Jinks didn't do anything."

"I know, honey, but would you just take him home, please?"

"But it wasn't his fault."

David was in no mood to argue; he snapped back at his daughter. "Missy, I'm not asking you. I'm telling you. Now take Jinks back to the house. Right now!"

Missy was not used to David raising his voice at her, and for a moment it looked as though she was going to cry again, but she didn't. She pouted, and then she took Jinks' hand and started home. As they left, David started down the steps to apologize to Evan, but Marty had beaten him to it. She was standing near the now-quiet Butler, speaking to Evan.

"Actually, arguing is pointless, Mr. Robbins. The fact is, we should have asked before we let Jinks approach the horse, and we didn't." Her voice was calm and relaxed.

"Goddam right," Evan said.

"I'm sorry, Evan," David said, "it was my fault. I just didn't think."

"Forget it, Paddock. No harm done."

"That's right. Butler's fine, isn't he?" Marty said, taking the horse's bit in one hand and patting him gently on the nose with the other.

Evan leaned forward and rubbed Butler's neck. "Oh . . . probably throw him off his feed. Arabians are temperamental, you know."

Marty nodded. "But he needn't have worried. Jinks wouldn't hurt him."

"All the same, keep the ape off the beach when I exercise. One spooked horse is enough."

Marty released the horse and looked up at Evan. "Don't worry, Mr. Robbins. Jinks will not bother your horse again."

Evan grunted. "I hope not. What a wasted workout. First Bartley, then an ape. I'd have been better off to have left Butler in the barn." Giving David a nod, Evan kicked the horse gently and galloped toward the more compact sand at the edge of the surf.

Marty watched Evan ride away, and then turned to David. "I'm sorry, David. I know I shouldn't have argued with him, but he really angered me. All he cares about is his horse. What about Missy? He didn't say a word about her. She could have been trampled."

"Don't worry about it," David said, "I should have gone down with Missy instead of being so careless. Besides, Evan always spouts off. Forget it, he's harmless."

"Oh, I'm sure," Marty said with a sigh. "I guess part of it is that I'm just overly sensitive about Jinks. Maybe it's because I've put so much into him, but I noticed during the tour that I'm becoming less and less tolerant of ignorant criticism. Even during the little demonstration yesterday, I didn't say anything, of course, but that child Brenda was being so obnoxious about Jinks I wanted to strangle her."

David smiled. "Don't worry—everybody wants to strangle Brenda. I think you have a right to be sensitive considering what you've put into this. By the way, did you know that you are signing with your left hand? As you speak, I mean. I noticed it when you were talking to Evan.''

Marty looked down at her left hand and rubbed the back of it. ''Yes, I . . . I guess it's ingrained.''

David frowned. ''You're not left-handed, are you?''

''No, but when I learned Ameslan, the left hand responded easier, so I concentrated on using it predominantly. And, I guess I talk to Jinks so much it happens automatically.''

David nodded. ''I'm really fascinated with this signing. Maybe you can teach me on the sly if Missy doesn't pick it up.''

''Fine,'' Marty said, ''but she's very fast. She already knows several combinations. I'm sorry you had to yell at her before about Jinks.''

David waved off the apology. ''She'll forgive me, don't worry. Especially when she finds out we're going to Sunken Forest today.''

''Sunken Forest?''

''It's a thick woods further out on the island that makes up the main part of the National Seashore Preserve. Missy loves it there, and I imagine Jinks will too.''

Missy placed the two bowls on the kitchen table. Jinks sat there watching, a large cloth napkin stuffed into the top of his shirt. He held a spoon in his right hand, and patiently waited as Missy poured Cheerios into the bowl she had set in front of him.

''Anyway, don't worry, Jinks, it wasn't your fault. That stupid old Mr. Robbins is always grumpy most of the time. We'll just stay away from him, okay? And, thank you for not giving me away last night, Jinks, even if Clyde did have to go and spoil everything. Where were you when we came home? In Marty's room?'' Jinks stared at Missy for a moment, and then reached

85

into his bowl, withdrew a single Cheerio, and tossed it into his mouth. "No, silly," Missy laughed, "You're supposed to wait for the milk."

Responding immediately, Jinks stood on his chair, grabbed the milk carton from the table, and flooded milk into his bowl. Then, putting down the carton, he extracted a single Cheerio from the many that floated on the top of the bowl and, opening his mouth very wide, tossed the piece of cereal down his throat.

Missy giggled. "No, not like that. You know what I mean. You're so silly. You're supposed to eat it with your spoon."

Jinks jumped up and down on the chair, chattering happily. Then he picked up another Cheerio from the bowl, placed it on the spoon he held in his hand, and, with a quick flick of the spoon handle, tossed the Cheerio into his open mouth. Missy laughed aloud, squirming with pleasure at the chimp's antics, and Jinks, responding to the attention, scampered up onto the table, and over to where Missy was sitting. Leaning back on his haunches, the chimp signed dramatically, moving his hand from Missy, into his mouth, and back again.

Missy laughed as she understood. "You want me to try?" The chimp chattered again with excitement, and Missy reached into the box of cereal beside her. "Okay, open wide. I don't think I'm a very good shot, though."

Jinks backed off slightly with his mouth open as Missy stood on her chair and tossed cereal in the general direction of his face. Most of the round pieces missed, landing everywhere except in Jinks' mouth. However, finally, after Jinks dipped his head in the line of a throw, a Cheerio sailed right between the chimp's open lips, and the two of them went wild with satisfaction.

Then Jinks pulled Missy up onto the table with him, and, breakfast totally forgotten, the two of them, amid squeals of laughter and chatters of excitement, were tossing Cheerios at one another's mouths when Pam, tying a robe around herself, came in.

"*Missy!* . . . . What on earth?"

Her mother's voice brought Missy's merriment to a halt instantly, and she jumped down from the table, pulling Jinks after her.

"Missy, what is going on here?" Pam said loudly as she approached the table. Random Cheerios crunched beneath her slippers.

"Nothing," Missy answered quietly, leading Jinks to his chair where the chimp sat obediently. "We're just eating breakfast, that's all."

"Eating breakfast!" Pam surveyed the table and the area around them and glared down at her daughter. There were Cheerios everywhere. "Get over on the other side of the table and sit down where you belong, young lady. Where is your father?"

Missy scooted past her mother and into her regular seat, but before she could answer, David and Marty came up to the front door of the house.

"I'm right here," David said, as he entered the living room. "What's the problem?"

"I would say, from the looks of things, that it was a Cheerios fight," Pam answered with disgust. "What time is it anyway?"

David rolled his eyes, giving his daughter a look. "Too early for you to get all upset. Go back to bed. I'll take care of this. It's just a few Cheerios. No big deal."

"Jinks," Marty said, coming up behind the chair where Jinks was sitting quietly, "did you—"

"It wasn't his fault, Marty. Really. I was just kind of playing around. You know, throwing Cheerios into my mouth, and he sort of followed my example. And I guess we just kind of got carried away."

"That is an understatement," Pam said, stooping to

pick up bits of cereal from the floor around her. "When I came out of the bedroom, David, they were jumping around on top of the table, throwing cereal at each other. On top of the table, David."

David and Marty immediately bent to retrieve scattered Cheerios as David spoke. "Okay, okay," he said soothingly. "Let's just pick them up and have breakfast. Missy knows she was wrong. As she said, they just got carried away. Go on, it's not even seven o'clock yet. Go back to bed, Pam. We'll take care of this. Unless you'd like to come with us after we eat. I thought I'd take Marty and Jinks to see Sunken Forest."

Missy's face brightened. "Really, Daddy?"

"Really. It'll give the two of you a chance to run off some of your steam."

"Why don't you come with us, Pam?" Marty said, placing a handful of Cheerios on the table.

"No, thank you," Pam said, standing. "Taking a five-mile hike after being rudely awakened at dawn is not exactly my idea of a good time. Besides, I have to take Missy to a birthday party later today, and I still haven't gotten a present." Pam turned to her daughter. "If you go with Daddy to Sunken Forest, young lady, just be sure you're back here in time to get ready. In fact, you'd better get back in time to rest, so you won't be too tired."

"Oh, I won't be too tired," Missy said, twisting her face in incredulity. "Why don't we take Jinks to the party? He can be the present. Then you won't have to go shopping."

Pam's eyes widened as she cut off a yawn. "Absolutely not. After seeing how you handle a box of Cheerios, I can just imagine what the two of you would do with cake and ice cream. I hope this isn't an indication of what to expect every morning."

Missy shook her head. "It isn't. Don't worry,

Mommy. I promise."

"I'll keep a closer eye on Jinks, Pam," Marty said. "From now on I'll keep him with me."

"You shouldn't have to, Marty, if Missy can behave herself." Pam yawned again. "Now, if you'll excuse me, I think I'll take your advice, David, and go back to bed. I hope you all enjoy your walk in the hot sun."

Missy waited until her mother had disappeared into the bedroom, and then she jumped up to help her father and Marty gather cereal from the floor.

"Are you still mad at me, Daddy?" she asked softly. "Please don't be. I'll pick all these up. We were just fooling around a little. And you should have seen Jinks. He was so funny. I threw the Cheerios right in his mouth."

"He was, huh?" David said. He attempted a stern look, but it wasn't convincing, so David gave it up and glanced at the Cheerios in his hand. Then he winked at his daughter and turned toward the chimp who was still sitting quietly in his chair. "Open your mouth, Jinks."

Jinks' features immediately became animated, and he stood on the chair, opening his mouth to present the gaping target. Marty shook her head and looked on, smiling, while David tossed several Cheerios directly into Jinks' mouth. Missy giggled with delight.

After breakfast, David was a little concerned that there might be a problem with Jinks and the leash; but the chimp allowed it to be put on as long as Missy carried the end of the strap. However, as they walked toward the eastern end of the island it became apparent that the leash was only a formality. Standing upright, even with his shoulders hunched, Jinks was taller than the little girl beside him. The strap did serve its purpose, though, because the bathers didn't seem to be the least disturbed that Jinks was on the beach. In fact, they shouted and waved, and Jinks and Missy happily waved back.

David glanced at Marty. "do you ever grow tired of the attention Jinks gets?"

"I did at first," Marty said. "I guess I've just gotten used to it. Seems normal now." She tilted her head into the sun. "Let them stare all they want. I'm happy just soaking up this sunshine."

"Well, you'll get plenty of that before we get back. It's a good two- or three-mile hike to the forest."

Marty frowned slightly. "I hope that really is the reason Pam didn't come along. You don't think she's purposely avoiding me, do you? I mean, she didn't get up to go with us this morning either."

"Forget it," David said. "First of all, Pam's not what you'd call a morning person, and the walk to Sunken Forest and back is pretty tiring. Besides, she has to take Missy to a noon birthday party . . . I'm sure she just didn't want to make the walk. Plus, Sunken Forest is no big deal. I mean don't get overly excited about seeing it. It's just woods with a path through it."

Marty smiled. "David, it's so nice here, I'd enjoy it if it were a single bush in the middle of a sand dune. And I'm sure Jinks will love it."

"We'll soon find out," David said, pointing to a space in the dunes far ahead of them. "There it is, where the sand dips inward along the dunes."

There were guided tours through the Sunken Forest Preserve, but David decided the group would go on its own so that Jinks would not have to be leashed. They took pamphlet maps from a box at the start of the path and entered the secluded, thickly shaded woodland, where the interior, punctuated with piercing shafts of light, presented a sharp contrast to the sunlit beach outside. The wooded area ran the full width of the island. Other than the small hamlet of Bartleyville on the bay side, the only signs of civilization in the forest were the narrow wooden-planked paths that the service naturalists had built, and an occasional cleared out area with benches.

As they walked past holly and sassafras trees, the thick growth of twisting cat briar, and ever-present poison ivy, David could see that Marty had been absolutely right about Jinks. The chimp seemed to enjoy the cool shadows even more than his companions. In fact, from the moment they entered the forest, his entire demeanor changed, as if the wooded atmosphere had awakened some instinctual flame. He dropped to his hands when he moved, and his refined walk reverted back to a scampering lope. The forest also seemed to bring forth his need to vocalize. Jinks would rush ahead of the others on the path, and then, in place of his usual signing, would turn and call to them in sharp, high-pitched barking sounds. Then he would rush back to them, his breathing loud and heavy with excitement.

After following the path along the tall marsh grass at the bay side of the forest, Jinks bounded back into the woods. Missy ran after him, and Marty and David didn't see them again until they reached the first interior rest area. Jinks and Missy were jumping up and down on one of the benches, so David and Marty sat down on the empty bench opposite the cavorting pair. Missy was giggling at her own chimpanzee imitation.

"Jinks' refinement seems to be slipping away, Marty," David said. "Must be the call of the wild."

Marty laughed. "The bad part is that he's knocking some of Missy's culture away at the same time."

David nodded. "Yeah. But it's simply the call of 'let's act silly and have fun.' I hope bringing Jinks here isn't destroying years of programmed training."

Marty shook her head. "I'm not worried. He's just excited. He acted just like this when we were in Africa. I think it's roots, and all that."

As Marty spoke, Jinks bounded onto the bench back, then up into a tree and out of sight. Marty jumped to her feet.

"Jinks, come back here." The chimp answered with loud hoots and they could hear him moving through the foliage, but he remained out of view. Marty sat back down. "That little devil! He must have heard you. Jinks' one bad characteristic is that he is an incredible showoff. He is now having a little joke and demonstrating how the woods have ruined his training."

David looked at her doubtfully. "I have to tell you, Marty, that I still find it hard to believe that your chimp can understand English that well."

"I know. Actually, it's a combination of things that are causing his actions. This is just another example of one of his new bursts of independence."

"He isn't listening to you?"

"Not always. Adolescent rebellion. I know it's just a part of his natural growth process, but it still bothers me."

"Ah, yes," David said, grinning, "the pangs of disciplining a teenager."

"Something like that," Marty admitted.

Missy screamed. David jerked around. Missy had crawled up to a standing position on the bench, and was leaning over the back, apparently to see where the chimp had gone. Now, as David looked, the bench overturned.

"Missy!" David shouted and lunged forward. Jinks appeared from the tree above. And, hanging from a limb by one hand, he swooped down, caught Missy with his other hand before she hit the ground, and pulled her clear. The bench crashed forward. David reached the bench just as they dropped to the plank-covered ground.

"Are you all right, honey?" he asked, kneeling down

to his daughter.

Missy's face was white, but she nodded, and stared wide-eyed at Jinks. The chimpanzee moved to Marty and sat down obediently at her side. Marty scowled down at him.

"Don't come sidling up to me, Mister Wise Guy," Marty said, as the chimp placed his paw in her hand. "I don't know whether I should scold you for running off, or thank you for helping Missy."

David looked over at Jinks. "Well, I thank you, Jinks," he said, "I guess you're a little more human than I thought you were." The chimp looked at David with unblinking white-rimmed eyes, and David stood up, taking Missy's hand. "And you, little girl, had better be more careful, or we'll have to reverse things and put *you* in the leash. Jinks can hold the other end so he can look after you." Missy laughed, as David had intended. He righted the bench, and they all started on the path toward the oceanfront exit.

The walk back was uneventful, but as they slowly splashed along the edge of the surf, David couldn't help thinking about the Sunken Forest incident. The fact was that Jinks had saved Missy from a bad fall. And that was what bothered him. The act of saving someone seemed to him to be very human, with moralistic overtones which he assumed monkeys did not have. He thought of mentioning his feelings to Marty, but when he glanced at her, she was staring silently out over the ocean. He decided not to interrupt her thoughts.

During the act in the playground, euphoria had replaced the nagging tug on the senses. And this time the afterglow had been stronger than before. This time had been different. The danger had added a new tingling edge of excitement. The action would be discovered—its power would cause wonder and dread.

But something else was different as well. Before, deep within the recesses of awareness, there had been a guardian—a sense that the act had been terribly wrong . . . an unholy deed that must never happen again.

But now the guardian was gone, buried by the living pleasure of the kill.

And now the gnawing returned, stronger than ever. There had to be another, and soon. More . . . now! . . . And with the tingle of danger to magnify the thrill. Perhaps daylight this time . . . still taking care, still taking great care . . . but in the open, for all to see afterwards, for all to fear. Soon. . . .

EIGHT

The sky had become overcast by the time they approached Dune Beach, and the oceanfront almost empty of sunbathers. It looked as though rain were imminent. However, there were several fishermen casting into the dark blue ocean, and even from a distance David could see Clyde Bartley seated in his favorite spot with his fishing pole.

To prevent erosion of the oceanfront, the town of Dune Beach had sunk double rows of large cement pilings from the dunes out into the ocean on both sides of the public bathing area. Unfortunately, the erosion continued unabated, but the wide round pilings, their root-like bases buried in the sand, stood as monuments to the effort. In between the pilings, wide slabs of rock pointed upward at different angles, running from the high-tide mark out to the end of the piling rows, about twenty feet into the ocean. It was there that Clyde Bartley, liked to fish for blues and striped bass.

By the time they were parallel with him Clyde had seen them, waved, reeled in his line and climbed back over the rocks to meet them. He placed his pole against a piling, and leaned against a stack of driftwood logs in the sand nearby as he lit a cigarette. Then he smiled at Missy and the leashed chimp.

"Looks like you and the monkey are getting on pretty

good, Missy," he said, pleasantly.

Missy beamed. "Oh, we are, Clyde. He's my guardian."

"Oh, he is, is he? How's that?"

" 'Cause he watches over me. Marty says that's what they do."

"Well, I guess that's what guardians do, all right," Clyde said. "The cousin over in Bayshore became one for his neighbors' kid when the parents got killed in a car crash. Situation's reversed though. The cousin does all the watching and the kid acts like a monkey." Clyde had been grinning good-naturedly, but his expression grew more serious as he kneeled down to the little girl. "Say, Missy, I know you'd rather I didn't mention this, but there may be a problem. I'm afraid I have to let the cat out. You didn't happen to see Brenda after I spoke to the two of you last night, did you?"

Missy's eyes widened in warning to Clyde, and she gave her father a quick glance.

"When was this, Clyde?" David said, frowning.

Clyde looked regretfully at Missy, and turned to answer, but Missy ran to her father before the handyman could respond.

"It was late last night, Daddy, after you went to bed. I would have asked you but I was afraid you might say no . . . and Brenda was so upset earlier I had to do it . . . I promised I would."

David put up his hand in protest. "Whoa. Slow down. What did you promise?"

"To take her to see Jerry's garden because of what happened when she got embarrassed after Jinks knocked over the vase."

"Wait a minute. You mean, Jerry invited you to bring Brenda?"

"No," Missy said sheepishly after a moment's hesitation. "He didn't know about it either."

David rubbed his forehead and sighed. "Missy, I'm not sure I follow all this, but one thing is pretty obvious. You've been sneaking around without permission, and I'm not very happy about that."

The first fat drops of rain began to fall. Missy looked down at the fresh wet marks in the sand, avoiding her father's eyes. "I knew you wouldn't be. I'm sorry," she said.

David nodded. "Well, we'll talk about it later . . . now I think you better answer Clyde's question." He looked up; the rain seemed to be only a sprinkle.

Missy looked back at Clyde. "No, Clyde, I didn't see her any more. I went right to bed just like I told you I was going to. Really, Daddy, I just showed her the garden, and then we saw Clyde, and then I came home."

Clyde stood up.

"See, Daddy," Missy continued rapidly, "Brenda wanted to go to the playground, but I wouldn't go . . . 'cause I knew you wouldn't like it, Daddy . . . so I came straight home. Right, Clyde?"

Clyde nodded and David allowed a partial smile to cross his face. "Okay, okay. . . . Don't lay it on too thick. As a matter of fact, I think you better get home right now before it really starts raining."

Missy hesitated. "Can I take Jinks?"

"Marty?" David said.

"Sure," Marty responded.

"Thanks, Marty. Come on, Jinks!" And the two of them ran through the sand toward the red wooden fence that separated the beach from the dunes. David turned back to Clyde.

"What's this all about, Clyde?"

Clyde took a final drag on his cigarette, and then shredded it between his fingers. "I'm not sure, Davy.

But from what I hear, Brenda Felding has been missing since last night and her mother is pretty frantic.''

"Well, what happened last night? How is Missy involved?''

"Oh, it's nothing,'' Clyde said, "I just caught the two of them out prowlin' around. You know, kid's stuff. It does show the influence the Felding girl's having on Missy, though.''

David raised his hand and frowned. "Okay, Clyde. I get the message.''

"All right, all right, it's none of my business. I'd appreciate it if you didn't go too hard on Missy, Davy. See, I kind of promised her I wouldn't say anything about seeing her last night, but I figured I better ask—you know, just in case. Anyway, roamin' around late like that wasn't Missy's idea, you can count on that. She's a good kid. And, this whole missing-person thing's probably nothing. You know how that Felding kid is. Not that her mother's much better. I'm surprised the woman missed her kid at all.'' Clyde shifted his attention to Marty. "You see, Mrs. Felding usually reverts to certain rabbit-type habits during the night, if you get my meaning. And you can be sure her daughter ain't what she's thinkin' about while that's going on. Typical, though, just like I was saying yesterday.''

"It sounds like Brenda's behavior would improve quite a bit if she were just given a little more attention and affection from her mother,'' Marty responded.

Clyde's head jerked in agreement. "Damned right. It's no wonder these kids are monsters. Look at the example that's set for them. I'm tellin' you, the people who come out here don't give a shit about anything except their own pleasures. And the kids aren't the only ones who are hurt. They're also destroying the island. The way I see it, the kids are their problem, but I'm not going to let them ruin all this God-given beauty. I'm just not going to let that happen. Oh, I know people aren't really listening to me. But at least I make them think about it a little. And I'll tell you something else. They better not go too far, or I'll stop talkin' and do something about it.''

"Clyde," David said, looking at the handyman doubtfully, "I appreciate how you feel, but to tell you the truth, other than talking to people, I don't think there's a whole hell of a lot you can do about it."

Clyde's eyes narrowed, and he smiled slyly. "Oh, don't kid yourself, Davy. There are ways. I could get this island to empty pretty fast if I really wanted to.''

"I'm sure Fire Island has environmental problems because of people's carelessness, just like everywhere else. But if you want an outsider's opinion, Mr. Bartley, I think it's gorgeous here. I don't see the problem as being that critical,'' Marty said politely.

"Fire Island isn't like everywhere else. It's very fragile. You're looking at the surface, but there's a lot more to it than that. I've lived here all my life, and I can see what's going on. There's a big difference between looking and seeing.''

"I'm sure you are more aware of the problems than I am," Marty agreed, "but I'm not so sure anyone knows the critical point in a situation such as this. How will you know when things have gone 'too far'?'' Marty asked.

"Signs," Clyde said. "There are always signs, Miss Goodman. Don't you worry. I can tell. Nature's not to be tampered with, if you know what I mean. You mess up the balance, and it can turn on you. Which reminds me. You were going to tell me about this talking monkey business. The way I hear it, your pet just kind of moves his hands around a little.''

"Yes," Marty said. "The movement is called sign language. Jinks doesn't really talk vocally.''

Clyde grunted. "How come you like monkeys so much, anyway?"

"Well, I don't know that I've ever thought about it, really."

"Think about it."

Marty gave David a quick glance, but answered Clyde, her voice calm and unperturbed. "Well, I suppose for the same reason you like Fire Island. I find studying and working with chimpanzees satisfying . . . just as I imagine you find working and living here satisfying."

"Why?"

"What?"

"Why study monkeys?" Clyde said. "What's the point?"

"So we can learn, Mr. Bartley," Marty said. "So that we can learn from what they do. Studying chimpanzees can help us to learn about our distant past, and it can help show why we act the way we do in almost every phase of our lives."

Clyde's eyes widened slightly. "You're talking about evolution, aren't you?"

"There's a great deal more involved than evolution, believe me."

"You think God made people out of monkeys, Miss Goodman?"

Marty smiled. "I'm afraid I don't believe in God, Mr. Bartley. I'm a scientist, and God is just a little too simplistic an answer."

Clyde frowned. "Too simple, huh? You know why the ocean has never destroyed Fire Island, Miss Goodman?"

"No."

"Poison ivy."

"Excuse me?"

"Poison ivy holds it together. Funny, isn't it. That

little weed that we can't touch has twisted its way so thoroughly into the sand that it's become the main support of Fire Island's existence. And it'll probably keep right on growing and holding the island together naturally despite the ocean's constant beating.''

"That's fascinating," Marty said. She caught David's eye, but he shrugged and leaned against the woodpile.

"What's the point, Clyde?" David said.

"The point is that it's only a theory," Clyde said. "No one really knows. A person would have to destroy all the poison ivy first to find out for sure. And then, if it were true, that would be the end of Fire Island, wouldn't it? So, far as I'm concerned, it can stay. I'd rather just let things develop naturally. You know what I mean, Miss Goodman?"

"I think so, Mr. Bartley," Marty said. There was a slight edge to her voice. "However, there is nothing unnatural about teaching Jinks to use sign language. I'm only providing a tool through which he can use the intelligence he already possesses."

Clyde lit a cigarette. "Does that monkey of yours really talk, Miss Goodman?"

"Please call me Marty. I hate being so formal."

"Only if you'll make it Clyde."

"All right . . . Clyde. Yes, in terms of understanding English and having his own language which he transmits with his hands, you could say he does talk."

"Well, Marty, to tell you the truth, I find that pretty hard to believe." Clyde looked at David. "What do you say, Davy?"

David stood up. "I know, Clyde. It is hard to believe. It still shocks me when Jinks responds to conversation as he does, but I have to say it's true. The chimpanzee actually talks with the sign language of the deaf. He seems to know what's going on most of the time."

"If it's any consolation," Marty said, "he surprises

me sometimes too, and I've been with him since he was a baby."

Clyde jerked his head. "Well, if Davy says it's true, I'll go along with it. But I'll tell you something, Marty— it ain't natural, and I don't like it. People are supposed to talk, not monkeys."

Marty's smile was slightly condescending as she answered. "Well, I wouldn't worry too much about it."

"You wouldn't, huh?" Clyde seemed irritated. "Let me tell you something. You can study all you want. I agree with you, studying the things around us leads to understanding. But it's a mistake to tamper with nature. And when you start teaching that monkey to talk with his hands, you're tampering, as far as I'm concerned. You're upsetting the balance. You say he can talk. I guess that means he can think too, doesn't it?"

"No, Clyde, it doesn't," Marty said, "not like a human being, in any case. Believe me, Jinks' learning is extremely elementary."

"How can you be so sure about what's going on in that mind that you've tampered with?"

"Clyde, give me a little credit for knowing my field. The main thing this sign-language training does is give us a clue to how we possibly first learned to communicate."

"It does, huh? Well, I think you'd be a lot better off and smarter too if you left well enough alone. If monkeys are going to talk, they'll do it on their own. I may not be a scientist, but I'm smart enough to stay out of the poison ivy."

It had begun to rain harder. Marty seemed not to notice. She stood smiling silently at Clyde for several moments. Finally, becoming uncomfortable, Clyde gathered up his fishing gear and spoke again.

"I hope you're not offended, Marty," Clyde said, "but I speak my mind as Davy here can tell you. And that's how I feel. I ain't no two-face."

"Nor am I, Clyde," Marty answered. Her voice was even, but firm. "It's my opinion that it's about time research and scientific fact put an end to ignorant, uninformed superstition once and for all. And that's what I'm dedicated to."

Clyde's face reddened. "Ignorant superstition, huh? Sorry, Marty, but you're dead wrong, and I'll tell you why. Even though I've spent a lifetime on Fire Island, the natural beauty that exists here in spite of the summer spoilers still has an effect on me. And I know that what exists here couldn't just happen. Something has to be responsible. Call it what you want. It's out there. And it watches. Like Missy says. A Guardian. And I figure this Guardian watches to make sure things take their natural course. And I'm telling you that when you start teaching that monkey to talk with his hands, you're tampering with nature just like the people who put fluoride in the water or fool around with nuclear energy . . . anyway as far as I'm concerned. You're upsetting the balance. Sure, there are things we don't know. And there are answers, too. They're out there. And when the time is right, they'll become obvious. But some answers we're not supposed to know, because we're not ready. It's not time. If we did know the truth, it'd be too much for us. We either couldn't or wouldn't know how to handle it. Look at inventions. Great discoveries are made only when the time is right, not before. Mess up the balance and you pay for it every time. Your Jinks may act human, but he's not, Marty. He's a wild animal, and a big one at that. And if the wrong thing sets him off, he'll react like a wild animal. You think about that."

"I don't have to think about it, Mr. Bartley," Marty said loudly. "If there is one fact I am sure of in my life, it is that Jinks is not a wild animal! And I find it pretty narrow-minded of you not even to give him a chance.

Why don't you spend some time with Jinks? You just might discover you're wrong."

Clyde snorted. " 'Fraid I'm not much interested in talking to monkeys. You take my advice. Stop fooling around with monkeys and get married. Have children. Teach them. It'll be a hell of a lot more normal."

"Well, if you want my opinion," David said, stepping between Marty and Clyde as Marty took a deep breath, "I think we all better get off this beach before we get soaked. I don't know if you two noticed, but it's raining like hell out here."

Clyde held his palm out and grinned. "By God, you're right, Davy." He extended his hand to Marty. "No hard feelings, Marty?"

"Not on my part, Clyde," Marty said, accepting Clyde's hand. "I think all talk is healthy—human or otherwise."

As David and Marty hurried off the beach, Marty whispered to him. "I hope I wasn't rude, David, but your friend's grass-roots philosophy got to me after a while."

"You weren't rude," David said, as they mounted the steps leading from the beach. "I'm sure Clyde knows that if he's going to dish it out, he's got to expect to get it back."

"Maybe," Marty said, stopping at the top of the platform, "but I don't think he's used to being answered back by a woman." David shrugged. He glanced back out at the ocean. Clyde had not moved. He was standing in the rain in the same place they had left him, looking in their direction.

The afternoon turned out to be wet and dark. Pam had taken Missy to her friend's birthday party and Marty had gone to her room to rest. David decided to stretch out in the hammock on the porch and read *The Times*. Soon, however, the soft rhythm of the rain made him drowsy. He put down the paper . . . then he slept. That was why he didn't hear Winnie Dukirk at first. It was only slowly that he became aware of the call, "Wubbie . . . Wubbie . . . here, Wubbie. . . ," seeping into his consciousness. And he was just starting to wake when Winnie screamed. It was a sound of terror.

David swung out of the hammock and ran to the front door. Winnie was standing on the sidewalk in front of the house. She screamed again. She was staring into the shrubbery that lined the Paddock's property. David pushed the door open and stuck his head out into the rain.

At first, he only saw shrubs. Then he saw Jinks. The chimp had crouched far into the bushes. In his left paw was a very dead Wubbles. The dog's head looked shattered; the top part of the skull seemed to be completely gone.

Jinks' eyes shifted frantically from the screaming Winnie to David and back again. Otherwise he was motionless.

"Do something, David!" Winnie cried. "Get Wubbie away from him!"

"Just wait a damn minute," David snapped back at her.

Jinks' hair was on end, and David had a feeling the chimpanzee was in no mood to hand the mangled body over to him. He stuck his head back into the house and yelled. "Marty! Get the hell out here! Jinks has got the neighbor's dog!" Then, without waiting for an answer, David opened the door and stepped out.

Jinks screamed loudly and sank further into the shrubs. And, suddenly, almost desperately, the chimp did a horrifying thing. Quickly, with his right paw, Jinks tore a wad of grass from the ground beside him. He wiped the grass around the inside of Wubbie's skull, and then stuffed the grass into his mouth. He screeched at Winnie, and at David. Then Marty stepped into the rain.

"Don't go near him, David. He'll think you're after his food." She walked past David, and her voice became strident and commanding. "Jinks! That is not yours. Give me that dog. Now!" Without hesitation Jinks jammed one last fistful of glistening grass into his mouth. Then, reluctantly, he dropped the limp body of the dog into Marty's hands, and bolted away around the house. "Jinks! Come back here! *Jinks! Come back to me right now!*"

The force behind Marty's voice must have overpowered Jinks' fear, because the chimp reappeared and slowly approached his mistress. He stopped in front of her, his head down and his shoulders slumped humbly. Marty stared down at the crushed body of Wubbles. Then she stooped, placed the dog gently on the sidewalk, took the chimpanzee's arm, and pulled him toward the house.

"You need me?" David asked.

"No," she said. "Better see what you can do for your neighbor."

"What the hell was he doing with the grass?" David said.

Marty sighed. "Well, I'll have to punish him, but the fact is he would have done it no matter how well he was trained. To a chimpanzee, it is the supreme delicacy."

"What is?"

David was listening to Marty and watching Winnie Dukirk at the same time. Winnie was kneeling over the dead dog, sobbing, stroking the wet, blood-matted fur. Leonard was coming out the Dukirks' front door and running toward his wife.

"Brains," Marty said, lowering her voice so the Dukirks could not hear her. "Jinks was eating the dog's brains."

NINE

Leonard Dukirk was not happy about his wife's dog. David volunteered to bury Wubbles, and the Dukirks accepted gratefully. While David solemnly completed the task with a shovel, Leonard comforted his mourning wife.

Then they had a ceremony in the Dukirk's backyard, in the rain. Leonard said a few words about how wonderful Wubbles had been, and then David scooped on the sand and patted it level. Winnie ran into the house crying. Leonard looked after his wife for a moment and then turned to David.

"I'm going to sue your ass off for this, Paddock," he said.

"Well, thanks a lot, Leonard," David said, jamming the shovel into the sand beside him, "considering I have done all the dirty work. I didn't kill your dog, you know."

"No, but your guest's pet did. I hold you responsible."

David nodded his head angrily. "Fine, you do that. But remember that there are no witnesses to the killing, and there is no proof. Just because Jinks was eating the dog doesn't mean the chimp killed it. Maybe he just found it lying around and was hungry."

Leonard stood silent for a moment, squinting at

107

David through his rain-smeared glasses. "I don't think much of your flippant remarks, you know," he said.

"Well then, I'll just take my shovel and go home," David said sarcastically. "Frankly, I'm not too crazy about being threatened with a lawsuit, Leonard. And to tell you the truth, I never thought much of your dog either. And if you're really planning to sue my ass off, you can also kiss it."

Leonard glared at David, and then strode past him toward the house. David looked at the grave and shook his head.

Marty and Jinks were on the porch when David got there. He placed the shovel against the screening and wiped the rain from his face as Marty crossed to meet him.

"Well?" she said, her face full of concern.

David glanced at Jinks, who was sitting in the hammock swaying comfortably back and forth. "You tell me. What's the story?"

Marty seemed surprised. "Oh, David, it wasn't Jinks, believe me. I know how it must appear, but Jinks is no killer. I swear it. He had to have found the dog dead. And, as I said, he was only following his instincts. Any chimpanzee would have acted the same way."

"Maybe so," David said, "but at the moment it's this particular chimp that may put my ass in a sling."

"The Dukirks aren't taking it well?"

"What do you think, Marty? Winnie just found the thing she loves more than anything else in the world, including Leonard, with a gigantic hole where the top of its head should have been. And it really was awful, you know."

"David, I'm just trying to talk this out so that we can understand what happened."

David nodded and sighed heavily. "I know. I'm sorry. Marty, it's not that I don't believe you, but are you sure? Did you ask Jinks? I mean if he can sign, he can tell you, can't he?''

"Yes." Marty nodded. "He can. And I did ask him."

"And?"

"He found the dog. He said he didn't kill it."

David groaned. "Big surprise. The catch is, of course, that if he's smart enough to comprehend this whole thing, he's smart enough not to admit it."

"David, he didn't do it," Marty said loudly.

David rubbed his forehead and sighed again. "All right. All right. It's just that it couldn't be worse. I mean, he was on the front sidewalk eating the dog, for Christ's sake."

"I know," Marty said. "I'm just thankful Missy wasn't here."

"Missy. . . ," David said. "What about Pam? I can't wait for her to find out about this." David glanced at Jinks again and then back at Marty. "Look, the best bet we have right now is to play this innocent . . . just as you said. Somehow the dog got hurt, and Jinks just happened to find it. And we go to the party tonight as if nothing had happened."

Marty took a quick breath. "Oh, David, that's right! The mayor—what are you going to tell him?"

David shook his head. "I don't know." At the sound of approaching voices he glanced outside. "Damn! Wishful thinking. Looks like Leonard didn't fool around."

"What do you mean?" Marty said, turning to look in the same direction. Three men were coming up the sidewalk toward the Paddock house. One of the men wore a police uniform; one was Clyde Bartley.

"The one on the left is the mayor, Ernest Nilscoff," David said quickly, lowering his voice to a whisper. "The cop is Joe Baker. Harmless, and does pretty much what Nilscoff tells him to. I don't know what the hell

Clyde is doing with them. Better let me handle this."

"Should I take Jinks to my room or anything?" Marty said.

"No, leave him here," David said, attempting a smile to ease Marty's apprehension. "We've got nothing to hide, remember? Go sit on the hammock with him. I'll try to cue you somehow if I think we're in real trouble. Nilscoff likes to sound off, and sometimes that's all it is."

Marty nodded and joined Jinks. David allowed himself a look of exasperation as he watched Marty walk to the hammock, then he transformed the expression into a light smile and pushed open the front door.

"This visit must be pretty important for you to make it in the rain," he said loudly to the approaching men. "Come on, get inside here before you're completely soaked."

The mayor came in first; Joe Baker closed the umbrella he had been holding for the two of them and followed Nilscoff onto the porch. As Clyde passed, David tried to catch the handyman's eye, but Clyde was pushing the hood of his yellow poncho off his head and missed David's eyes. David closed the door.

The mayor was the first to speak. "So this is the chimp."

"Yes," David said, moving toward the hammock. "This is Jinks. And our houseguest, Marty Goodman, of course."

"Of course," Nilscoff said, crossing to Marty. "I've been looking forward to meeting you, Miss Goodman." The mayor extended his hand. "I'm Ernest Nilscoff. The mayor of this little community."

"How do you do," Marty said, standing and shaking hands. "David mentioned that we would be seeing you later this evening."

"Well, Miss Goodman, something's come up, and we

figured that it might be better if we discussed it before this evening. This is Officer Baker, one of the men who help to keep things in order in Dune Beach. I understand you've already met Clyde." The policeman nodded politely to Marty and Clyde stood silently beside the officer, his expression grimly sober as he directed his gaze from Marty to the chimpanzee.

"What is it that couldn't wait until later?" David said, deciding the best approach in dealing with Nilscoff was to be straightforward.

The mayor pursed his lips, forcing a silence for a few seconds before he spoke. "You heard about the Felding girl being missing, didn't you?"

David was caught off guard by the remark. He frowned. "Yes, Clyde mentioned it this morning."

"Well, they found her," Nilscoff said, his expression grave. "Her body was washed up by the tide on the bay side. Near the marina."

"That's too bad," David said quietly.

"Goddam right it is!" Nilscoff said angrily. "She didn't just drown. I wish to God she had. The poor girl was mutilated. Some bastard killed her. Her throat had been savagely lacerated, and her skull was crushed." The mayor's words seemed to fall like stones. David stared at Nilscoff dumbfounded. "That's right. You heard me correctly. We've got a Goddamn child murderer among us. How's that for a mothering mess?"

David could not answer. He shot a nervous glance at Jinks and then at his houseguest. Marty avoided his eyes as she sat back down in the hammock beside the chimp.

"Now look, Paddock," the mayor continued, "this is murder. And I told Clyde, and I'm telling you. We're not pulling any punches. No one is being accused, but we're going to check out every possibility. We all know that the odds are it is a chance thing done by some freak. This town draws some weirdos in the summer, and it only takes one. On the other hand, we have to look at all the facts. That's why, even though I didn't like it, we had to talk to Clyde.''

David looked from the mayor to Clyde and back again. "Come off it. You know damn well Clyde didn't do anything like this.''

"You're not listening, Paddock. I didn't say he did. I said I had to talk to him . . . just as we have to talk to you.''

"What does *that* mean?''

Nilscoff backed up a step and nodded to the policeman. "Joe. . . .''

Officer Baker cleared his throat. "According to Clyde, Missy and Brenda Felding were together last night. Is your daughter here, Dave? It might help clear things up if we could talk to her.''

David shook his head. "No. She went with Pam to a birthday party at the Stantons. But Missy has already told me she has no idea what Brenda did after Clyde ran into the two of them. Missy came right home with Clyde and that's all she knows. Right, Clyde?''

Clyde looked at the mayor before he answered, and Nilscoff nodded. "Relax, Davy. It's not Missy they're concerned with. They just want to check with her on something I said. Don't get me wrong. I'm not placing the blame either. But, like Nils here says, facts are facts, and one thing I remember about last night is that Missy was surprised when she came onto the porch.'' Clyde jerked his head toward Jinks. "According to her, when she left to meet Brenda, the chimp was sleeping in the corner over there. Well, there was no chimp here when I brought her home.''

"And that's where we are right now," Nilscoff cut in, taking over. "We want to know where the chimpanzee was last night when Brenda Felding was being killed.

We know he was not on the porch, where he was supposed to be."

"I thought you weren't accusing anyone," Marty said.

"It's not an accusation. It's a question," Nilscoff said. "Do you have an answer to it?"

Marty stood up and the chimp clambered out of the hammock and stood beside her. David shifted uncomfortably and said nothing. His houseguest's face was expressionless.

"Yes, I do," Marty said evenly. She took Jinks' hand in her own. "Jinks was with me, in my room."

Nilscoff nodded. "Can you confirm that for me, Paddock?"

"No, he can't," Marty said before David could answer. "I got up to go to the bathroom during the night, and when I went out to check on Jinks, I found him awake. And, although I trust him completely, I thought it would be better if I took him back to my room. As far as I know, no one else in the house was awake. It sounds like that must have been while Missy was out with Brenda Felding—which would explain why Jinks was awake. Missy probably disturbed him when she left. I will ask him if you would like, or perhaps you would like to ask him yourself."

Nilscoff allowed a half-smile to cross his face as he exchanged a look with Officer Baker. "Thanks, but no thanks, Miss Goodman. I'm afraid I wouldn't be able to attach much credibility to what your pet might have to say about all this."

"Suit yourself," Marty said. "In any case, your question is answered. Jinks spent the rest of the night with me."

"As a matter of fact, I think I can confirm that," David said, stepping closer to Marty. "We all got up to see the sunrise this morning, and when I went to wake up Marty, both she and Jinks were in her room."

Nilscoff pursed his lips, nodded again, and started toward the door. "Okay. That's good enough for me. Joe, you have anything else?" Officer Baker shook his head, and Nilscoff looked at Clyde. "Looks like it's back to you, Bartley. Your wife hear you come in after you brought Missy home last night?"

Clyde's face reddened. "No. But forget it, Nilscoff. You're not pinning this on me. I spoke to Jerry just before I went inside. He'll vouch for me."

"Okay," the mayor said smiling. "let's go pay Dile a visit. Since the kids were around his property, I think we should talk to him anyway."

"How about Missy?" David said, joining the men at the door. "You still want to talk to her?"

Nilscoff shook his head. "No, I don't think so just yet. I found out what I needed to know for right now. There's no reason to upset her. In fact, Paddock, I don't think I have to tell you what the news of this will cause around here. I'd rather try to keep it quiet until we've had a chance to check a few more things out. Why don't you just not say anything? Maybe we can keep the lid on until tomorrow. My real concern is tonight. This party is sort of the social event of the summer, and if that crowd gets hold of this while they're all together, they might turn it into a panic. It's going to be bad enough if the news leaks tomorrow."

"You still want us to come, then?"

Nilscoff nodded. "Absolutely. I'm satisfied." The mayor took a couple of steps toward Marty. "Sorry I had to ask, Miss Goodman, but I'm sure you understand considering the circumstances. And I hope we'll see you tonight. I think it's crucial that people are satisfied that the chimp is harmless before they find out about this Felding business."

"Whatever David says. I'll be happy to go along,"

Marty said.

"Fine," Nilscoff said. "We'll see you tonight then, Paddock . . . and you won't say anything about this?"

"Whatever you say," David agreed, opening the door. It had stopped raining, but no one mentioned it as the three men stepped out onto the sidewalk. David closed the door and watched silently as the men started up Holly Lane. Marty helped Jinks back into the hammock and then crossed the porch and stood beside David.

"Well?" David said, continuing to stare out at the sidewalk.

"I know, David. It's a horrible situation."

"Was he with you?"

Marty frowned. "Yes, of course he was with me. What do you think? That I was lying?"

"How can you be sure he was there all night?"

"*David!*"

"All right, Marty," David said, his voice full of dejection. "Christ, what a mess!"

"You mean because of the dog?"

David turned and looked into Marty's face. "This is serious, you know, Marty. Nilscoff may have bought it today, but when he finds out about the Dukirks' dog, it's all over."

"I know," Marty said. "Why did you decide not to tell him? He's bound to find out."

"You're Goddamn right he is. I expected Leonard to come running over here at any moment. He must have been too busy comforting Winnie to notice that Nilscoff was here. But don't you worry. Leonard'll get to it. It's only a matter of time. I don't know why I didn't say anything. I just couldn't, that's all. I've got to have time to comprehend what's happening here."

"Well, I know one thing," Marty said, meeting David's stare. "Jinks is innocent. I'm just sorry that the dog thing has put you in such an awkward situation."

David took a deep breath and exhaled slowly. "Okay, so that's it. We go to the party . . . and play it casual and innocent, just as Nilscoff asked."

"You don't think your neighbor will go to the mayor before then?"

David shook his head. "No, it's pretty late in the day. I think he'll deal with Winnie now and hit Nilscoff tomorrow."

"What about Pam and Missy?"

David started to pace. "I know. That's the other problem. Well, we have to take Jinks to the party. There's no way around that. Pam will have to stay here tonight with Missy."

"David, I haven't really seen Pam all day. Considering the circumstances, don't you think she might be upset about the two of us going to the party without her?"

"Who the hell knows? If she does, that's her problem. I'm not going to leave Missy here with a baby-sitter when there's a Goddamn killer running loose. I mean, let's face it, Marty. Someone killed Brenda Felding and ripped that dog's head open, and that probably happened right outside this front door." David stopped pacing and thought for a minute. "I'm going to tell Pam about the Felding girl. Don't worry. She'll realize the situation with Jinks and all, and go along. And Clyde's only a couple of doors down the street. I'll have him keep an eye on the house while we're gone. If Pam knows that, she'll feel safe enough. Just don't mention Wubbles . . . that'll be too much for her. I'll eal with that after we get through this party tonight. Sound okay?"

"I guess so," Marty said. "I guess you feel you can trust Clyde, then."

"No question about it. Clyde may be gruff and

narrow-minded, but he's no killer. Take my word for it."

"And what about Jerry Dile, the man the mayor was going to see? He did sound pretty strange."

"Forget it," David said. "Jerry's just a fat old eccentric who likes his privacy. Do you think I'd let Missy visit him and his garden if I thought he was dangerous?"

Marty's expression clouded. "Then who is responsible for these horrible things, David? Who could it be?"

Jinks gave the hammock a shake. David looked over at him; deep, unreadable brown eyes stared back. David turned his head and looked out at the wet sidewalk. The rain had begun to fall again.

"I haven't the slightest idea," he said.

It wasn't the same with the dog. The act had been too easy . . . the victim too small. Only a slight surge of satisfaction and it was over, the body crushed and limp. There had been too little time. The delight was cut short.

It would be better to return to the cover of darkness, where there was time to dwell on the act. And a larger victim . . . a longer death . . . yes. The stupid people would recognize the power behind the act.

Wait for darkness, and then hit again, only this time, a larger victim. A victim to struggle. . . . A victim to refuse to die easily. . . .

TEN

Pam was appalled when David told her about Brenda Felding. Nonetheless she understood the need for Jinks to make an appearance at the party, and, although a little apprehensive, she agreed to stay home with Missy. By evening, the rain had stopped, and so, after a phone call to tell Clyde they were leaving, David and Marty walked Jinks to town.

As David and his guests turned the corner to the main promenade, people were everywhere, as was usual in the evening. Most were wearing bright clothing accenting deep tans. Jinks got lots of attention. He almost strutted along the sidewalk, flaunting his spotless white suit. And, although David was not in the best of moods, he couldn't help but smile when they met the mayor in front of Eaton's Stationery.

Nilscoff's white suit duplicated Jinks' exactly. After quickly informing them that no progress had been made in the Felding case, Nilscoff expressed the hope that people wouldn't think he was dressed like a monkey. Marty diplomatically assured him that people would probably think just the opposite. David loved the coincidence and said nothing.

Most Fire Island society parties were, in David's opinion, superb examples of excess. Silverman's gathering was no exception, and by the time they arrived at the sprawling beach house of the bubble-gum magnate, the party was swinging.

The main bar was in the shape of a huge bubble extending upward from a gigantic wad of pink plastic. Whatever the shape, champagne and liquor were flowing freely. The food served was abundant and superb. Lucullan *hors d'oeuvres* were circulated on trays. There was steak tartare and Beluga caviar, flown in from New York by seaplane. There was lobster and filet mignon, asparagus and endive, napoleons and apricot tarts. Excess extended to the mobs of people. The guests were all dressed extremely expensively, in scandalously revealing or gold-embroidered burnooses. And, as the champagne flowed endlessly from the gaudy bar, conversation flowed and flooded among the guests.

David was edgy. He sipped his champagne and followed along while Nilscoff led Marty and Jinks around from group to group. The mayor's spirits seemed brightened by the party, and he led Marty and Jinks like a white-suited ringmaster, introducing Jinks and urging him to perform.

The group Nilscoff entered now included Tom Urnstein, a town councilman; Marvin Rosen, the druggist; Rosen's wife; Gil and Perry, a gay couple who were florists; and a few other people David knew from Dune Beach. After introductions, Urnstein was the first to speak.

"I like your outfit, Nils. What is it? Monkey see, monkey do?"

"Pure coincidence, Tom," Nilscoff answered. "Does show good taste on the chimpanzee's part, though, don't you think?"

"It does if he's working for Good Humor. Next time you come around this way, bring your cart. I'd like a vanilla cone with sprinkles." Everyone laughed, and Gil spoke to Marty.

"What is the name of the people who worked with the chimp—Washoe was she called?—and started this sign-language thing? I remember reading something about it a few years ago."

"Gardner," Marty replied, "Allen and Beatrice Gardner. They had watched a film on a chimp that people had tried to teach to speak vocally, and they noticed that while the vocalization attempts of the chimp weren't successful, he was constantly gesturing. So, they decided to work on the theory that maybe it wasn't that chimps couldn't learn language. Perhaps it was just that they didn't have the mechanisms to vocalize. And things developed from there."

Gil handed Perry a cigarette. "That's interesting . . . and ingenious of the Gardners. How far has the research advanced? Think we're on the threshold of *Planet of the Apes?*"

"I'm afraid not. The whole thing is pretty elementary."

Marvin Rosen spoke up. "Well, I'm glad to hear that. I hated all those ape movies."

Marty laughed. "Don't worry. This is not just entertainment. It's a great deal more than that."

"How so?" said Gil.

"Well, for one thing, gesture is probably the way human beings communicated before they developed the capacity for speech. And these chimps may be able to provide us with living examples of how that worked. You see, if you look at a chart of the function centers of the brain, you find that the two largest areas are devoted to helping us move our vocal instruments and our hands. Now, without getting too technical, the right hemisphere, which controls our general movement, is slightly smaller than our left hemisphere, which gives us our ability to speak. In chimps, the size of the hemispheres is exactly the same. From our studies, we can

121

theorize that man—"

Mrs. Rosen interrupted. "You mean people, not man, don't you?"

Marty smiled. "Right. Sorry, sometimes the ingrained scientific language sneaks by my female sensitivity . . . anyway, ancient people such as the ones Leakey was discovering in Africa probably had duplicate hemispheres, just like the other primates of their day. In fact, Australopithecus, an erect, tool-using ancestor of ours who existed about three-quarters of a million years ago, had a brain exactly like that of a chimpanzee. You see, both hemispheres of the brain are equal in intelligence, but we feel that through evolution, *homo sapiens'* left hemisphere probably evolved and tipped the balance slightly in favor of speech . . . and, consequently, suppressed our need to communicate by gesture. It probably also helped to stabilize our more violent tendencies too, by the way, since the larger left hemisphere in humans is our rational side and tends to dominate the more primitively emotional right hemisphere."

"Tom," Nilscoff said to Urnstein. "I've noticed at town meetings that you always talk with your hands. Think it means you're a throwback?"

"No, Nils," Urnstein replied, "it just means I'm more balanced than you are. Right, Miss Goodman?"

"Please . . . my name is Marty. Neither one, really. Remember, my explanations are very simplistic."

"Well, please keep them that way," Nilscoff said. "Tom has trouble understanding anything that isn't simplistic." Urnstein started to reply, but stopped politely as Marty continued.

"The one thing we have learned from all this though is that chimpanzees are far closer to us than we imagined. Researchers at the Primate Center had hoped that when Washoe had her baby, Sequoyah, the mother would teach her infant the sign language. Unfortunately, Sequoyah developed a respiratory infection at eight weeks of age, and the researchers were unable to save her. However, the part I think you'll find interesting is that when the research scientist approached Washoe with a hypodermic so that they could tranquilize her in order to remove the baby for medical treatment, Washoe began weeping and signing, 'my baby . . . my baby.' Obviously, she knew they were bringing the needle so that the baby could be taken. And, when she was told her baby had died, Washoe stopped signing completely, and refused to eat or respond in any way to those around her. Her mourning process duplicated that of a human.''

"How sad," said Mrs. Rosen.

"Certainly leads to fascinating speculation about what's going through a chimp's mind, doesn't it?" said her husband. He smiled at Jinks. "Wonder what our friend Jinks here really thinks of us?"

"Better not ask," Urnstein said. "I don't think I could take being put down by a chimp. These Gardners that came up with this. Are they any relation to Herb Gardner, Marty?"

"Yes," Marty said. "Herb is Allen's brother."

"Who's Herb Gardner?" Mrs. Rosen asked.

"Playwright," said Rosen, standing and taking a drink from a passing waiter's tray. ". . . Wrote *A Thousand Clowns.*"

"Talented family," said Perry. "How about Jane Goodall? Ever meet her, Marty?"

"No, I've always wanted to, but she wasn't there when I did field work at the Gombe Chimpanzee Reserve in Africa."

Sid Turner, the hardware-store proprietor, had been standing behind the sofa listening, and he leaned forward. "How long were you in Africa?"

"Not nearly long enough," Marty said. She shifted her gaze and met David's eyes for a moment, and then looked quickly away. "I had to leave before my field work was completed."

"Magnificent though, isn't it?" Turner said. "My wife and I went on a safari to Kenya last year. Of course, we didn't exactly rough it. Stayed in those lodges and went out in those minibuses to view the game. We thoroughly enjoyed ourselves, though."

"Yes, we enjoyed it when we went too," Mrs. Rosen said as Marvin sat down beside her. "The animals were just gorgeous."

"Yes, they are," Marty said, smiling cordially. "I think my favorite is a tiny miniature antelope called the dic-dic."

"Well, I've never been to Africa," Mrs. Rosen said, looking very daring, "but I agree with you. The dic-dic is my favorite too."

"Mine too," said Perry, putting his arm around Gil.

Everyone laughed. Nilscoff pushed Jinks, who had been standing quietly beside Marty, forward a little. Jinks looked back at Nilscoff curiously.

"Come on, Marty," said the mayor, "show us a little of what Jinks can do."

Marty seemed to be holding her own, so David decided he could circulate around the party for a while. Actually, the evening was going well. Many of the people at the party had seen Jinks on the beach earlier and continued to be captivated. Of course, they didn't know about Brenda Felding yet. Or the Dukirks' dog. David frowned. Deep down, he was desperately hoping that by the next day the police would have somehow solved everything. And, he also knew that the odds on that were not very good. He resolutely pushed the implications of his thoughts out of his mind. And whiled away the time stuffing his face and watching Marty and Jinks out of the corner of his eye.

At around eleven-thirty, he heard his name being called. When he turned, David found himself facing Frederick Butz. Butz, a Wall Street lawyer, had been David's tennis partner in the doubles matches at Dune Beach the previous summer. Unfortunately, Butz was the fierce competitive type who, in David's opinion, took all the fun out of tennis, so he hadn't signed up again. He was giving Butz a lame excuse as to why he wasn't playing this summer when Marty walked up beside them. David introduced her, and offered her his drink, which she gratefully accepted.

"So, how's it going?" David said, his voice a little anxious.

"Fine," Marty said, meeting his eyes. "I decided to leave Jinks with your mayor for a while, though. I wanted a breather."

"How do you like Fire Island?" Butz said. "Are you enjoying it?"

"Very much," said Marty. "I needed a rest badly. In fact, I haven't mentioned this to David, but I was thinking this afternoon how nice it would be to have a house here. Not that I would be able to use it very often, but it would be nice to know it was there. And I don't think I could lose as an investment. Is it hard to find tenants?"

"Are you kidding?" Butz said, "people come out here to rent for the summer while the snow's still on the ground. And you pull top dollar. I'd say it's wise thinking on your part. If there were ever a place to make an investment, this is it."

"It's an expensive place, I can tell you that," David said.

Butz took a pull on his scotch. "But look at the return. If you've got the money up front, you can't go wrong." Butz's face took on the expression David used to see just before he aced a serve on the court. "Listen, I have a house, if you're really interested, Marty."

"I didn't know you had two places, Fred," David said.

"Well, I didn't, but Mrs. Thayer—she was my God-mother—died this spring, and I was able to buy her place pretty cheaply." He turned to Marty. "Now I've got a house I don't need. It's listed with Charlie Bende. If you're interested, you could go take a look."

"How much is it?" Marty said.

"Well, why don't you go with Dave and look at it, and then, if you're interested, we'll talk."

Marty looked at David. "What do you think?"

David shrugged. "It's up to you."

"Good," Butz said. "Come anytime. Dave, you know where I live; I have the key. I'll have my daughter, Tammy, take you over."

"Thanks. Marty and I will—" Suddenly there was a scream from the crowd surrounding Nilscoff and Jinks. David dove into the ring of people, and caught a glimpse of dark, wet, splotches on Nilscoff's shirt. Frantic, David clawed his way to the center. Then he stopped short. People were laughing. Nilscoff was wiping chocolate mousse off the front of his white suit with a cloth napkin, and Jinks was looking calmly at the mayor and gesturing in large, clear signs.

"Oh, no," said Marty, coming up beside David, "Jinks didn't—"

"No, no. Don't worry, Marty," said Nilscoff. "My fault, really." He pointed to Mrs. Turner, who was bringing him another napkin. "I didn't see Blanche here. I was pointing out something for Jinks to name, and knocked the dish out of her hand. What the hell is he saying, anyway?"

Marty looked at Jinks who was signing dramatically. "It's nothing. Just Jinks' attempt at humor."

Nilscoff stopped wiping for a second. "Humor, huh? Well, what's his joke? Tell me what he said."

126

"He said you were a clumsy dirty."

"Well, he's right. I'm dirty all right. Some joke this cleaning bill's going to be."

"No, you don't understand the joke," Marty said, smiling. "He said you are a clumsy dirty . . . not that you are dirty. It's Jinks' only signing vulgarity. You see, dirty is his word for excrement."

Nilscoff stared at Marty in disbelief. "You mean that chimpanzee is calling me a clumsy shit?"

Marty nodded. "I'm afraid so."

Nilscoff turned and stared at Jinks for a moment, and then burst ito laughter. "I'll be damned!" he roared. "Dune Beach has got itself a swearing chimpanzee."

ELEVEN

David, Marty and Jinks arrived home late. David was well aware that his being tired was only one of the reasons why he did not say much as he and Marty bedded Jinks down on the porch.

"I thought it went pretty well, tonight," Marty said as she finished preparing the makeshift nest. "Didn't you, David?"

David hooked the front door, locking it shut. "Yeah. Now if tomorrow were over, we'd be all set."

Jinks settled into his nest, and Marty stood up. "Have you decided what you're going to do yet?"

"Yes," David said. "Nothing. Let's wait until Leonard makes the first move. Then we'll deal with it."

"Okay, David. I'll go along with whatever you say. I'm glad tonight went well. I think it will put Jinks in a much better position. The mayor really liked him. I could tell."

"Maybe. . . . We'll find out for sure soon enough."

"Things will look better after a night's sleep," Marty said, bringing her hand to her mouth to cover a yawn. "See you in the morning."

"Marty?" David's voice stopped Marty in the middle of the living-room doorway; she turned slowly to face him. "Are you really interested in buying a house here?"

"I . . . I had thought about it. I guess you can't help but think about how nice it would be to own a house at a place like this. I don't know how serious I am. I just thought it might be fun to look at your friend's house. What are you saying? Would it bother you?"

Absentmindedly, David picked at the wood on the doorframe with his fingernail. "I don't know how I feel about it," he said, his voice soft and cautious. "I do know there's a difference between you coming to visit and your owning a house here. And I also know, in spite of the trouble today, I . . . enjoyed being with you. That doesn't answer your question, though, does it?"

Marty looked at David for a moment and then touched his arm lightly. "I would say whether I buy a house or not is the least of our problems, so let's not worry about it."

David half smiled. "All right. . . . Good night."

"Good night, David." Marty turned and walked down the hall toward her room as David switched off the lights, and opened the door to the master bedroom.

Pam was still awake, in bed, reading a book.

"No trouble," David said, "right?"

Pam shook her head. "No, but I was a little nervous about going to sleep. Please don't close the door. It's stuffy in here tonight, and I want some air. Did you relock the front door?"

David nodded and pushed the door back open. His wife said nothing further, and seemed absorbed in what she was reading. He undressed in silence. Then, feeling the need to ease the tenseness out of his body before going to sleep, David went into the adjoining bathroom and took a shower. When he came back, drying himself with a towel, the book was in Pam's lap on the sheet, and she stared at him. David rubbed his wet hair vigorously and spoke through the towel.

"So, how's the book?"

"Okay, I guess. You know, the usual. Did Nils have any new information?"

David shook his head. "No, and the news will be out tomorrow. So get ready. I think Missy will be able to deal with it if we just explain honestly what happened to Brenda. I also think we better keep pretty close tabs on her for a few days."

"You mean you don't think it was just a random thing as Nils suggested?"

David threw the towel on the bureau, avoiding his wife's eyes. "I don't know. It won't hurt anything to be careful. The point is it happened, and it's not solved."

Pam sat up slightly. "Do you think we should leave?"

"Let's talk about it when we see what happens tomorrow."

"All right," Pam said, settling back on the pillow. "How did things go with Jinks? Was it a good party?"

"No problem," David said, talking to his wife through the bureau mirror as he brushed his hair into place. "Jinks was fine. They loved him. It was a good move to take him. You didn't miss much, though."

"Did Marty enjoy herself?"

David shrugged. "I guess . . . although I doubt if that crowd is her idea of a good time."

"Well, I'm sure she wasn't bored," Pam said, placing her book on the nightstand next to the bed. "After all, she was with you."

David put down the hair brush and picked up the towel. Then turned toward the bed. "What's that supposed to mean?"

Pam smirked. "Well, it looks to me like you two are getting along pretty well. And, from the time, I'd say you must have enjoyed yourselves. Should I be suspicious about why you need a shower before you get into bed with me?"

David threw the towel into the bathroom and went to the bed. "What did you say?"

"Come off it, David. I saw you rolling around on the beach with Marty last night."

"Pam, we went for a swim. Big deal. Why didn't you say something when we came in last night if it bothered you?" David's wife looked at him and said nothing. "Is that why you've been avoiding the two of us all day?"

Pam stared at him silently.

David sat down on the edge of the bed. He tried to speak quietly. "Pam, she was feeling tired from her lecture tour and we went for a swim, all right? That's it. A swim. Period. All right?"

"All right, David."

"Don't just say 'all right' if you don't believe me."

"Okay, I believe you. I'm sorry I said anything. Let's drop it."

David crawled into bed and turned his back to his wife. "Listen, Pam, when the time comes for you to start worrying, I'll let you know . . . don't worry. I'm not going to lie to you."

"Oh, David, try to see my side of it. You know how I felt about this whole thing. Then I come home at night and find you bare naked with her on the beach. I mean, let's face it! How long has it been since you took me for a night swim in the ocean?"

"A long time. And that's because I hate it. You know I hate swimming in the ocean at night. It's too Goddamn cold. I was just trying to be nice because nature girl Marty wanted to go for a swim."

"Okay, I'm sorry I said anything," Pam said, snuggling next to David. "I guess I'm just too sensitive."

As Pam moved against him, a familiar warmth began to ease its way into David's body. He slowly turned over on his back and yawned. "Let's forget it . . . I'm just tired, that's all."

Pam smiled, and her hand moved under the sheet and across David's thigh. "How tired?"

"Why?" David said, smiling lazily, "You want to go for a swim?"

"No, but I'll settle for something else . . . if you're not too tired."

David rolled toward Pam and slowly slipped the sheet off of her deeply tanned body. "I'm never that tired," he said.

Over the years, David had come to realize that there were a couple of things that held him and his wife together. Missy was one of them. The other had been there from the beginning, since he had first spent the night with Pam in spite of Marty. Even now, that original sensuality remained and drew on them like a magnet.

David didn't switch out the light beside the bed. They never did. Nor did he close the door, although the thought did cross his mind. However, as Pam's lips moved down his body to join her hand, the growing feelings of pleasure crowded other considerations out of David's mind, until his only desire was to give himself to the pleasure as it spread and overwhelmed him.

And that was one reason why, a little later, David did not notice the shadow that moved out of the darkness of the hallway and into the frame of the bedroom door. The other reason was that David was no longer facing the doorway. Rather, he was sitting with his back to the hall and Pam's legs were wrapped around his waist as she rode with their passion, her body straining against his, her voice moaning and murmuring softly into his neck.

Pam's ragged intake of breath suddenly stopped in a sharp gasp. David's eyes opened. Then she gave a kind of high pitched, cut-off cry, and fell back from him against the headboard, her eyes wide and staring past David. He turned his head and looked over his shoulder.

Jinks was standing just inside the doorway. He was standing tall, stretched to his full height; his eyes bulged and the hair was standing on end all over his body. And, at the bottom of his torso, his member extended from his body in a swollen erection.

"Get rid of it!" Pam cried, pulling the sheet up over her body and pushing at David. "Oh my God, get that disgusting animal out of here."

David, stumbling out of bed, wasn't sure how the chimpanzee would act, so he tried to imitate Marty's style as he moved cautiously toward him.

"Back to the porch, Jinks," David said, stopping in front of but not too close to the chimp. "You know you're not supposed to be here. Now, go back where you belong."

The chimp did not move. David hesitated, not sure what to do next. Then Marty was at the doorway, and with her appearance, Jinks immediately became compliant. Unfortunately, the noise had also awakened Missy, and she was right behind Marty. It suddenly came to David that he was standing in the middle of the room naked.

"Jinks, what do you think you're doing?" Marty shouted, grabbing the chimp's arm as David hurried over to his pants. "Get out of this room this instant."

With his mistress present, Jinks' excitement seemed to vanish, and he obediently turned and left the room. At the same time, David tangled his feet in his cut-offs and fell. Missy burst into laughter, and David exploded.

"Missy, get the hell back to bed! Right now," David yelled, getting to his feet and yanking on his pants. Missy immediately disappeared down the hall, and David zipped up and followed Marty and Jinks out to the living room.

"I'm sorry, David," Marty said.

"Just take the ape to your room and keep him there, all right?" David said, a little too loudly.

Marty nodded and without a word led Jinks toward the porch. David stared after them for a moment, and then turned back toward his bedroom. The door closed. He tried it; it was also locked, from the inside.

"Pam, it's me," David said, turning the doorknob roughly, "open the door!" No answer came from within, and David knocked angrily. "Pam, everything's taken care of. Now open up, will you?" David waited several seconds more. Finally, when his wife still did not respond, he kicked the door violently.

"Fine," he said, moving to the front porch, "*don't* open the Goddamn door." On the porch, David fell into the hammock, and then, as an afterthought, gave one final yell into the other room. "I hope you suffocate!"

TWELVE

Dawn was just breaking as Evan Robbins walked down to his stables, but even so he could see that the door was ajar. Frowning, Evan slowly opened the door and took a few steps inside. Then he stopped, his eyes panning the interior of the stable. It appeared empty.

"Butler?" Evan called softly. "You all right, boy?" Only silence answered Evan, and apprehensively, he began moving cautiously through the stable.

Slowly, Evan inched forward until he reached Butler's stall. He looked over the edge of the stall door. The horse's hind quarters were lying on the floor. Something was very wrong. Hurriedly, he moved inside. It was only as he looked down and saw that he was standing in a pool of blood, that the horse's whole body came into view.

There before him, covered with blood, was Butler, his eyes clouded and open in the shattered skull. The horse's trachea protruded from a huge gouge in its neck. The prongs of a pitchfork were buried deep into the side of the horse's face, and a long, broken, splintered, bloody portion of the fork's wooden handle extended upward from the prongs.

Evan began to shake uncontrollably. He grabbed the broken pitchfork handle and pulled until the prongs gave and slid from the horse's face. He jammed the pitchfork into a supporting beam and screamed.

The morning turned out to be wet and dark, and Marty awoke with a start, having slept later than usual. Jinks was sitting next to her bed waiting patiently for her to get up. The sight of the chimp reminded Marty of the late night scene that had taken place with Pam and David, and she groaned briefly as she rolled into a sitting position.

Jinks pulled excitedly at her hand, signing for her to get out of bed. Marty shook her head helplessly and smiled. The dread of having to face Pam and David probably had just as much to do with her sleeping late as the overcast day did. However, knowing that she was only postponing the inevitable, Marty allowed Jinks to pull her to her feet. Slowly she began to dress. Although she was prepared for the worst, when Marty finally led Jinks into the living room, the only person she encountered was Missy. The master bedroom door was closed, Pam presumably still asleep inside, and David was snoring on the front porch, stretched out on his back in the hammock.

Not only was Missy up, but as they prepared a breakfast of juice, cereal, and toast, she announced that she had a surprise for Marty and Jinks. Apparently, Missy had arranged things the previous day. As soon as they finished eating, she was going to take them to Jerry Dile's for a tour of the garden. Marty was not only pleased, but relieved, deciding that it was probably better if she and Jinks were out of the house when Pam and David got up. So, after a hurried breakfast, the three of them crept slowly past David and out of the front door.

As they came through the open gate, Jerry Dile was there waiting for them. He shifted shyly under Marty's gaze, his heavy, nervous breathing escaping in short, wheezing gasps from his tiny mouth between two, round, puffy-fat cheeks. He was monumentally obese. Short stubby fingers brought a round, battery-operated amplifier to his neck, and Jerry's voice greeted them as Missy led Jinks and Marty into the garden.

"Watch the chimp, Missy," Jerry's voice cracked. "Don't let him hurt any of the plants."

"Don't worry, Jerry," Missy answered, taking Jinks' hand, "he'll be careful. He promised. Didn't you, Jinks?"

Jinks nodded and looked with eager curiosity around him. Then he signed to Jerry.

"Is he talking now, Missy?" Jerry asked, his small sunken eyes gleaming as he stared at Jinks. "Is he? Is that you meant?"

"Yes. See, it's sign language, Jerry."

"Well, what's he saying?"

Missy stared at Jinks a moment and shook her head. "I don't know. What do those signs mean, Marty?"

Marty smiled. "He wants to know if this is Africa. I guess some of your beautiful flowers and foliage remind him of the chimpanzee reserve in Tanzania."

Jerry's eyes widened slightly. "Africa? He said Africa . . . with his hands that way?"

"Well, actually," Marty said, repeating the sign, "it's an amended version of the word 'home' that Jinks uses to say Africa. You see, I've told him that Africa is his original home."

"Smart chimp. Africa, huh?" Jerry's voice crackled with momentary distortion through the amplifier, and then he continued. "Yes, there's a little of Africa here . . . a little of Africa. This way. We'll start with the orchids since the chimp likes the tropics. This way . . . careful of the plants."

In the corner of the garden, near a wall of bamboo plants, was a stunning array of orchids. Jerry Dile pointed toward various specimens as he announced their names and watched to see Marty's reaction. Not that Marty had to fake her reaction for Jerry's benefit. She could not remember ever seeing floral beauty in such a concentrated form. When she said as much, Jerry merely smiled and pointed out the elaborate sprinkler system and the portable solar panels that were mounted near small reflectors so that he could control the water and heat.

As Jerry continued his tour, the foliage and vegetation seemed perfect everywhere Marty looked. Occasionally, Marty was even able to supply the name of a particular specimen before Jerry announced it, and this seemed to please her host tremendously. In fact, by the time they had worked their way through the greenhouse and back to the gate, Jerry seemed totally at ease and was talking rapidly, in spite of the frequent shrill squeals that his amplifier transmitted.

"You were right, Missy," Jerry said, as they stopped near the gate, "your friend Marty is nice. Very nice, very nice. Jinks, too. Oh, yes, Jinks, too."

Marty smiled politely. "We're honored that you allowed us to see what you have here. I don't think I've ever seen anything more beautiful. Thank you very much."

Jerry smiled, looking very pleased, as he watched Jinks make several signs in his direction. "You can thank Missy . . . she talked me into it. What's your Jinks saying now?" As Jerry spoke, Jinks stepped toward him and signed again, ending the signs with his hand on his neck.

"Well. . . ," Marty said, her expression clouding slightly, "I'm afraid Jinks has an insatiable curiosity as well as a child's lack of discretion. He's asking about the amplifier you use for speaking. I apologize if his questions make you feel uncomfortable."

Jerry's eyes widened and his breathing became slightly labored, but he shook his head. "No, it's fair . . . I asked how *he* talked." Jerry lowered the small, round metal object so that Jinks could look at it, and then he brought it back to his neck again. "I use this to talk, Jinks. Sometimes it doesn't work too well, though . . . maybe I'd be better off using your method." Jerry looked at Marty. "People'd still stare, though, wouldn't they? They'd still stare." Marty said nothing; the corner of Jerry's tiny mouth turned up slightly as he attempted a smile. "Missy, take Jinks and get him some bananas. You know where they are . . . careful of the plants though."

"Okay," Missy said, and as she led Jinks away, Jerry spoke to Marty again. This time the high pitch was gone, and a raspy monotone came through the amplifier.

"Thank you for your concern. . . . You have a concern, a concern for others."

Marty shook her head. "Don't give me too much credit, Mr. Dile. I once had surgery which demanded extensive therapy before I could function normally again. I can, to a certain extent, appreciate how you must feel."

"Not your throat?" Jerry said, frowning until his tiny eyes almost disappeared under the thick flesh above them.

"No, my surgery was in the brain. A stupid accident buried metal in my skull, disturbing my nervous system to the point where my body convulsed uncontrollably. Unfortunately, although the surgery stopped the convulsions, I could not coordinate the simplest actions for a long time after that. You know, things like missing my mouth when I ate and sticking my fork in my forehead. Stunts like that draw quite a bit of attention. Believe me, I know what it is to be stared at."

Jerry's frown remained. "Why tell me all this?"

"Because you were kind enough to open your garden to me," Marty said pleasantly, "and sometimes when you've suffered from an impairment that draws unwanted attention, it's nice to know you're not alone. That there are others who know how you feel."

"But you've overcome it."

Marty frowned. "Well, for appearance's sake, perhaps. But the scars are there."

Jerry's body shook slightly, and his amplifier squealed. "I have not . . . not adjusted," he said, his thick fingers pulling again and again at the folds of skin at his throat. "And you don't know how I feel. . . . This was no accident. It was greed. I . . . I have no voice because my trusted business partner sliced my throat open and left me for dead . . . to rot on the floor of one of our mines. But I crawled out. I would not die like that . . . like a rat in a hole. It was only later that I found I couldn't stand to live like this either. Stared at, everyone looking at me . . . you know the way, an abnormal. So I sold everything and came . . . finally . . . to my garden. I just won't be stared at . . . that way."

"What happened to the man who caused your suffering?"

Jerry's voice became a harsh whisper that hissed through the amplifier. "He found out that I was not dead, after all," he said. His small mouth twitched, and his beady sunken eyes held Marty's gaze. "You are very nice, Marty. You come visit again. I'd like it. . . . You won't be afraid to come again will you?"

Marty frowned. "Afraid? Why should I be afraid?"

"Wait 'til they all talk to you. They will. You'll hear. They think I'm a criminal. They came to me about the girl . . . the one who was killed." Jerry's voice rose in pitch as he became more agitated. "Do you think I'm a criminal? Do you?''

Marty glanced quickly in the direction of Missy and
Jinks who were coming back toward them carrying
several bananas, and then shifted her gaze to Jerry.

"I don't think anyone who could be so nice to Missy,
and who has the sensitivity to create this garden, could
be destructive or malicious," she said.

"You should live here, Marty," Jerry said, smiling
broadly for the first time. "You'd like it. . . . And you
could visit the plants any time. They'd like it. I know
it.''

"As a matter of act, Fred Butz, a friend of David's,
has a house he wants me to look at, but I'm not sure I'm
interested.''

"Look at it . . . look at it," Jerry said, "and give
him a check as a binder. They go fast here. You have
David take you to look at it . . . and give him a check or
you'll lose it.''

"We'll see," Marty said. "Anyway, thank you for a
thrilling tour and a lovely visit.''

"We got some, Jerry," Missy said, stopping in front
of them and proudly holding up the bananas. "Jinks ate
some there, and these are for later. Okay?''

"Fine . . . that's fine," Jerry said, his voice high and
squeaking again. He opened the front gate. "You just
bring him back when he wants more. And your friend
Marty, too, of course. Oh yes, bring Marty, too.''

"Thanks, Jerry," Missy said. She led Marty and
Jinks through the opening in the tall shrubbery, and the
gate closed behind them.

"Any time," Jerry's voice squeaked behind them,
". . . any time.''

David did not wake until late morning. When he
pulled himself out of the hammock, he discovered that
Pam was the only other person in the house. She was in

the living room reading, and she refused to talk to him, except to tell him that Marty had left a note in the kitchen. David went in, found it, and fixed himself something to eat. Then, after cleaning up the dishes, he leaned on the kitchen doorframe, sipping coffee and staring into the living room at his wife.

"He probably just heard us, and got curious, you know. . . . That's all," David said. Pam said nothing. David tried to keep his voice light. "Come on, Pam, it's not such a big deal, is it?"

The last brought Pam's attention from the book in front of her. "You had better not be serious, David."

David shrugged and moved into the living room. "All right. What do you want to do? Ask them to leave?"

Pam's look was hard and expressionless. "Whatever you like, David."

"Fine," David said, holding her stare. "Thank you. That's very helpful."

"What do you want me to say?"

"I think we could discuss it instead of walking around glaring at each other. What the hell does *that* prove?"

Pam put the book down and folded her arms. "All right. Go ahead. Discuss."

David hesitated, not sure of what to say, and then sighed. "Forget it. . . . Just go back to your book."

"No. You want to talk; let's talk. First of all, I think Marty's chimpanzee is a disgusting, filthy animal and I can't stand having it in the house. I think last night's incident was inexcusable, but I think you're trying to play it and everything else down because of Marty. I told you I thought having her here was a mistake, David, but I thought I was just afraid of facing her. I was wrong. That was only part of it. I know now that what I was really afraid of was what would happen between the two of you. And don't lie to me. I can see it. Or maybe you haven't even admitted it to yourself.

But, believe me, that chimpanzee could do anything short of attacking our daughter and you'd ignore it if it meant Marty would stay a little longer. And if you'll look at yourself honestly, I think you'll agree with me."

"Well, you're wrong, sweetheart," David answered loudly. "I think you're full of shit up to your earlobes."

"Your anger just proves my point," Pam said evenly. "I have no intention of continuing this when you answer me like that."

"Come on, Pam! What do you think I am? Some kind of horny kid? Of course, I still have feelings for Marty, and being around her makes me confront them. But I'm attempting to deal with them. That was the whole point of all this. To get things resolved. Isn't it better that I attempt to do so?" David's wife had picked up her book and was reading it studiously. "Pam?"

"You just stated how you feel about my opinions," Pam said without looking up.

David shook his head, running his hand through his hair. "All right, you're not full of shit. I apologize for my crass, unfeeling remark. Now. Isn't it better that I attempt to work out these feelings . . . for that matter, isn't it better if we both do?"

"I told you," Pam said, looking up blandly, "you may do whatever you like. Just make sure that ape doesn't ever come near me while you and Marty work things out."

Missy came bursting through the front door.

"Daddy," she said, running into the room, "I took Marty and Jinks to see Jerry, and look, he gave me all these bananas." Missy held up the bundles of bananas for David and Pam to see as Marty and Jinks followed her into the room. The chimpanzee was eating a banana.

David forced a smile at Marty. "So, you met the mysterious Jerry Dile, huh?"

"Yes," Marty said, "and he was nice. And the plants—it's incredible! They're gorgeous. I don't see how he gets the rare ones to grow here."

"I know," David said, "it's unbelievable. Magic green fingers, I guess. Anyway, consider yourself honored. There aren't that many people who have seen those plants."

"So I understand," Marty said. "I'm very grateful to Missy. It was a wonderful treat."

Missy smiled and handed Jinks another banana. "Jerry liked Marty, Daddy. She knew the names of the plants and everything. He said she could come back whenever she wanted to. And I can bring Jinks again, too, if I want."

"That's very nice of him," David said, looking towards Pam. She had gone back to her reading. "It isn't raining out, is it?"

"Not yet," Marty said. "Why?"

"Well, since it's too cloudy for the beach, I thought we might go look at the Butz house if you'd like."

Marty's face brightened. "It won't hurt to look, will it?"

Pam looked up from her book. "What about the Butz house?"

"Marty is considering buying a house here as an investment. Pretty good idea, don't you think?" David said, giving his wife a smile.

Missy came running from the kitchen where she had deposited the bananas. "Really, Daddy, that would be great. Then Jinks and I could play all the time. Can we go look at it? I bet Jinks would like to see it."

"No, better not," David said. "Why don't you stay here with Jinks and work on your sign language. Then when Marty and I get back, you can show us what you've learned."

"Okay," Missy said.

"You'll be here for a while, won't you, Pam?" David said innocently, walking over to the sofa. Pam stood up and nodded tight-lipped. "Good. . . . Then you can keep an eye on Missy—and Jinks, of course—until we get back. I don't think we'll be long."

"Unless you'd like to join us," Marty said. "You're welcome to come along. I'd like that. We haven't really seen that much of each other since I've been here, Pam."

Pam walked over to Marty. Her expression was cold. "No thanks. You and David go ahead. I want to finish this book."

"Pam," Marty said, touching the woman who had once been her roommate lightly on the arm. "I'm really sorry about Jinks scaring you last night. I know I can't undo it, but I promise you it wasn't malicious. He just has an unending curiosity. It won't happen again."

"It's not important, Marty," Pam said. ". . . Go look at the house, all right? I'd rather just sit on the front porch and read. Really."

"All right," Marty said as Pam walked past her to the porch. "Missy, why don't you play cards while we're gone? Jinks loves it."

"Good idea," Missy said. She seemed relieved to have an activity to take her away from the tension among the adults in the room, and ran to get the cards from the desk. And, as David and Marty left, Missy and the chimp were settling down in front of the fireplace. "Let's try slapjack," Missy was saying.

"Pam doesn't look too happy," Marty said as they turned into Holly Lane. "Last night really put the icing on the situation, didn't it?"

David shrugged. "What are you going to do? I know it was just one of those things. In fact, I'm sorry I wasn't a little more understanding last night. I could have handled things a little better."

"Don't be ridiculous. You had every right to be angry. But, actually, his excitement was just a normal reaction. After all, he is an adolescent going into puberty . . . and I take it the two of you weren't actually sleeping. The scene probably stimulated him."

"Well, no, we weren't sleeping," David said awkwardly. "Pam was all upset when I came in. You know, about us, and about all the time we've been spending together . . . and I—"

"David," Marty said quickly, "you don't have to explain. I'm just saying that what Jinks saw probably stimulated him. We've found the same thing happens when we show these signing chimps pictures of naked humans in seductive poses."

David looked at her doubtfully and grinned. "Come on."

"No, I'm serious. Anyway, I just wish to God it hadn't happened. It doesn't look like Pam and I are speeding toward a reconciliation, does it?"

"Well, I'm not going to get to bent up about it," David said. "She's not going out of her way to help the situation."

They were passing Jerry Dile's gate.

"I have to admit," Marty said, "I was glad Missy got me out of the house this morning. I had a feeling Pam's mood wouldn't be the best. And the garden really was incredible. Your Mr. Dile is quite a character . . . he told me the story of the voice box."

"You're kidding!" David said admiringly. "How the hell did you get that out of him?"

Marty smiled. "It's my honest face. People open up to me. Anyway, you were wrong. It's not cancer. His business partner in Africa tried to kill him. Cut his throat."

David whistled. "No shit! You mean the rumors are true?"

"I don't know about that. He didn't go into much detail. But I sensed that he got revenge . . . which would explain why he left Africa. And maybe why he has never gone back."

"You don't think he's dangerous, do you? I can't believe it. I mean he seems like just a nice shy fat old guy who's a little eccentric."

Marty nodded. "I think you're right. Whatever happened in the past has nothing to do with what he is now. He seemed like a very shy and sensitive person. My guess would be that beneath Jerry Dile's eccentricity there's a warm and generous human being."

Butz, as he had promised, had his twelve-year-old daughter, Tammy, show them the house. It was located on the bay side and was a small one-story cottage. But, though tiny, it had been modernized, re-jacked on a new foundation of locust posts within the last five years, and was virtually maintenance free. It also had a warm, bright atmosphere. Marty was bubbling with excitement when Charlie Bende appeared at the cottage front door and called David outside.

"Come on in, Charlie," David said, coming out onto the steps, "I think Marty's interested."

"No thanks, David. Can't stay. Fred'll handle it. I just came by to tell you Nils wants to see you right away."

"Yeah, I know," David said irritably, "it's about Dukirk's dog. You tell the mayor I'll see him as soon as I have time."

"I think you better make it now, David," Charlie Bende said calmly. "Evan Robbins' horse was killed last night."

David was stunned. "You're kidding."

Charlie shook his head. " 'Fraid not, Dave. Situation's pretty serious. Nils is waiting for you in his office."

David hesitated. Marty came out the front door to join them.

"David, I love it!" Marty said, nodding hello to Charlie Bende. "Really. I know we need to talk a little more about it . . . but I would really like to consider it."

"Charlie Bende . . ." David said, gesturing to his houseguest, ". . . Marty Goodman."

"Pleased to meet you," Charlie said, shaking Marty's hand. "I'm afraid I need David's help for a few minutes, but I just talked to Fred, and I'm sure he'll be happy to discuss the house with you."

"Wonderful," Marty said, losing a little of her enthusiasm. "Is something wrong, David?"

"No," David lied. "Charlie just needs my advice on something . . . I'll meet you in front of the hardware store in an hour, okay? If you think you might want the house, go talk to Fred. See what's involved and how much he wants." Marty nodded, and as David hurried away with Charlie, he called back over his shoulder, "It's up to you, Marty. If you want the house, put a binder on it. But watch Butz—he'll steal you blind if you let him."

. . . . Not enough . . . it was not enough. Why? It was so powerful, struggling, kicking, fighting to stay alive. And yet the urge refuses to ease. Something was missing. Something that has nothing to do with the daring of an attack in daylight . . . or the size of the victim . . . or the lashing out . . . striking. . . . And still the nagging drive remains, scraping at the nerve endings. Something else is needed for the feeling of euphoria to come . . . something else is needed to make the gnawing go away. . . .

THIRTEEN

David went to see Nilscoff alone. Charlie Bende left him at the corner, and told him to stop in at Homer's, the bar where most locals gathered, as soon as he was finished. Nilscoff's door was open when David got there, and three people were inside. Nilscoff was sitting behind his desk, Leonard Dukirk was on a chair to the side of the desk, and Evan Robbins was on his feet, coming directly at David.

"You son-of-a-bitch!" he shouted. Evan was moving very quickly, and David's reaction was purely instinctual. He pulled his arm back with an alarmed jerk just as Evan reached him, and then pushed forward defensively, the flat of his palm hitting Evan in the chest. The blow broke Evan's momentum and thrust him backwards. He stumbled slightly and fell against the wall behind him. The blow must have stunned him; he stood there rubbing his shoulder.

"I'm sorry, Evan," David said. David noticed he was shaking slightly. ". . . But I'm not going to stand here and let you attack me."

"Where is she, Paddock?" Evan shouted at him. "Your friend and the Goddamn killer ape?"

Nilscoff stood up. "Calm down, Evan. I'll handle this." He motioned to a chair opposite Leonard Dukirk. "Sit down, Paddock. As I'm sure Charlie told you, we have a problem."

David ignored Nilscoff. "Look, Evan. I'm sorry about your horse. I came here to see if I could help."

Evan wiped his mouth with the back of his hand, and then leaned against the wall and folded his arms. David sat down and nodded to Dukirk.

"I figured you'd be in New York today harassing your aged tenants," David said. "Just happen to drop by, Leonard, or did you decide to have the papers for suing me drawn up before you left for work?"

Leonard adjusted his glasses. "This happens to be a very serious situation, David. If I were you, I'd listen."

David turned to Nilscoff. "Okay, go ahead. . . . What happened?"

The mayor cleared his throat. "Well, Evan's horse was killed sometime after one o'clock last night. Evan checked the stables, as he always does, before he went to bed. This morning he found the horse lying in its stall with its throat ripped open and its skull crushed. Looks like the weapon used was a pitchfork. The prongs and part of the broken handle were sticking out of the horse's face."

David looked at Evan. "You didn't see Jinks, did you?"

"What the hell else would kill Butler, Paddock?" Evan shouted. "Christ almighty, the horse wasn't just killed, it was slaughtered. I know it was that Goddamn ape. You saw it go for Butler the other morning."

Nilscoff cut in. "Evan didn't see anyone or anything, Paddock. Of course, he called the police. They're looking into it."

"I'm sure he told them and you about the incident with Jinks the other morning," David said. Nilscoff nodded. "Then why haven't the police been to see me?"

"They will," Nilscoff said. "That's why I sent Charlie for you this morning. Leonard told me about his dog, and adding that to Evan's horse and the Felding girl, I figured we'd better talk things over before the police got to you. This thing is entirely out of hand, Paddock. I've asked Baker to have some higher-ups look into this . . . but ultimately, I'm the mayor, you know; and this town and what happens in it are my responsibility. Now, what's the story, Paddock? Was your friend Goodman lying to me the other day? What the hell is going on with this chimpanzee?''

"Wrong question," David said, "what you mean is, do I know anything about these killings?"

Nilscoff folded his hands in front of him on the desk. "Meaning?"

"Meaning your conclusions are wrong. I don't know what's doing the killing around here, but I know it's not Jinks."

"Go on," Nilscoff said.

"As I said, the other morning at dawn when I went to wake Marty, the chimp was with her in her room. Now, of course I can't guarantee the chimp was there all night, but Marty assures me she brought him into her room just as she told you she did. And I do know about last night. I slept in the hammock on the porch after we got home from the party last night. If the chimp had gone by me, I would have known it."

"You didn't stay awake all night, Paddock," Evan said, jamming his hands into his pants pockets. "Maybe the ape went out during the night."

"No dice. I locked the front door before I went to sleep, and I remember rousing this morning when Missy unlocked it and went outside. And let's be sensible for a minute. Jinks may be a smart chimpanzee, but I don't think he's intelligent enough to unlock a door, sneak out, find your stable and kill your horse, then tiptoe back into the house without waking me, lock the door, wash the blood off himself, and then go back to sleep.

Do you? Marty keeps very close tabs on the chimp, you know. I can't imagine him going in or out of her room and her not knowing it."

"Maybe she does know it," Evan said. "Covering for the chimp . . . she could clean him up."

"Oh, come on, Evan!"

"What about the back door?" Nilscoff said.

David felt an edge of doubt creep into the corner of his mind. He hadn't considered the back door. He wasn't sure whether it had been locked or not. Either night. "Locked too," he said.

"What about the windows?" Dukirk said.

"Screened, Leonard."

"Could have left by the sliding door which leads from your house to the front deck, couldn't he?"

"No, the bedroom door was locked too. Pam locked it."

"Are you sure?"

"Yes, I'm sure," David said loudly. "Sorry, Leonard. The chimpanzee did not leave the house last night. Find a new killer."

Nilscoff stood up. "Paddock, let's get down to it here. The chimp was eating Dukirk's dog. That's a pretty strong indictment, the way I see it."

"Wrong," David said. "The explanation is very simple. Jinks found the dog dead . . . and Marty says brains are a delicacy to chimps. He couldn't help himself."

Nilscoff raised an eyebrow. "How do you know he found the dog dead?"

David kept his expression blank. "That's what he told Marty . . . in sign language."

"Well then, it must be the truth. If the ape says so," Leonard said sarcastically. He and the mayor exchanged a look.

Nilscoff sat back down. "Why didn't you tell me

about the dog yesterday, Paddock? According to Leonard, it must have happened before we got there.''

"It did," David said. "I didn't say anything because I knew you would draw the wrong conclusions, just as you have done. You were very upset about the Felding murder, and I wanted to give you a day . . . so that you would be able to view the whole situation in the proper light.''

Nilscoff stretched his fingers. Then he looked from Evan to Leonard, slowly and deliberately.

"All right, Paddock. There's no proof connecting Jinks with Evan's horse, and maybe the police won't find any. Frankly, I hope you're right. I kind of like him. He has nice taste in clothes.'' Nilscoff smiled and went on. "But it really doesn't matter, even if Jinks is innocent. The facts are the chimp ate part of the dog, the people of Dune Beach are going to get scared about these killings, and I have to take some positive action. So, we're going to lower the odds a little. I want Goodman to get her chimpanzee out of Dune Beach by tomorrow night, Paddock. Then if another slaughter happens, at least we'll know you were right. I'm giving you two days so that she can make arrangements, but you tell her to keep that animal right with her all the time until she leaves. I don't want her to hate me or this town. And maybe you're right. Maybe we are jumping to conclusions. Tell her it's a precaution. Tell her to board the chimp somewhere on the mainland, then come back to Dune Beach and enjoy herself.''

"And if the chimp is still here beyond your deadline?" David asked.

Nilscoff leaned back in his chair. "Well, the dog'll be a good place to start. I'll serve as Leonard's attorney. We'll have the chimpanzee impounded for eating the dog, and take the case to court. If I get a conviction, I'll argue that the chimp is a public danger and try to have him put to sleep. And I'm not kidding, Paddock. I want that chimpanzee off Fire Island before I have a panic on my hands."

David stared at the mayor without expression. "Anything else?"

"That's it. You better go. I'm holding you personally responsible for that chimp's whereabouts and actions from now on . . . starting right now."

David stood up, and turned to Evan. "I truly am sorry about Butler, Evan. I hope you believe that." Evan looked at the floor, and Nilscoff rose from his chair.

"Then you'll go along, Paddock?"

"I'll talk to Marty," David said.

"I think you'll see it my way, Paddock," Nilscoff said, extending his hand.

"I'll think about it, Nilscoff," David said. He ignored the mayor's hand, turned, and left the room.

David walked to the corner, toward Homer's. Charlie Bende was there, sitting at a table in the corner of the dimly lit bar along with Sam Kline and Clyde Bartley. They had obviously been discussing something related to David; they abruptly stopped talking as he got a draught at the bar and approached them. He pulled up a chair and Sam Kline smiled at him, his eyes friendly and understanding.

"How'd it go, Dave?"

David half-drained his glass before he answered. "Either Jinks leaves in two days or we go to court and they try to get the chimp exterminated."

Sam whistled. "Will you do it?"

David sighed. "Up to the owner. I'll give Marty the message. It's her decision."

"What do you think, David?" Charlie said. "Did the chimp kill the horse?"

"I don't know," David said, "I can't imagine him

going out of the house without Marty or myself knowing it. Oh, he's certainly strong enough, but he seems so tame. . . . Really, he's like a funny kid, you know what I mean?"

Clyde gave David a look and emptied his mug of beer.

"Well, something did, that's for sure," Sam said. "I went to see the horse, Dave. Of course, I just looked. Didn't do anything medical, but I can tell you this. Something or someone really did a job on the animal. Entire top of the skull was crushed. Brains all over the place. Throat was gouged. Big, gaping jagged tears. Looked like the pitchfork was jammed in the neck and then pulled downward. Sliced the jugular. Probably bled to death first. . . . Then the handle was used to smash away at the skull. The blows apparently split the handle."

"Spare me the details," David said, swallowing the rest of his beer, "I better go. Not only do I have to tell Marty the good news, but I understand the police may be wanting to talk to me."

"David," Charlie Bende said, "I think you better know that Fred Butz talked to me about the cottage just before I saw you this morning."

"And?"

"And he said I should keep the bids open . . . he wasn't going to sell the house to your friend."

"News travels fast, doesn't it?" David said. "Instant conviction by rumor."

Charlie shrugged. "What can you do?"

"You going to turn on me too? You starting to think I'm housing a crazed beast?" David said half-jokingly to the others at the table.

"Fat chance, Dave," Sam said. "Who'd buy the drinks?"

"Could be a bad sign of attitude, though, David,"

Charlie said. "Maybe you should do as Nils asked."

"Maybe. . . ," David said, looking from Charlie to the handyman across from him. "You've had words with Robbins about exercising his horse on the beach and Nilscoff knows it. He bother you this time, Clyde?"

Clyde shook his head, and the corners of his mouth turned down. "Nope. He's not interested in me. He was just groping that first day when he found out about the Felding girl."

"Well I wish he'd stop groping for Jinks," David said. "How about it? You got any opinion on this?"

"Yup, Davy, I do," Clyde said, pushing his beer mug away from him. "The monkey did it. No question about it. And if I were you I'd get it the hell out of the house and off the island before anything else happens."

"What makes you so sure it's Jinks?" David asked.

"I just have a feeling, that's all."

"Very sound, medically speaking," Sam Kline said.

"Yeah, go on, Sam," Clyde said, his head jerking in the affirmative, "You just wait and see if I'm not right."

"Well, I hope you're not, Clyde," David said, "but thanks for the advice." As he pushed his chair away from the table and headed out of the bar, David felt depressed.

When David picked Marty up at the Butz house, she took the Jinks news quite calmly, although she expressed concern about the killing of Evan Robbins' horse. However, she was furious about Butz's refusal to sell her the house.

"Can he do that?" Marty said as they turned the corner and started home. ". . . Just refuse to sell me the house?"

David nodded. "Charlie says there's nothing you can do."

"Damn! Actually, it's a good thing you didn't go

with me to the Butzes', David. I'm afraid I created quite an unladylike scene when your friend told me the real reason why he wouldn't consider selling me the house. But, damn it, he deserved it! These people around here are really choice, aren't they?"

"Some are. Not all, Marty. What about Nilscoff? What do you think?"

"I think he's an ass. Jinks happens to be a very well known chimpanzee, David, and I have no doubt that he has more pull than some two-bit resort town lawyer."

"There's nothing two-bit about Nilscoff," David said. "In New York, he's a pretty influential lawyer."

"Good for him," Marty said. "He can try anything he wants. Jinks and I stay until we get good and ready to leave. . . . Unless you feel otherwise, of course, David."

David didn't know how to answer Marty. He only knew there was a tight gnawing feeling in his chest that refused to go away. They walked in silence until Jerry Dile's voice through the shrubs brought them to a halt.

"That's a very nice lady you have with you, David," Jerry's voice squeaked. ". . . Very nice."

David stopped and smiled. "I told you you'd like her, Jerry. Thanks for showing her your little Eden."

"My pleasure . . . my pleasure. Did you show her the Butz house, David? . . . We need people like her here, you know."

"We just came from there, Jerry," Marty said.

Jerry's voice went up in pitch. "Did you give him a check as I told you? . . . Did you?"

"No, I didn't have a chance . . . the house is not for sale. Anyway, not to me."

"What's that mean . . . not to you?"

"There was another killing, Jerry. Evan Robbins' horse was destroyed last night. It seems the suspicion is falling on Jinks, and so Butz refuses to even consider the possibility of selling the house to Marty. Nice, huh?''

For a few moments, Jerry said nothing, and then his voice came blasting shrill and loud through the foliage. "I told you they were rotten, Marty . . . didn't I tell you? . . . With their high and mighty stares. They don't care. They don't want explanations. That chimp wouldn't hurt anyone . . . anyone can see that . . . except know-it-alls like Butz. And Evan's not much better. He wouldn't take my vegetables. Did you know that, David? Did you? Said I was putting something in them . . . might harm his horse. Can you imagine? . . . Thinking I would put chemicals in my plants?''

"*David!*" A scream came from further down the path. It was Pam, standing in front of their house.

"Oh Christ, now what?" David muttered, giving Marty an anxious look. "Got to go, Jerry. . . . Something must be wrong at the house.''

FOURTEEN

David and Marty trotted toward the Paddock house. Pam, obviously infuriated, began shouting at them before they reached her.

"Marty," she yelled, "I've had it! I'm sorry, but I want Jinks out of this house!"

"What's the matter now?"

"I'll tell you what's the matter, David. I went into the living room a few minutes ago, and that filthy monkey was masturbating in front of your daughter! That's what's the matter. And I will not put up with this any more. I mean it, David. I've had it. I want the chimpanzee out!"

"Pam . . . I'm sorry, I—" Marty said.

"Don't give me that! You were probably out trying to make my husband while your chimp was corrupting my daughter. Why don't you just get together with Jinks? Or have you tried that already?"

David grabbed Pam's arm and led her into the house, noticing that Winnie Dukirk was standing in the front door of her home across the way, drinking it all in.

"Where's Missy?" David said as they came into the living room.

Pam jerked her arm out of David's grasp. Jinks was sitting on a nest he had constructed in the middle of the room, and was grooming himself.

"She's in her room . . . crying probably, because her mean mother put her there."

"Look, Pam," David said, trying to remain calm, "it's not that serious. Jinks is in puberty. He can't help it. Marty says things like this are quite common."

Pam looked at David incredulously. "I don't give a damn what Marty says! Who do you listen to, anyway? I'm your wife, remember? I find this disgusting monkey sitting on our sofa whacking off in front of our eight-year-old daughter, and you tell me it's not serious? David, are you aware that the police were just here? They wanted to talk to us about Marty's animal in connection with Wubbles . . . and Evan Robbins' horse being killed. The chimp had Wubbles dead on our front walk, and Winnie says you knew all about it. And you didn't tell me? Brenda Felding, the dog, and now Evan's horse! *David* . . . what the hell is the *matter* with you? Letting our daughter play with that beast when you know it may be a killer! Are you *insane*, for Christ's sake? Taking those chances just because of Marty and old time's sake?"

"Pam, Goddamn it, that's enough! Just calm down." David realized he was shouting and lowered his voice. "What am I? What do you think I am? . . . Do you think I'd let Missy near Jinks, if I thought there were a problem? The chimp is no killer. And as far as this other business is concerned, what's the big deal, for crying out loud? So what if Missy saw it? He's only an animal, for Christ's sake. I'm sure Missy has seen dogs climbing on each other before. It won't kill her. I'll explain it to her. I think if anyone is being disgusting around here, it's you. And I think you owe Marty an apology for that rotten comment you made outside."

There was silence in the room as Pam glared at David. David noticed that Jinks was now standing a few feet from him instead of sitting in his nest and he thought of the animal reference he had just made. Then Pam was speaking again.

"I am going into the bedroom, David," she said. "When I come back out, I don't want that chimpanzee to be in the house. Do you hear me? I want him gone." Pam turned and stormed into the bedroom, slamming the door after her.

David shouted, "Well that's just *reasonable as hell*, Pam! Thank you for talking this out with Marty and me so that we can deal with the situation calmly and logically!"

Marty moved in from the porchway and came to David. She touched his arm.

"Take Jinks outside, David. I want to talk to Pam." David looked at her doubtfully. "Please, David. Let me try."

"Okay," David said. "Come on, Jinks." The chimp looked at Marty, who nodded to him, and then he followed David out the front door.

Marty stood looking after Jinks and David for several seconds. Then she took a deep breath and walked to the bedroom door. As she opened it, the wood squeaked slightly, and Pam turned from the sliding glass doors where she had been staring out at the ocean waves. When she saw it was Marty, Pam said nothing, and turned her head back out toward the ocean. Marty slowly crossed the room and stood beside Pam. The sky was wide and dark; a heavy storm was moving directly toward them. Marty allowed a brief, sad smile to cross her face as she thought of how appropriate the weather was to the circumstances. Finally, after they had stood staring out at the darkening sky for what seemed like a very long time, Marty spoke.

"Pam, I can't tell you how sorry I am that Jinks has behaved the way he has. But it isn't his fault, it's mine. I should have considered what was happening at his present age. I know you're really not interested in the reasons why he's doing these things, but I want you to know that his behavior is perfectly normal . . . for a chimpanzee, that is. He's entering puberty and just doesn't have the ability to restrain himself sometimes. But that doesn't mean he's malicious or dangerous. I'm not irresponsible, Pam. I wouldn't allow Jinks to be around Missy or anyone else if there were even the remotest possibility of him being harmful. I know there isn't. In fact, this kind of overt sexual behavior isn't restricted to just Jinks or even male chimpanzees for that matter. A female chimpanzee named Lucy, who was being raised in a human environment much as Jinks is, became excited while looking at a picture of a nude male in *Playgirl* magazine." For the first time, Pam turned her head toward Marty; the hardness of expression had melted slightly. "It's true . . . I swear. Lucy looked at the picture . . . and proceeded to masturbate while continuing to stare at the naked male centerfold."

Pam held up her hand in protest and nodded with weary resignation. "Okay, Marty, enough. I believe you. I know I'm overreacting. But it doesn't matter. The point is I just can't deal with this situation. I knew I couldn't. I knew before you ever got here. I tried to tell David."

"I know, Pam," Marty said quietly. "I'm not so sure that it was such a good idea myself anymore. And the whole Jinks problem is just compounding everything."

Pam sighed. "You . . . you still love David very much . . . don't you?"

Marty held Pam's eyes and nodded. "Yes. . . . I do. I wish I didn't. I had even convinced myself that I didn't, but I do."

"God . . . can you believe this?" Pam said, looking away. ". . . It's like a soap opera."

"I think the truth is always like the soaps, Pam. Tragedy and confused emotions, and everybody scraping away in a futile attempt to be happy . . . but trouble always catches up with you. . . . Just as it's caught up with us."

"I knew it would, too. I could see it in David's whole attitude the minute he got a hint that you might be coming. He wasn't . . . bored any more." Pam's eyes started to cloud, and she blinked quickly to keep from tears. "I'm not you, Marty. I've tried to have a good relationship with David, but I just am not cut out to go off exploring new frontiers. I'm just not that type of person, and once we get beyond the physical thing . . . I think I just am not interesting enough for David. I think he feels he's not really involved with . . . I don't know . . . with life. I guess that's the real reason I resent Jinks. He represents the exact thing that David admires and that I lack."

"Pam . . . you don't lack anything. You're different. Don't you think I've ever wished I had your appeal . . . your beauty? It's very easy to fall into tearing away at yourself, but let's be honest. You didn't force David into anything. He made his own choices. And you have a lovely daughter. I'm not so sure that David would have been so crazy about my lifestyle either. Oh, I'm dedicated, all right. But you give a lot up for my kind of dedication. It forces you to live in a certain kind of vacuum, cut off from naturally evolving relationships. And the truth is that, deep down, I know I would have chosen this way of life even if nothing had happened between you and David."

"So what are you saying?"

Marty shook her head. "I don't know. I can't separate it all out. Maybe it just isn't possible."

"All right, Marty," Pam said, turning and walking into the center of the room. "Discussing whether you

164

should have come here or why things happened isn't going to solve anything really, is it? I think this boils down to the fact that you and David must make some kind of choice. You're the ones who wanted this to happen, not me, so fine. I'm going to let you work it out." Pam pulled a suitcase from the closet. "I'm taking Missy back to the mainland. As you said, I can't separate it all—and maybe if I leave you two alone for a while I won't have to. David won't be happy about my taking Missy, but that's just a price he'll have to pay for helping to create this mess. I'm sure you're right about Jinks being harmless, but there is some kind of danger here. I don't want Missy exposed to it."

"Wouldn't you like me to go send David in, so that the two of you can talk?" Marty said.

"No," Pam said quickly. "I really don't want to talk any more. I just want out. Maybe we can all talk in a few days. I don't know."

"Pam," Marty said, crossing to the bedroom door, "I'm not sure who's to blame for all this, but in many ways I do feel you're getting the worst part it. . . . And I'm sorry."

Pam had been throwing clothes into her suitcase. She stopped for a moment and looked up. "No one's to blame, Marty. You put it very well, before. We're all just being pulled along, grasping for a little comfort wherever we can find it. You're right. The whole damn thing is just one big soap opera."

Jinks and David walked to the beach platform to watch the approaching storm. The oceanfront was deserted and David sat down on the top step. The surf was breaking against the sand in huge, spiraling waves. Grayish-black clouds were rolling toward him above the ocean, and, as Jinks plopped down beside him, and stuck his face into the whipping wind, David realized it was about to start raining very hard. He was wearing a knit tennis shirt and considered going back for a poncho, but decided it would be better if he stayed out of the house for a while. And, as he sat there and waited patiently for the clouds to reach him with their torrential rains, David turned his head and spoke aloud to the chimpanzee beside him.

"Well, things are going quite nicely, don't you think, Jinks? My wife is totally pissed, my kid is in tears, Marty's upset, I don't know how I feel, and you're an oversexed chimp that people think is a killer. And we're about to get drenched. So what's the story, Jinks, huh? Come on, I need some answers. How about these killings? Is it you, or do we have some maniac out there among the dunes. . . . Or even worse, is it someone right here in Dune Beach, and we can't even see it?"

The sound of David's voice brought the chimp's head around, and Jinks stared at David for several seconds. Then he slowly turned his face back into the wind as the sky opened, and a ragged bolt of lighting cut through the air and knifed its way downward into the churning sea. It was immediately followed by a loud clap of thunder. Jinks' body went rigid, and he shot up into a ramrod-straight standing position, his face raised to the angry sky.

"Relax, Jinks," David said, as huge drops of water began to pelt the platform. "It's just a storm." The chimpanzee seemed not to hear David. He began to rock back and forth slowly from foot to foot and the hair on his body rose as low moans rose in his throat. His face was tight with a rictus grin and his eyes looked glazed and distant. Not sure what the chimpanzee was going to do, David eased himself back onto the platform as Jinks' moans grew louder. Then the rain was pouring down as the lightning and thunder crashed around them, and Jinks started to screech loudly in an ever-increasing tempo. He stretched his arms until he was able to grasp the wooden railings that bordered the steps. His feet began to pound violently as his screeching became piercing screams of rage.

David realized it was hailing; the rain became hard and bounced like tiny glass fragments against the wooden slats of the platform. And then, without warning, Jinks leaped forward in a powerful lunge beyond the steps onto the sand below.

"Jinks, come back here!" David yelled. But the chimpanzee was already racing down the beach, his arms waving violently over his head, into the hail and rain. When he reached the cement pilings at the far side of the bathing area, Jinks grabbed one and spun around it. As the hail slackened and became a steady rain again, Jinks stood on the piling staring out into the ocean. Suddenly, as the wind shifted, David could hear the animal's savage howl cut through the rain.

Then the chimp was moving again. He raced to the large stack of driftwood beside the piling, grabbed a log, and, dragging it behind him, bounded back towards the steps. When he reached the steps, he turned and raced back to the pilings. Then he turned into the surf, and moved down across the jagged rocks, the water slapping against his legs. When he reached Clyde's fishing spot, he climbed onto it. Then he raised the gnarled timber over his head with both hands and, as if issuing some sort of primeval challenge, hurled it into the sea. He stared after it for a moment, turned, and loped slowly back along the rocks to the woodpile. He grabbed another piece of wood and repeated the entire process. And again. And again. David stood unmoving on the platform above Jinks, watching in fascination. The rain slackened at last. It was only slightly sprinkling again when Jinks ended his strange performance and Marty came up beside him. David jumped.

"Did you see that?" David said, wiping at the water dripping from his face.

"The end of it," Marty said. "I wish I had seen it all. It's actually quite rare among captive chimpanzees . . . especially to that degree."

"What was it?"

"A charging display. It's a way adult males release pent-up tension brought on when they are excited or startled . . . as by a sudden heavy rain. I've never seen one . . . a full one, anyway. Jinks has only done that once, just before a rain storm during one of our visits to Africa. I only saw the beginning, because he disappeared into the woods." Jinks came slowly up the steps, dripping wet, and sat down beside Marty. Marty patted his head; he began to groom himself. "That time he disappeared totally, and I was worried sick. I searched all around the camp for hours. Finally he just walked out of the undergrowth beside me. He was covered with splotches of blood. God knows what happened. But I was pretty relieved to see him, to say the least. I don't think I've ever been so frantic. In fact, I had a strange reoccuring dream for a long time afterwards. . . . While searching, I found him with a female chimpanzee and he refused to leave her when I called to him, and I . . . I attacked the female chimp out of frustration, beating her mercilessly. A shrink would have fun with that one, wouldn't he?"

"Marty, we're not talking about dreams, here," David said, upset. "I thought you said he was tame. That was a raging, wild animal down there just now. What would have happened if people had been on the beach? Someone would have gotten hurt."

"I know," Marty said quietly, "I'm surprised he actually went into a full display. No matter how civilized I try to make him, instincts triumph, I guess. But it just means he's no longer a baby, David. Don't worry, I can still control him with no problem . . . charging display or no charging display."

As David looked skeptically at Marty, it suddenly came to him why he was standing in the rain. "Damn, I can't believe I forgot! What happened with Pam?"

Marty shrugged. "She's gone."

"*What?*"

"She packed some things, got Missy, and the two of them went to catch the ferry for the mainland. She said she'll be back in a few days. She needs time to think . . . and she said this would give the two of us time to work things out."

David shifted awkwardly. "You're kidding. Did she at least listen to you?"

"Yes. As a matter of fact, we had a good talk. What can I tell you, David? She's very upset, and justifiably so. I can see her side of it. She . . . she's suffering from lack of self-confidence over this whole thing, you know. She thinks you're bored with her. That she's not an interesting enough person for you."

David frowned. "What?"

"Well, that's what she said. She was leaving with Missy when I started out here. What do you want to do? You might be able to catch her if you hurry."

David didn't speak for a moment. It had stopped raining and a cool breeze was blowing. The sun began to emerge from behind the scudding clouds.

"I think I would like to go and change into dry clothes, first of all," David said finally. "Then why don't we take a walk? I need to work off some tension. I'm tied up in knots inside."

"You think a walk will help solve anything?" Marty said with a sigh.

"Well, it's either that or run down the beach and hurl logs into the ocean . . . which I'm considering, now that I see how good Jinks seems to feel."

Jinks looked at David when his name was mentioned, and Marty smiled. "All right, sounds good. I could use a walk too, I guess."

A half hour later, although the weather had cleared, the beach was only partly filled with people. Those that were out sunbathing stared at Jinks with wary suspicion.

"Well, at least we know one person who's getting his wish," Marty said after they had walked for a while.

David frowned questioningly. "Who's that?"

Marty pointed to the few scattered bathers. "Clyde. It looks like people are leaving, just as he's always wanted."

"Yeah," David said, with a lightness he did not feel, "he and Jerry Dile. There's one good thing to come out of this—it'll be a little quieter, and Jerry's plants can grow in peace."

Marty smiled. They fell into a companionable silence as they walked past Sunken Forest and along the more isolated section of the beach. It was as if they had agreed to avoid discussing Pam, and Jinks, and the killings.

Just before they reached the Cherry Grove community, Marty suggested they get some sun, so they stopped and rested for a while. It had turned into a hot, humid day. David realized that they must have fallen asleep when he suddenly opened his eyes, because the sun was much lower in the sky than he remembered it. He heard Marty move beside him, and rolled onto his side, turning in her direction. Jinks was lying quietly in the sand near them, but Marty, although she was asleep, was groaning, and her body was in motion.

She was on her back. Her skin had a deepened color from its exposure to the afternoon sun, and her left arm was in the air, signing rapidly. Her eyeballs shifted rapidly in the sockets under her closed lids, and David figured she was dreaming. He felt guilty watching her, but he couldn't take his eyes off of her movement.

Her legs tensed as her heels dug into the sand. Then her face contorted, and her left arm moved erratically, flaying wildly and randomly in the air. Her back arched as she strained, pulling her swelling breasts tight against her chest, and the tendons protruded in her neck. Suddenly, her mouth flew open. Then the muscles slackened, and her body started jerking. Audible sobs broke from her throat, and tears appeared from under her closed lids and slid slowly down the sides of her head, disappearing into the hair at her temples. David reached over and touched her shoulder.

"Marty," he said softly, "Marty, wake up . . . you're dreaming." Marty's eyes shot open, staring at David with an unfocused gaze, and then she turned and grabbed him, sobbing loudly. David put his arms around her and held her tightly.

"Oh, David," Marty whispered. Her body convulsed with emotion.

"I'm right here, Marty," David said, as Jinks, hearing his guardian's voice, moved to beside them. "It's all right. You were dreaming. It was just a bad dream." Marty snuggled against David, and when she spoke, her voice was small and childish.

"Hold me, David. . . . Just for a minute."

"You want to tell me about it? What were you dreaming?" Marty looked at David, and she started to speak, but her voice broke, and she began sobbing again. David rocked her gently. "Shhh . . . it's all right. You don't have to talk. Everything's okay." Marty held David tightly, and slowly her crying eased. When she finally spoke, it was quietly, but with determination.

"No. I need to talk, David. And I'm not sure I can explain this to you, but I'll try. I . . . I'm not really dreaming, David. It's more than that. . . ." Marty's voice broke, and she turned her head away. "There's something wrong with me, David, and there's nothing I can do about it. . . . And because there's no solution, I'm having trouble coping with it."

"Since when can't you cope with something?" David said, attempting a smile. "You're the most coping person I've ever known."

"Since the accident," Marty said. "More things changed than just our relationship, David. As a result of the accident, I was also changed . . . or rather, the delicate balance was changed, as your friend Clyde would say."

David frowned. "I'm not sure I understand you, Marty."

"It's funny," Marty said. "I try not to think about it because I want to forget it. But I was talking about surgery and suffering today with Jerry Dile . . . and I guess it sort of brought it all to the surface again."

"Marty, in spite of what you might think because of Pam, I stayed with you every step of the way after the accident. I know it was tense, and there was extensive surgery, and the recovery was very slow, but the doctors assured me that you were fine. They guaranteed that with enough care and time you would be your old self."

"Almost . . . *almost* my old self, David," Marty said. "You see, the pieces of metal that were lodged in my brain not only caused hemorrhaging, but also damaged my nervous system somehow. You knew that my body would convulse violently each time the drugs they were giving me wore off. But what you didn't know is that, in order to stop the disruption in the nervous system, the surgery the doctors performed involved severing my *corpus callosum*, the bundle of nerve fibers that connects the two hemispheres of the brain."

"Your what?"

"My *corpus callosum* . . . it's three and a half inches

172

long and a quarter of an inch thick to be exact, and it links our two mental sides. Severing it is an accepted medical procedure in cases where convulsions are extreme and uncontrollable.''

"And. . . ?" David nudged as Marty paused.

"And the convulsions stopped. And I slowly recovered. But I still needed extensive therapy. By that time you . . . weren't around. You see, that bundle of nerve fiber unifies the two sides of our brain into a single functioning unit. Naturally, when that connection no longer exists, they each function separately, and they function differently.''

"I . . . don't understand."

"The left hemisphere controls the right side of the body and the right hemisphere controls the left side of the body—which adds to the complexity of the problem. And so after the connecting nerves were severed, my problem became one of synchronization. In many cases, the left side of my body literally did not know what the right side was doing.''

"Marty, I had no idea—"

"I know," Marty said quickly. "That's why in one strange way I was glad the thing happened between you and Pam . . . because it kept you away from me when I was so . . . helpless. I felt like such a fool not being able to do the simplest things, and I couldn't have stood you seeing me like that. You can't imagine how frustrating it was. The coordination of the two sides of my body that was involuntary before suddenly had to be sustained by learning voluntary control . . . and it took a lot of therapy and exercise.''

David spoke slowly. "Well . . . your recovery was certainly more complex than I realized. . . . But you did recover, Marty. I mean you're all right now, aren't you?"

"Yes. Anyway, I got well, except that involuntary

things happen sometimes—like just now—and it scares me. I try to be strong, but I've had to be strong for so long that sometimes. . . ." Marty began to cry again.

"Shh. You don't have to talk."

"Oh, David," Marty said, her voice desperate, "I'm so tired of being alone. The house was to be my new start, a permanent place to come home to, I need it so badly. Jinks is growing away from me . . . I can feel it. My parents are dead . . . I've no close friends, really . . . if I lose Jinks, I'll have nothing."

David brushed at the sand clinging to Marty's hair and ran his hand affectionately across her back. "Don't worry. There are other houses. If you really want a house, we'll talk to Charlie Bende. He'll find something."

As David stroked Marty's hair, he smiled gently into her eyes, and Marty responded by raising her face to kiss him lightly. David was caught off guard. Confused and unsure of himself, he mumbled Marty's name in a gentle protest as her arms went around his neck and they fell back into the sand.

Suddenly, Jinks was there. His unexpected screech startled David, and he yelled as the chimp's hairy powerful paw tore at David's shoulder and Jinks tried to wedge himself between them. As Jinks pulled at David, Marty's arm fell from his neck and she sank back in laughter. David started to get up, but Jinks was pushing at him, catching him in the chest, and he fell backwards into the sand.

"All right, Jinks, relax!" David yelped. "I'm not hurting her, for crying out loud!" David struggled into a sitting position, but didn't go any further because the chimpanzee was standing over him. Marty, meanwhile, had raised herself onto one elbow and was still laughing. "Marty, will you please call him off, damn it?"

"Don't worry, David," she said, choking on her

laughter. "He won't hurt you. He's just a normal adolescent chimp." Marty sat up. "Jinks, come here. Let David get up." The chimpanzee left David, and plopped down next to his guardian.

David stood up and waded into the water, splashing the sand off of his body. He called back, "What do you mean, normal adolescent?"

"Well," Marty said, moving to the water and following David's example, "young chimpanzees can't stand to see their mothers mating, and they always try to pull the male off whenever they see it happen. They don't hurt the adult male, but their pulling and shoving does make things a little difficult."

"I can imagine," David said. "Well, tell him he was mistaken. We were not mating."

Marty suddenly stopped splashing herself and straightened up. The amusement drained out of her face. "No, we weren't mating, were we, David?" Her voice had lost its warmth. Marty walked out of the water, and David slowly followed. He stopped in front of her and exhaled heavily.

"Marty," he said, "you asked me to be sure. I can't hurt you ever again, and I just don't know what I—"

"I think you do know, David," Marty cut in. "I think you know. You made your choice ten years ago. You may be a little bored now, and intrigued by what could have been, but I don't think Pam has to worry, David. Ultimately, your choice will remain the same. And even if I'm wrong, and you do decide differently, I think it's better if you do it without me around. I'll leave tomorrow. Besides, it's really been spoiled for me here now. Ignorant suspicion has set in, and I could never forgive the people here for that. Come on, we'd better get back."

David attempted to speak, but Marty shook her head and put her hand gently over his mouth. Then she took

Jinks' paw, turned, and walked down the beach away from him.

The need threatened to obliterate all other feeling. It was the fiend crying out in hunger to be fed . . . the fiend raging within, its internal howlings plummeting the brain into torment.

This crushing need was agony. The victim had to be a human being. That was the something that had been missing from the kill! That was the thing that had brought euphoria. The victim must not be simply human, but a child.

But there was great danger now. They were watching, hoping for a mistake. Great care had to be taken. The gnawing must be eased, but the choice must be right . . . a choice that not only gave relief, but also flaunted the ability to kill with cunning and with power. . . .

FIFTEEN

David and Marty hardly talked after they returned from the beach. Even Jinks' antics didn't shake the moody silence between them, and David was relieved when Marty retired to her room early.

Once alone, David began to feel guilty about the casualness with which he had treated Pam's departure, so he made a phone call. But when there was no answer at their home on the mainland, he decided he might as well go to bed too. Remembering what he had told Nilscoff, David checked both the back and front door locks. Jinks was lying on his newspaper nest on the front porch. Then David turned off the lights and went into his bedroom.

The heaviness of sleep was just starting to weigh on his senses when the bedroom door opened. It was Marty. There was a very faint outline of light around her trim, naked body in the doorway. Then the faint light disappeared as she stepped into the room and closed the door behind her.

Without saying a word, she crossed the room to the bed, pulled back the sheet, and crawled into bed. She turned to him and spoke in a soft whisper.

"I know what I said, David," she said, her warm body not quite touching his, "and tomorrow I can live with your indecision and the whole twisted mess . . .

but not tonight. Please . . . just for a while, I need what could have been."

David was on his back, and he turned to face her. "Marty—"

"Don't talk. Please," Marty whispered, snuggling against him. "Just hold me. There's no need to say anything."

"But I want you to know . . . how sorry I am that things got so. . . ." Unconsciously, David gently traced the edge of Marty's cheek with his finger in an old gesture of affection. She grasped his hand in hers and kissed it lightly.

"I know you are," she murmured, and David could feel the wetness of Marty's tears as they slid down her cheek against his hand. Then his arms were around her and their bodies strained against each other in an attempt to regain the old closeness that was buried in memory.

And for a long time, David was only aware of feeling. It was more than sensual. More than the need for sexual satisfaction. Perhaps they could make everything all right again. If they could only give each other enough pleasure, perhaps they would somehow get lost and never have to come back.

David could never remember being so excited at the touch of a woman against him. Not even Pam, with all her sensuality, had brought out such feelings in him. He did not want it to stop. Again and again he kissed hungrily at Marty's body, searching out her soft, tight breasts, her firm stomach, her churning thighs in an effort to bring her deeper into the web of pleasure he felt surrounding them. And she responded with a need and excitement that matched his own, covering him with her mouth in darting kisses that began with a soft tantalizing wetness, hardened into passion, and then moved on, leaving his senses screaming for release and yet not wanting the pleasure to end.

But, of course, it did end. There came a moment when, as their mouths strained in passion to express what they had not spoken aloud, their bodies seemed to melt together in an explosion of pleasure that overwhelmed them until it slowly faded and the warm glow of pleasure that had them in the blur of feeling dissolved into reality.

And then David was alone again. As he drifted into sleep, Marty had whispered something about not wanting to be with him if Pam should happen to return in the morning, and quietly she had slipped out of the room.

Then David's eyes were open and he was awake breathing hard. He turned on his side, pulling the sheet around him, and butted his head into the pillow. The room was dark, and he knew it was still night. Flashes of the dreadful dream he had been having kept coming back.

It had been night on the beach, and Marty was teaching him to swim. The water was cold, and there was moonlight, and Clyde was beyond them, fishing— only instead of sitting in his usual position he was standing on the water. Then Missy was crying for David, and he looked toward the beach, and Jinks had Missy on the sand and was attempting to mount her. Pam was screaming and David frantically swam for shore but Marty's arm was around him and held him. He yelled to Clyde but the handyman didn't seem to hear and walked away from them across the waves, further and further into the darkness, and then Marty was signing to Jinks and Jinks returned her signs. And leaving Missy limp in the sand he lunged for Pam, and Pam attempted to run but Jinks caught her by the hair and pulled her back to him, and then he had her head between his hands and her strangled screams stopped as he twisted her head around and sank his teeth into her neck, and David was screaming at him and tearing at Marty but she was smiling and pushing him under and he was choking and his mouth was filling with water and the water was hot and he was drowning and it was hot and he was drowning when he suddenly surfaced into consciousness.

David was dripping with sweat and he shuddered with the fear the dream had caused in him. Then he heard it—a distant cry of pain. It seemed to be coming from the beach. David held his breath and listened. The sound came again and it reminded him of the faraway moaning of a cat. The cry came again, louder, and David ripped the sheet off of his body. It was not a dream this time. The sound was a muffled scream, and it was unmistakably human.

David vaulted out of bed, and pulled open the drapes that covered the sliding glass door. There was a fog, but he thought he saw a figure moving on the beach. It seemed to be carrying something in its arms. David flipped the lock, pulled open the door, and stepped out into the damp air. The figure paused and let out a heart-breaking cry. Then it disappeared down the beach into the fog.

David moved quickly and methodically. He pulled on a pair of cut-offs and grabbed a flashlight from the top drawer of the nightstand. He tested it. Then, satisfied, he went through the open glass door and headed toward the water.

It was a moonless night, and, because of the late hour, there were no house lights among the dunes. The fog hid the stars, and David could only see a few feet in front of him. When he came onto the sand, he walked cautiously. He headed east, after the figure, shining the light in a sweeping motion from the dunes across the sand in front of him and out into the ocean. David listened, but heard nothing except the surf spiraling in, crashing, and then hissing away, spiraling in, crashing, and then hissing away. It was low tide.

He reached the far cement pilings, and saw nothing. He made one last sweep with the flashlight across the beach and out over the water, and then brought the light to a sudden stop. There was something on the rocks between the pilings out in the water. He brought the light back and held it there. Something small appeared to be lying across the rocks, the water lapping at its limp form.

There was a shuffling movement in the sand behind him. David spun around. The beam of his flashlight fell on the face of Clyde Bartley, who was standing directly behind him.

David let out a sigh of relief. "Clyde! What the hell are you doing out here?"

"I like the beach at night," Clyde said, his face set and serious. "I didn't know you did, Davy."

"I don't. I saw something moving on the beach and came to check it out."

Clyde's head jerked. "Well, I was just out walking the way I do sometimes . . . that is, until I came onto what you just spotted." The handyman pointed out over the rocks with his own light. "You better have a look. I hid when I heard you on the beach. Figured it might be the killer comin' back."

Aiming the light at his feet, David slowly crawled out on the rocks. The wet stone was slippery, and it took him a while to reach the body. When he got there, his legs were soaked from the water that churned around him. He shone the light on the figure.

It was a girl, or had been. As the light hit her face, David saw that it was Tammy Butz. There was no doubt she was dead. Water pulled at the shreds of skin that hung from her torn throat and washed at the blood that seeped from her crushed skull. The tide slapped across the slab; her head shifted loosely in the water.

David fought his rising nausea and scrambled back over the rocks to the beach. "My God, no, Clyde!" he hollered, "I can't believe it. . . ."

"Believe it," Clyde said sternly. "That ain't no blue-fish out there. I tried to warn you, Davy . . . I told you. One of us better go for the police, I guess."

"You go," David said, his voice hard. "I know what you're thinking . . . but I don't believe it . . . and I'm going to find out the truth right now." Clyde yelled something, but David didn't hear it clearly for he had already turned and was running down the beach toward the landing at Holly Lane.

When David returned to the house, he knew he wasn't thinking clearly. The flashlight still in his hand, he crossed through the living room and out onto the screened-in porch. Jinks was right where Marty had bedded him down earlier that evening. He roused slightly as the flashlight beam hit him.

David shut off the light. He paused for a minute. Then he turned and edged his way down the hall to Marty's room. Carefully, he grasped the doorknob and eased the door open. On the far side he could just see a form lying in bed.

Stealthily, David moved into the room and approached the bed. For a moment he stood there, refusing to think as he stared down at the woman who had been in his arms only a few hours earlier. Then, as he bent over Marty's still form, her body spun toward him in a sudden, jerking heave.

Marty's left arm shot into the air at David's face, and her eyes, bulging open, glared upward. David gasped and, backing away, raised the flashlight. Then, slowly, as the tension left her arched back and her arm fell to the bed. He realized that Marty was not awake, but having one of her dreams. And, as Marty's eyes closed and her breathing became even again, David backed out of the room, closing the door behind him. Then he edged his way to the end of the hall and shone the light on the back door. It was locked, just as it had been when he checked it earlier.

David turned off the flashlight, and stood in the darkened hallway trying to sort out his thoughts. All of the checking proved nothing, really. His suspicions were still very possible.

The last killing had been the answer. It had brought with it a sweeping moment of calm. But it was a vacant calm. Instantly the gripping drive returned . . . stronger, more urgent than ever before. The answer had been found, and now the need was ungovernable. The senses ached again. More. There must be more. There had to be a way to kill again. . . .

There was no question now. The drive could not be satisfied. For so long, the unholy thing had remained dormant, coiled within the bestial core of darkness. Now it was fully awakened. Each death tended only to deepen the appetite. . . .

SIXTEEN

Marty was sitting at the dining table, feeding Jinks his breakfast, when David returned from the police station the next morning. She was spooning some oatmeal into Jinks' dish as David came into the living room, and she looked up and smiled, a slight blush coming into her cheeks.

"Well, where were you off to so early this morning? When I didn't find you here, I thought that last night might have been too much for you, and you ran for the hills." David said nothing. The smile disappeared from Marty's face. "What is it, David? You don't look so good. You're not sick, are you?"

David didn't answer right away. He pulled up another chair and sat down. When he finally spoke, his voice was tired and depressed. "I found Fred Butz's daughter down on the beach last night, with her throat ripped open and her skull crushed. I've been at the police station since just before dawn this morning."

Marty's left hand jerked to a stop halfway from the main bowl to Jinks' dish with a spoonful of oatmeal, and the cereal splattered across the front of the chimpanzee. David looked at Marty and held her gaze.

"Oh, David. . . . No!" she said, wiping at Jinks with a napkin. ". . . It can't be. How did you—"

David interrupted her. "I don't have any answers,

186

Marty. Some time after you left the room last night, I heard a noise outside the house. I thought I saw a figure on the beach so I went out. . . . Actually, Clyde had already found her when I came along. I don't know any more than that. I only know I'm exhausted from questions put to me by Nilscoff and the police. I need some sleep. . . . They want to talk to you."

"Me?" Marty asked quickly. "I told you. They don't have to worry. We're leaving. In spite of last night, I meant what I said, David, really. I've thought it over, and I think you've gone through enough. My leaving will ease your problem with Pam and with the town. If you decide we should see each other again, we'll deal with that when the time comes. I've also been thinking about the bad publicity the accusations against Jinks could bring to the entire program of educating chimpanzees. It will be bad enough as it is, when the papers get hold of all this."

David rubbed his forehead. "I'm afraid it's a little more complex than before, Marty."

"You mean because of the Butz girl?"

David nodded. "There are no longer any games. The police want to see you right now. Joe Baker and another officer are waiting outside to take you down to the station house. Nilscoff knows about the Butz house deal, and he thinks the whole thing is just one too many coincidences."

Marty looked away from David. When she spoke, there was no trace of emotion in her voice. "What do you think, David?"

David sighed. "I think you better go talk to the police."

"That's not answer," Marty said, turning back to him.

"I know it isn't," David said.

Marty stood up and glanced toward the front door.

"Well . . . there doesn't seem to be much choice, does there? Come on, Jinks."

"I'd go with you, but they said no dice. They want to see you alone, without my interference."

"Don't worry, David, I can handle it alone. I've been taking care of myself for quite a while now."

"You can leave Jinks here, if you want," David said.

"No," Marty said. David could see she was holding back tears as she took Jinks and headed for the door. "I wouldn't want to expose you to any unnecessary danger."

David did not respond to Marty's sarcasm. He simply sat at the table until he was sure his houseguest and the police were well up the block, and then he moved to the phone and dialed Sam Kline's office. The nurse informed David that the doctor was on the mainland and would not be back until late afternoon.

"Would you like to leave a message, Mr. Paddock?"

"Do you know what ferry the doctor is coming back on?"

"Yes, I believe he was going to catch the four o'clock."

"Fine," David said. "I'll see him at the ferry."

David hung up the phone, got himself a beer, and sat back down at the table. It didn't matter whether Sam Kline was on the four or a later ferry. He'd meet them all until he came. He needed to talk to the doctor.

When Marty returned, David was still sitting at the table, nursing his fourth beer. Marty led Jinks to the table and the two of them sat down. No one said anything for several long moments.

"I told them everything I know, David," Marty said at last. I was straightforward and truthful."

"And?"

"And nothing. Obviously, they are convinced of the guilt, but they have no proof and cannot hold us. They have changed their tune, though. Now we're not to leave the island until they tell us we can go. Can they force Jinks and me to stay?''

"I don't know," David said.

"I listened very carefully to everything that was said, David, and I'll admit that it looks as if Jinks and I are involved somehow. But you're wrong . . . all of you.''

David spoke loudly. "Marty, look at the facts, at what's happened. Just what the hell are the other possibilities?''

"I don't know. But there *are* others, that I'm sure of, David. And they don't lead to Jinks.''

David drained his beer and set the can on the table. When he spoke, his voice was low, almost a whisper. "Marty, I have to be honest with you. I don't think the Butz killing leads to Jinks.''

David watched the shock enter Marty's face as she realized what he was saying. When she spoke, her voice was filled with rage.

"You expect me to sit here and listen to this. Do you know what you are saying? *Good God*, David . . . do you know what you're saying to me?''

David tried to keep his voice level. "Yes. I'm saying I care about you and what happens to you. I want you to listen to me, that's all.''

Sorrow crowded at the anger in Marty's face and her eyes welled up with tears. "Please, David. . . . Please tell me you don't believe I could mutilate a child. How can you believe that? My God, do you think after what we shared together last night, I went out and—and—''

"No, I don't believe that. I don't, Marty.''

"Then what?''

"Marty, think. Get by your emotions and use your reason. Your scientific inquiry. It is not the you that we know I'm talking about. It's the you we don't know.''
David took Marty's left hand, which was twitching

badly, and held it between his own hands. "It's the you that controls this hand. Think about it. You said something was wrong yourself. Maybe there's more to the behavior than you realized. The question is whether or not it's possible for your body to do something without you realizing it. I'm not accusing you, Marty. I'm telling you what I've thought of, and I'm asking you, as a scientist, to consider it as a possibility."

"Are you finished?" Marty said. Tears were streaming down her face, and yet her jaw was set and her voice sounded cold and without passion.

"No," David said. "Can you tell me that whatever controls this hand could not lash out beyond your control and beyond your knowledge of its actions? Can you?"

David let go of Marty's hand. She raised it to her face and looked at it a moment. Then, she jerked her hand back and smashed it across David's face with stunning force. Tears came to David's eyes and he felt his mouth fill with saliva. Marty stood up. Jinks, who had sat curiously quiet at the table, rose and stood beside his guardian.

"Just so there's no mistake, David. There was no schizophrenia involved in that action. I was fully aware that I was hitting you. Never . . . never would I have imagined that you could twist my abnormality into an accusation of murder. It disgusts me to think that I came to you in the night like a lovesick girl. God, how could I have been so wrong? How could I have spent all these years thinking I loved you when you're capable of this?"

David made no attempt to touch his throbbing face. And when he spoke, his voice was filled with a sad weariness. "Marty, I'm not some kind of heartless bastard. I know what I'm saying hurt you. God almighty, the last thing I want to do is to cause you more pain. I . . . I doubt if I could express to you what last night meant to me, being with you like that. You put me in touch with feelings that—I don't know—made me feel alive again. I know part of it was the realization of a long fantasy of being with you again. But it was much more than that! For just a little while last night, we were totally happy. And I know you felt it too. And maybe the fact that that exists will help carry us through all this . . . because I do care for you, Marty. What I feel for you is strong and real. But the facts are unavoidable. In everything that has happened, you and Jinks are involved. Somehow. So am I, it seems. There has to be a reason why the shadow stopped outside this house last night. It's almost as if some force was trying to reach out to me for help while an opposing force pulled the understanding away. I knew your initial reaction would be anger. But I hoped that when I confronted you, something would give . . . you would suddenly gain some new insight. All I'm asking is that you think about it. Work it out. Show me the flaws in what I've said.''

"I don't have to think about it, David. It's absurd. You couldn't be more wrong."

"I hope you're right," David said. "Now that I've presented it to you, I hope to God you're right, because then what you have to do won't be so difficult. All you'll have to do is forgive me for being capable of understanding it. But you have never, ever shied away from anything, Marty. You've always pushed for the facts . . . right up to the last possibility. That's what I'm trying to do, and that's what I'm asking you to do. Be completely objective. About me, about Jinks, about everything that has happened these last few days . . . and about yourself."

"If you're so sure you're right, why didn't you mention these amazing insights to the police and your friend the mayor?''

"Marty, I said I care about you and what happens to you, and I meant it.''

"I am going for a walk, David," Marty said after a moment. "You're right. My initial reaction is overwhelming anger. I am amazed and saddened that I so badly misjudged you. I felt I could trust and confide in you. And I'm not sure I can forgive you for hurting me this time . . . because the truth is that your conclusion is really based on the sick premise that since I'm abnormal, I must be guilty. I showed you a weak, vulnerable side of myself yesterday, and instead of giving me understanding, you have attacked me where I am most sensitive. I won't be defeated though, David. Not by you or anyone else. I've beaten back the odds before and I'm not about to stop now. I need time to think. You're right also when you say I should be objective. I can be and I will be. I know Jinks and I are not involved and if this thing isn't figured out, there'll be more deaths. More deaths to blame us for.''

David made no attempt to stop Marty as she left with Jinks. Her anger didn't necessarily mean she was innocent. He knew that. Yet the nagging notion that he had done the wrong thing would not leave him alone. Maybe Marty was right, and there were other answers. But what were they?

He pushed the chair back from the table and walked to the front porch. His eyes fixed on the hammock as he mulled over Marty's reactions, and David suddenly realized he was exhausted. He glanced at his watch. There were still hours before the ferry carrying Sam Kline arrived. Until then, there was little he could do except wait. Wait for Marty to consider what he had said . . . wait for the doctor to help substantiate his theory, or knock holes in it.

David went to the hammock and fell into it, but he

couldn't sleep. Being in the hammock reminded him of Pam locking him out . . . and that of moving with Marty's responsive body in such pleasure . . . and that of the horrible dream that had awakened him . . . and that of Tammy Butz's crushed skull shifting in the surf. . . . David closed his eyes to shut out the horror of the images that came to him. He would fight his way through the guilt, frustration, and confusion in order to find the sleep his body needed.

SEVENTEEN

Marty hurried down the steps to the beach at the end of Holly Lane and crossed the sand to the surf. She had not allowed herself to cry until she was out of the Paddock house, and now her sobs were covered by the pounding waves near her feet. Jinks had followed her across the sand, and waited patiently beside his mistress until her sobbing subsided. Then she placed her hand on the top of his head, scratching it affectionately.

"Well, Jinks," she said, sniffing hard to clear her nose, and wiping at her face with the back of her hand, "What now? God, what do I do now?"

The chimpanzee looked curiously at Marty for a moment, and then turned his head toward a man who was slowly walking down the beach in their direction. The man carried a long fishing rod; as he drew closer, Marty saw that it was Clyde Bartley. Her first impulse was to leave before he reached them. However, she stood staring at the approaching figure of the handyman. Instead of rushing back to the platform, she stood quietly holding Jinks' hand in her own until Clyde came up to them. At first Marty thought he was going to walk right by them, but he didn't. He stopped and looked first at the chimp and then at Marty. Then he spit and jerked his head.

"You picked a pretty good place to come to for crying, I'll give you that," he said. "The wife comes out here sometimes when she gets a real jag going. Seems to help her. Hope it does you some good. A little late for tears, though, ain't it? Fact is, I feel kind of sorry for you and your monkey here, but I tried to warn you."

"Yes, you did," Marty said, keeping her expression blank. "I remember. I remember most of the conversation we had. Quite clearly."

Clyde squinted with a certain wariness, and then jammed the end of his fishing rod into the sand beside him and took out a cigarette. He pulled a match across the seat of his pants and lit the unfiltered Camel as he spoke. "How is it they're letting your pet run around like this? I figured by now they would have come to their senses and have him caged up."

"There's no proof, Mr. Bartley. It takes more than prejudiced opinion to establish guilt."

"It does, huh? What kind of proof? Another murder? Is that what they want? Is that what you want?"

Marty glanced down the deserted beach and then back to Clyde. "I'm not so sure there will be another murder. It's strange, I could never imagine what kind of emotion would bring a person to the point of actually killing another living thing . . . unless it was war, of course. That's different, I guess. I suppose, once you have killed, it's different after that. But, you would know about that better than I would, Mr. Bartley. Didn't you say something about spending time in Africa . . . killing Germans?"

"Damn right. I served my time, and I'm not ashamed of it either. I know what you young ones think. All this pacifist bullshit. But I served my country, and you do what you have to do. And it ain't murder, either."

"I'm afraid you're wrong, Mr. Bartley. Sneaking up behind someone and killing him is murder, whether it's here or during a war in the middle of the jungle."

Clyde's face reddened. "Just what the hell are you driving at?"

"Jinks is not guilty, Mr. Bartley. Nor am I. But someone is, and we have turned up as the perfect setups to take the blame. And look at the beach. Look at the Fire Island that you love. People are leaving in droves. This beach is deserted . . . just as you've always wanted."

"I think you're the one who better leave," Clyde said loudly. His body was shaking slightly, and he pulled his fishing rod roughly out of the sand. "And I mean right now, before I forget you're Davy's friend."

"I'm not allowed to leave," Marty said, keeping her voice even. "Jinks and I are to remain on this island until we're told we can go."

"Then you better open your eyes, take a good look at that monkey of yours, and don't let him out of your sight. Because I'm telling ya, I don't care what Nilscoff and his bunch do. If I catch that pet of yours anywhere . . . or if he even looks like he's considering coming near me or anyone else, I'm going to kill him. And I mean it. Now you get your smart little liberated ass off this beach right now, and take him with you . . . *and keep him with you!*"

Marty glared at Clyde, her eyes wide and unmoving. Then, pulling Jinks after her, she walked quickly back toward the dunes, leaving Clyde staring angrily after her. She hurried up the steps and started down the Holly Lane sidewalk, passing the Paddock house without stopping.

She realized David was right about one thing. The answer was to be objective. To consider the possibilities.

And there were possibilities. David was just too close to see them. One was Clyde. He had the capability and the motive, even if he did seem to be far too upright to commit such atrocities. And there was another possibility. He also seemed sincerely nice, but Marty already knew his mental stability was questionable. And there was a strong possibility that he had been pushed to murder long before he settled into his private seclusion on Fire Island.

Marty stopped in front of the gate that guarded Jerry Dile's garden and tried the latch. To her surprise, it moved. Apparently, reputation, rather than a lock, kept people out. She eased the gate back, and, keeping Jinks at her side, stepped through the opening into the garden.

As the latch snapped shut behind them, Jinks screeched a warning. Marty jumped back in startled fear as Jerry's heavy body moved out of the bushes next to them, the breath escaping from his mouth in a rasping hiss. He was holding a hoe defensively over his head, but lowered it slowly as he recognized the intruders.

"Oh, it's you, Marty," he said, after one hand brought the amplifier to his neck. "It's you and Jinks . . . you should have said something before coming in . . . I didn't know. . . . And I have to be careful. There's too much going on, too much happening. I have to be careful."

"I know. I'm sorry," Marty said, taking Jinks' hand in her own, "I should have thought."

"It's all right. I'm glad you came . . . Does Jinks want a banana? Come on, we'll get him one . . . careful of the plants."

Marty followed Jerry through the maze of growth to a row of dwarf banana trees. "I'm sure Jinks would love one. I know I should have asked before coming, but I was upset and. . . ."

Jerry pulled a small bunch of bananas from a nearby tree, and handed Jinks one of the riper ones. "No . . . no, not at all. I'm just edgy, that's all. . . . Just too edgy."

Marty chose her words carefully. "Then you heard about the Butz girl being killed?"

"Oh, yes. . . . Here, Jinks, you help yourself," Jerry said, placing the entire bunch of bananas in the chimp's hand. Jinks had eagerly consumed the first one. "Nasty business. . . . But don't worry, you're safe here. You can stay if you like."

"Thank you, that's very kind, but it's more than that," Marty said. "I came here because I thought you would understand. You were right about the viciousness of the people. They don't want to understand. It's not just Jinks they suspect. It's me. And they don't want to listen."

Jerry nodded and seemed to blink faster as his eyes narrowed. "I told you . . . they don't care. You said you suffered . . . so you know. It shouldn't surprise you. Look at me . . . they came to me at first. The freak . . . if there's trouble it must be the freak." Jerry lowered the volume of his voice and stepped closer to Marty. "You stay here . . . they won't bother you here."

"But it infuriates me. They have no right to judge me. It makes me want to strike out at them, somehow."

"I know, I know. . . . You think I don't know?"

"Only I'm not sure I could." Marty paused for a moment, and then went on. "You . . . didn't tell me really. Were you able to strike back at the man who hurt you so badly?"

Jerry frowned and stepped back slightly. "Why do you ask that?"

"Because I can see how being hurt and infuriated works on the emotions," Marty said, tightening her grip on Jinks' hand. "Did you slash his throat the way he did yours?"

"We're not talking about that," Jerry screeched, rushing by Marty and back toward the garden gate. "That's not what we're talking about! I want you to go now, Marty. You and Jinks had better go."

"Jerry, listen to me," Marty said, following him. "Jinks and I are innocent. But you're absolutely right. I know what it is to suffer. And I also know most people don't give a damn about the crippled and the maimed. Especially these people. They want them shut away somewhere, so they won't be reminded of their own frailty. They want to come here to be carefree and happy. So they shut it out. They've forced you with their stares and gossip to shut yourself away. And I understand how you would be angry. How you would want to show them what it is to suffer. Because it hurts to suffer, and the pain doesn't go away. It stays there, eating away at you until you think you can't bear it anymore."

Jerry reached the gate, and jerked it open. All pitch was gone from his voice as it screamed loudly through the shiny, metal amplifier.

"You get out . . . you get out of here," he rasped. "I shouldn't have let you in. . . . Shouldn't have talked to you. I knew it. I knew it. Now you get out! I was nice to you. Get out! See how they treat you." Marty moved quickly through the entrance, the gate slamming behind her as Jerry's voice continued its harsh ranting. ". . . And stay out! I mean it. Don't come back here. I won't have it. You stay out. . . . You stay out."

Marty moved away from the crackling of Jerry's voice, and headed with Jinks back to the beach. She felt emotionally drained, but at least she had pushed a little. Maybe one of them would panic and make a mistake . . . something that would make it clear that she and Jinks were not to blame.

A noise outside the front door brought David awake, and he sat up with a start, swinging his feet onto the porch floor. However, it wasn't Marty that he encountered as the screen door opened. Pam set her suitcase on the floor beside her as David rose to meet her. At first she was tentative. Then Pam ran to her husband and threw her arms around him.

"David, it's just getting more and more horrible."

"Yeah," David said. "When did you hear?"

"Not until Missy and I got to the ferry. It was jammed with people who were leaving Dune Beach. The killing was all they were talking about . . . and then I was told you found her." Pam pulled back and looked at David. "God, it's terrible. What's going on, David?"

"I'm not sure," David said, "but it's not Jinks. It was a human I saw on the beach last night."

Pam moved away from David slightly, avoiding his gaze. "I'm sure you're right, David . . . Jinks wasn't the reason I left, you know that."

"Yes, I do," David said, "but I don't know why you came back. Where is Missy?"

"With Clyde. I wanted to talk to you alone and find out what was going on before I brought her home. She and Clyde were standing on the sidewalk talking to Jerry Dile through the shrubs when I left them."

Pam looked back at David. "I came back because I thought it over, David, and I'm not going to quit. I'm not going to give up on what we have without at least trying to save it. I know I'm not much of a wife sometimes, but I try, and I want to keep on trying. You were right in the beginning. There's no running from this one. The three of us have been involved in it from the start, and all of us will have to work it out. I'm not saying I'll be good at it, but I'm willing to talk. The way you wanted it . . . the three of us. I'm willing to try."

David pulled his wife to him. "Don't worry, Pam. It'll all work out now that you're back. Actually, I'm glad you and Missy weren't here to be exposed to the danger."

"David, what is the danger? Who is doing these atrocious things?"

David hesitated. He wanted to be straightforward, and it astounded him that thing could possibly become more complicated. However, he knew he had to lie to Pam about his feelings until he was sure.

"I don't know," he said with concern. "All I'm sure of is that last night whoever it is passed right by our house. And it's not that I don't appreciate what you're trying to do, Pam, but in a way, I wish you hadn't decided to come back. I don't think it's safe here. Not after what's happened."

"What about Marty? How is she taking all this?"

"Well, I don't think it's what she had in mind for a relaxing vacation," David said quickly, trying to keep it light. "There's quite a bit of pressure on her. The police questioned her. . . . She's not allowed to leave the island. She's pretty upset, I guess. She went for a walk on the beach with Jinks to get away for a while."

Pam frowned. "You mean the police still think it's Jinks?"

David nodded. "In any case, they're convinced he's involved somehow."

"God! What a mess."

"Mess doesn't even come close," David said, smiling weakly. "Look, it'll be time for dinner soon. Why don't we eat and talk this thing out? We'll make some sort of decision about what to do before the last ferry leaves."

"All right," Pam said, "whatever you think. You want some coffee?"

"No thanks," David said, heading into the bedroom

to get his wallet. "I have to go meet Sam Kline. He's coming in on the four o'clock ferry."

"Why?" Pam asked, following after him.

"He examined the Butz girl's body, and there are a couple of things he wants to ask me about since I'm the one who discovered her," David improvised.

"Why don't you just give him a call when he gets back?"

"No, he doesn't want to take the chance of talking over the phone. Too public, I guess." David tucked in his shirt and jammed his wallet into his hip pocket. "Look, I've got a couple of ideas about these killings that I want to discuss with Sam anyway. This will only take a little while. I'll be back for supper. Then, we'll talk this whole thing out—and I mean all of us, including Marty—and we'll decide what to do."

"Yes," Pam said.

"Good. I'll stop at Clyde's and bring Missy home. Better keep her at the house for the rest of the day, just to be safe. Jinks will be here with Marty pretty soon anyway, so she won't mind."

Pam smiled nervously. "Hurry back, all right?"

David kissed his wife lightly. "As soon as I possibly can."

Although he was sure there was no danger in leaving Pam and Missy alone, even if Marty and Jinks did return to the house, David took a precaution when he met Clyde and his daughter on the sidewalk in front of Jerry Dile's. He asked Clyde to look in on his family while he was at the dock.

"No problem, Davy," Clyde answered amiably, "I'll take Pam some fish over for supper. But I do think you better talk to your friend with the monkey, or at least rein her in a little. She's running around here laying into everyone with accusations. Even went after Jerry, for God's sake. He told me just before Missy and Pam came up to us. You better talk to her, David. I'm not going to stand still for that shit if it happens again.''

David gave a frustrated sigh and nodded. "She's upset over this whole thing. I'll talk to her, I promise. And thanks for the favor, Clyde. I appreciate it. See you later, Jerry,'' David called toward the shrubs beside him. There was no answer. Assuming Jerry Dile had already gone back to his gardening, David gave Clyde a wave and headed home with Missy.

The sun was preparing for its evening plunge when the ferry pulled into Dune Beach. Sam Kline had missed the four o'clock; David was sure he would have made this, the six o'clock. From the fence lining the dock, David watched the mob of people fleeing from the island shuffle for positions to board the ferry as Sam Kline stepped off the boat and onto the crowded pier. David was aware that several people were watching him and pointing in his direction, but he ignored the attention he was drawing. As Sam reached the outer perimeter of the crowd, David walked up next to him.

"Want a beer, Sam?"

The doctor looked at David questioningly. "Yeah, I guess I could use a beer. You buying?''

David nodded; the two headed up the sidewalk toward Homer's. The bar was relatively empty, but rather than sit at the counter, David got two draughts and ushered Sam over to their regular table. Sam took a long pull on his beer and smiled.

"Thanks, David. That's good. Now. Let's have it.''

"What do you mean?''

"Come on, David. You didn't meet me just to buy me a beer.''

David exhaled heavily. "Okay. I need some information, and I thought you might be able to help me.''

"I will if I can. Go on," Sam said, taking another pull from his glass.

"Well, can you tell me anything about an operation in which the *corpus callosum* is severed?"

The doctor frowned and cleared his throat. "*Corpus callosum?*"

"Isn't that the right name?"

"Yeah, I guess so. You mean the nerve fiber at the middle of the brain, right?" David nodded. "Well, I'm no brain surgeon, David, but I have read a little about it. It's used in rare instances to stop convulsions. Separating the two hemispheres apparently breaks up the surge of energy that causes the nervous system to go haywire."

"Right," David said, pulling his chair in closer. "Now what can you tell me about the two hemispheres?"

"Although they look alike, the two sides serve different functions. I'm no expert, but it's my understanding that the right side is mute and irrational and helps us deal with spatial relationships, whereas the left side is more rational and gives us our ability to think logically. It also controls speech."

David nodded. "What I want to know is whether, after the severing operation, it would be possible for the right brain to act in a totally independent way . . . as a different personality."

"If you mean, does the operation turn the person into a schizophrenic? The answer is no. Oh, I'm sure there are adjustments to be made. In fact, I remember reading about a case where a postoperative patient was incapable of arranging building blocks in a prescribed pattern because one of his hands swatted the other hand away as the two sides of his brain battled for control. However, this was an isolated case in a medical journal, David. Just because the operation divides the brain into two independent halves, it doesn't create a Jekyll and Hyde."

David hesitated a moment, and then pushed ahead. "But suppose the mute side could be taught a language . . . some way of communicating other than speech. What would happen?"

Sam Kline stared at David keenly. "Look, David, you're not a medical doctor. You may know sociology, but you're completely out of your element when it comes to brain surgery. And frankly, so am I. And amateur conjecture about mental problems is nothing but dangerous." Sam leaned in toward David. "Look, what you're driving at is your business, but if it has anything to do with finding a human suspect for these killings, you can forget it. I examined the Butz girl today, you know."

"And?"

Sam sucked at his teeth and shook his head. "It was the look. Nothing positive. A feeling. Same as the horse. I'll grant you there's a pattern. The killer is definitely leaving his sign. But I'm just not so sure it's a human attack. I worked for the Suffolk County police for a while years ago, and I've seen murders, a lot of them. And a human killing is different from one done by, say, a mad dog. An animal killing has an unrestrained savage quality about it. Now there's definitely an intelligence involved in these killings. You can tell that by the repeated throat injuries and crushed skulls and sometimes an instrument or weapon of some kind is used. But, I don't know—it's the look. Malicious savagery is all I can think of to describe it. And that's what the Butz girl looked like."

"Sam, I'd swear I saw a human figure on the beach last night."

"Well, I don't mean to disagree with you, Dave, but I think you're wrong. I'd bet on an animal."

Sam's comment hit David wrong, and he snapped angrily back at him. "What are you saying, Sam? That I'm lying to protect the chimp?"

The doctor looked at David. "No. But it was night and it was foggy and you could be mistaken about what you saw. Damn it, David, I know you're no fool. And if you say this chimp can talk and understand what people say, I believe you. But doesn't that also mean that we don't know just how intelligent it really is? Of course your friend thinks the chimp is innocent. It's like a kid to her! Are you absolutely sure about it, or are you maybe, just maybe, letting what she says influence your opinion?"

David let out a sigh. "Who the hell knows. I'm not sure of anything. I'm sorry I got angry. I'm just tired. Anyway, thanks for the time. I better get back; I told Pam I'd hurry."

"I'm headed in that direction," Sam said, standing. "I'll walk along with you if you don't mind."

"No, not at all," David answered, pushing in his chair, and throwing some change on the table. "You want to stop in for a drink? In fact, Clyde dropped off some fish, and I'm sure there's plenty if you'd like to join us for supper."

"I'll pass on dinner, thanks," Sam said, holding Homer's swinging entrance door open for David. "But I would like to stop in for a minute if the chimpanzee is there . . . and if you don't mind."

"Not at all," David said. "You think it might help you?"

"Well, let's just say I'd like to see your friend's pet at close range. I don't know that it will make any difference, but it might, now that I've examined a victim closely. It will probably just help to confirm for me that you're right. We'll use my stopping for a drink as an excuse."

David nodded. And, as he and Sam headed for the house, the more he thought about it, the more he wasn't sure. Sam Kline was experienced, and David valued his opinion. If he said it was an animal, there was a strong chance he was right.

. . . She must be stopped. . . . Do not wait for darkness. . . . She is not confused. She is the danger. . . . She does not understand yet, but she will. She is the danger. . . . She must be stopped. Now. . . . She is the one, the true enemy. The rest are stumbling in confusion. She is the danger. Stop her. Her usefulness is over. . . . Savagely and without mercy. . . . Stop her. Now. . . .

EIGHTEEN

It was late in the afternoon when Marty returned to the Paddock house with Jinks. She had walked for several miles before turning around and heading back, but the physical exhaustion didn't bother her; her emotional state was calmer. And she was determined to get through the present crisis just as she had been able to get through everything else in her life. It did not upset her that Pam had returned with Missy. She just accepted it as something else that had to be dealt with.

Missy was ecstatic to see Jinks again. And, as the two of them ran excitedly to the front porch, Pam attempted a cheerful smile.

"Well, at least there are two of us who aren't overwhelmed," she said, coming to Marty. "I'm sorry the situation has become so difficult for you, Marty. I certainly didn't make things any easier with my stupid behavior yesterday, I know. If I had been here last night, I might have been able to help in some way, but I'm going to try and make up for it. And I told David that I want to be a part of whatever is decided. . . . All three of us are going to have to work this out. But first things first. Right now, we're going to get supper ready."

Marty gave Pam a tired, sympathetic smile. "Fine. Where is David?"

"He went to see Sam Kline about something," Pam said, as she headed into the kitchen. "Sam is the doctor around here, and he wanted some information about Tammy Butz. I'm not sure what. David said he'd explain it when he got back. He should be here any minute."

Marty followed after Pam, and stopped at the kitchen doorway. "What did David say about the murders?"

Pam shrugged. "Nothing really, except he knows it isn't Jinks. He said we would all talk about everything after dinner and decide what to do."

"Good," Marty said. "I took a long walk and thought things out, and I'm ready to talk now, too. I have some ideas of my own that I don't think David thought of."

"Well," Pam said, holding up a metal tray, "our biggest problem right now is, who'll clean these fish? David usually takes care of it because it turns my stomach. Do you mind doing it while I get the rest ready?"

"Not at all," Marty said, accepting the tray of fish and gutting knife from Pam. "I'm an expert at this type of thing from my African experience, you know. Where shall I do it? The sink?"

"No, I can't take the smell. Do it out back on the patio. We just hose it down to clean up."

Marty nodded and turned toward the back door as Missy and Jinks bounded into the living room.

"Mommy, can Jinks and I go down to the beach, please?"

"No. We're going to eat soon. You know your job."

"Anyway, I need Jinks right now," Marty said, trying to be helpful. "He's going to help me clean the fish."

"Oh, me too. I can clean fish," Missy said proudly. "Daddy showed me. You just slit the belly and dump the guts."

Pam shook her head, smiling to Marty. "See what wonderful things David teaches our daughter?" She turned to Missy. "I think Marty and Jinks can manage the fish on their own, Missy. Your job is to set the table, remember?"

"Well, I can help after I set the table, can't I?"

"Set it first, and we'll see. I don't think it will take them very long. And make sure the napkins are turned correctly."

"Oh, Mom," Missy said, hurrying to the kitchen. "I'll be right out, Marty."

"Okay, Missy, we'll save a belly for you to slit," Marty said, smiling at Pam, and then heading with Jinks out to the patio.

Marty could have cleaned the fish very quickly, since she really was somewhat of an expert at it. But for Missy's sake she took her time. As she worked, she tried to decide exactly what she would say when David arrived. The only thing she was sure of was that she didn't look forward to the discussion. She wondered whether David would mention his suspicions to the doctor. Well, at least she now had some ideas of her own to confront him with. Out of nowhere, a picture of David naked, in bed, came into her mind, and she thought of the irony of Pam's wishing she had been there the night before to help.

That was when the attack came.

If she had been concentrating on the fish and her surroundings, she might have been able to stop it in some way, but she wasn't concentrating. The force of it knocked her backwards as it came at her. Tearing and ripping. In panic, Marty felt her throat being lacerated, her air choked off before she could scream. Frantically, she clutched for her throat, but she had lost the knife, and now it was being used against her in hard, hacking blows, blows that chopped at her attempt to save herself. And through the pain she felt and heard the knife's blade slicing into skin and cartilage. And through the blinding flashes of pain, as her body screamed for air, she knew that she was losing. And it was as the flashes became sheets of searing white, filling her vision and pushing her toward unconsciousness, that she saw and knew her attacker. And it no longer mattered. She was losing . . . and she was going to die.

Sam and David came into the house to find the dining table set but no one in the room.

"Pam?" David called.

"In here, David," his wife answered from the kitchen. "I'm glad you're home. I'll start dinner cooking."

"Sam Kline just stopped in to have a drink."

Pam came through the kitchen doorway, wiping her hands on a dishtowel. "Hi, Sam! Clyde brought some fish over earlier, and I thought we'd have them for supper. You're welcome to stay if you like. There's plenty."

"Thanks, Pam, but I better not. One quick drink, and then I better get moving," Sam Kline answered pleasantly.

"Where is everyone?" David asked.

"Well, Marty went with Jinks to the patio to clean the fish, and Missy was setting the table. She was right here a minute ago. I guess she went to help them. Marty should be done by now. I'll check." Pam went down the hall as David motioned Sam toward the sofa.

"Sit down, Sam," he said, "what can I get you?"

Pam screamed.

David bolted down the hall. Pam was leaning against the open back door, staring out. David looked past her. Marty was thrashing wildly and helplessly among the fish and their loose intestines on the multi-colored flagstones. She was making strangled gurgling sounds in her throat. Random hack marks covered the upper part of her body, and the lower portion of her right arm was lying beside her, completely severed at the elbow. Blood spurted from her sliced throat and from the stub of her arm. A gutting knife smeared with blood lay on the stone near her head.

David stood there paralyzed. Sam Kline shoved him forward.

"Tourniquet her arm with your belt, Dave!" he shouted. David reacted automatically, pulling the belt from its hoops and wrapping it tightly around the top part of Marty's arm. His fingers slipped as he fumbled with the buckle, but finally the notch caught. The flow of blood stopped. Sam took a quick look at Marty's neck and reached for the gutting knife beside Marty's head.

"Sam!" David shouted, "The fingerprints!"

"To hell with the prints, David! She's dying. I've got to get air to her."

Without hesitation, Sam picked up the knife and made a small cut in Marty's throat below her larynx, into her trachea. Then he pulled a pen from his breast pocket, unscrewed it, cut off the tip of the lower half of the pen casing, and jammed the makeshift hollow tube into the incision. He ripped cloth from his shirt tails, pushed it against the cuts on her throat above the pen casing, and shoved his arm under her, elevating her head and shoulders.

"Looks like there was a struggle. She must have stopped the killer from crushing her skull," David said.

"Get a 'copter here fast, or it won't matter," Sam shouted, "she'll die anyway. Pam, get me some ice and a sewing needle. A big one. And some thread."

David started past Pam, but she grabbed his arm and

gasped. "Oh my God, David. *Missy. Where's Missy?*"

"I'll find her," David said, "call the 'copter and help Sam." David ran for the front door, and as he came out of the house he was screaming. "*Missy! Help! Clyde! Somebody!* Missy, where are you? . . . *Missy!*"

David ran out onto the path, calling; then Clyde was beside him.

"What's wrong, Davy?" Clyde was breathing hard.

"Marty's been attacked, and Missy's gone. So is Jinks. You've got to help me find them, Clyde. I'll go towards town. You take the beach." Clyde nodded and ran down the sidewalk as Pam appeared at the front door.

"David, is she out there?"

"No," David said hurriedly. "Stay in the house!"

Not waiting for an answer, David started up Holly Lane, calling for Missy. People came out of their houses, disturbed by the commotion. David reached the bay end of the street and, finding nothing, he quickly turned around and headed back toward his house. A thundering helicopter passed overhead, its lights searching below for a place to land. David ran until, looking ahead, he saw something. Somehow he had missed it when he ran up the street.

Jerry Dile's gate was wide open.

David hurried through into the garden, dark and inviting in the gathering dusk. He was unable to see, and paused to allow his eyes to adjust to the dim light within the dense vegetation. Suddenly there was heavy, labored breathing within the darkness. A large figure emerged partially from the shadows. Then it spoke. "David." The high-pitched squeaky, metallic voice was unmistakably Jerry's.

David turned quickly toward Jerry. "Is Missy here?"

"Yes. Hurry. . . . This way. What is happening, David? She is very frightened . . . very frightened."

214

"Marty was attacked. That's all I know," David said hastily. Jerry led David down the narrow row of plants and into a greenhouse. The enclosure was filled with the heavy odor of thick, damp vegetation. Jerry pointed the beam of a small flashlight toward the corner of the glass building, and motioned for David to go on ahead. Pushing some branches aside, David saw his daughter and the chimpanzee crouched near some shrubbery. Missy looked very small and frightened as she stared up at him. She was crying. Yet she was holding Jinks tightly, her short little arms around the chimpanzee protectively.

"Don't hurt him, Daddy," she said. "He's afraid."

David knelt slowly, closing his arms around his daughter. "Are you all right?" he asked.

Missy nodded and put her arms around her father's neck. David blinked hard, but the sense of relief was too strong. The tears came anyway.

"Yes, I'm all right, Daddy . . . but Jinks is afraid. I didn't mean to go, Daddy, but Jinks came running down the hall from the patio and he pulled on me . . . and he was shaking. He kept signing 'hide Jinks, hide Jinks' over and over and Jerry's was the best place I could think of so I took him out the deck door and over the dunes. Then we circled back and I came here." Missy pulled back from David slightly. "Only now Jinks won't talk to me. Something's wrong with him, Daddy. I think he's sick." David looked at the chimp. Cowering under the beam of Jerry Dile's flashlight, Jinks was shivering violently. "See? Please help him, Daddy. He didn't hurt anyone. I heard what they said on the ferry, but I know it isn't true. Please, Daddy, don't let him die?"

David wiped at the tears running down Missy's face. "No, honey, Jinks will be all right." He stood up and took his daughter's hand.

"It's okay, Jinks," Missy said. "Daddy's here. And I'll take care of you." Jinks did not look up. He seemed to shiver even more violently.

Jerry leaned toward David so that Missy would not hear, and his voice spoke in a hissing whisper. "Is Marty dead, David? Did you say she was dead?"

"No," David answered quietly, "but it's close. We're not sure. We need to pray for her."

Missy looked up from the chimp to her father. "What? What's wrong with Marty, Daddy?"

"She's been hurt pretty badly," David said. "Come on, honey . . . let's go home."

A new experience. Surprise at the strength of her struggle . . . her determination to stay alive. And because of it, doubt entered into the act, introducing fear, confusing the movement, blurring the intent.

She had been stopped, but was it enough? Now she knew. She was alive . . . and she knew. It was time to retreat, to burrow down into the safe darkness, to wait and to watch. . . .

To act would be foolish. But waiting was the sign of true cunning. Waiting would confuse them. Let them wonder why the killing had stopped. Let them search, bewildered.

The waiting could be done. It had been done before. And the sensations had proven to be even stronger after the long wait had ended. That was the answer. Eventually, the waiting would end, and, just as before, the killing bliss would come again. . . .

NINETEEN

Marty did not die, but it was close. The throat slices had not hit an artery, or she would have died in the 'copter. But the doctor who operated, while Sam assisted, said it would be a long time before Marty would be able to talk again, if she were ever able to. And the right arm damage was permanent. It couldn't be remedied. Furthermore, Marty was only semiconscious, and no one was sure when or if she would regain consciousness.

Sam Kline gave David a status report in a phone call from the hospital that jarred David out of his sleep the following morning. David thanked Sam for calling, and, rubbing his eyes, dropped the receiver back on its cradle. He was still dead tired. After talking to the police they had rushed to leave Fire Island the previous evening. Then, when they had finally gotten to their home in Queens, things had not gone well.

Pam had refused to let Jinks roam free in the house, so David had locked him in the shed outside. He hated to do it, considering Jinks' condition, but he had no idea what was really going on, and he knew it was safer. Missy had started screaming in protest, and had gone into the worst temper tantrum David had ever seen from her. He had ended it by spanking her for the first time in his life and putting her to bed. Then he had gotten Pam a tranquilizer, spilling the pills all over the floor because his hands were shaking so badly. It had told him he was pretty close to cracking himself. After calling the hospital and finding out that Marty's condition was still critical, he had asked to be called the minute there was a change, pulled off his clothes, and fallen into bed.

David realized he would sleep no more, and pushed himself up as Pam stirred slightly and rolled to her side, her sleep unbroken. After dressing, David decided he'd better eat something before he left for the hospital. He gave Missy her breakfast at the same time. She pouted all the way through her cereal, but David was finally able to cheer her up by letting her go feed Jinks, and promising her that when they returned from the hospital, they would fix the shed up into a nice house for Jinks.

David hoped taking Missy to the hospital with him might help Marty to tell what had happened. Maybe she couldn't talk, but she could still sign with her left hand; he hoped that Missy would be able to understand what she said.

Sam Kline and another doctor, whose name David didn't catch, led them into Marty's hospital room. Ernest Nilscoff, Joe Baker, and a detective were also at the hospital when David arrived, but they waited outside the room, their faces crowded together at the small glass window near the top of the door.

Missy gripped her father's hand tightly and stared wide-eyed at the many tubes that ran to Marty's body from bottles of blood and glucose overhead. David had Missy stay just inside the door with the doctors, and sat in a chair next to the bed. His voice cracked as he spoke.

"Marty? . . . Marty, can you hear me? Marty, it's David." There was no response. David's eyes darted from the bandage covering Marty's amputation to the thick plastic tube fitted into her throat. His face

219

tightened. "Marty? It's David. . . . Can you tell me what happened?"

Marty's body stirred and her eyes opened, but her pupils were high under her lids and only the bloodshot whites stared out. Then the pupils centered, but even though her eyes remained open, it was obvious that they were not focusing. Marty's mouth opened; her dry, cracked lips bled a little. As her lips moved, she emitted a soft whisper of breath. It was obvious that even whispered speech was beyond her. Marty's jaw opened and closed several times. Then her body began to jerk, and water appeared around the whites of her eyes. The doctor with Sam moved forward.

"I think that's enough," he said quietly. "It's too soon."

David nodded and had started to back away when Marty's left arm slowly began to rise into the air. David glanced at Missy. His daughter was staring intently at Marty's arm. Suddenly, Marty's back arched and her arm stiffened. Her hand moved randomly, but it did not sign. However, as Marty's lips continued to move, David suddenly realized that the lips were slowly and silently forming his name.

"Yes, Marty," he said urgently, bending closer. "It's David. I'm here. Can you tell me what happened? Use your hand, Marty . . . don't try to talk. . . . Sign. Missy will understand you."

Marty's head jerked from side to side, and her eyes again rolled high under her lids. Her arm and hand moved, but still there was no signing. Tears began to flow from Marty's eyes and edge their way down the side of her face. David glanced at the doctors; Sam Kline motioned for him to come away from the bed.

"It's all right, Marty," David said softly, gently stroking Marty's damp forehead, "it's okay. You don't have to talk. Rest and get well. Everything's going to be

220

all right. I'm sorry, Marty . . . please hear me . . . I'm so sorry, but I'll make it up to you. I'll take care of you, Marty. I'll be here whenever you need me. You sleep now and get better. Everything's going to be all right."

As David spoke, Marty's body slowly relaxed, and her arm dropped back onto the bed. As her eyes closed, her body became still. The doctor with Sam crossed over, took Marty's pulse, nodded that she was okay, and then motioned everyone out of the room. In the hall, Nilscoff was the first to speak.

"So what's the story? Didn't look like you got much from here. Did your daughter pick up anything, Paddock?"

David's head snapped in the direction of the mayor. "Nilscoff, I swear to God, if you don't—"

"I'm afraid she's still in shock, Nils," Sam cut in, putting his hand on David's shoulder. "And until that subsides, whatever happened is going to remain locked inside her."

"And how long will that be?" Nilscoff said impatiently, ignoring David's stare.

Sam pursed his lips. "I can't answer that, Nils. Could be soon. On the other hand—"

Missy looked up at her father with a troubled expression. "Is Marty going to be all right, Daddy?"

David looked at the doctors. Sam Kline frowned, and the other doctor shrugged. David put a comforting arm around his daughter. "We'll just have to wait and see, honey," he said.

When David and Missy returned from the hospital, Pam was out of bed, but she was still in her nightgown. When she met them at the front door, David noted that, for one of the few times in her life, his wife didn't look very good.

"Well, how is she?" Pam asked anxiously.

221

"Alive . . . that's about all," David answered.

"Marty looks really sick, Mommy," Missy said. "She has tubes running into her."

Pam frowned. "You took her into Marty's room, David?"

"Yes. I needed her. It was important."

"Did you check on Jinks, Mommy?"

Pam shook her head tiredly. "No, Missy, I just got up."

"Can I go see if he's okay, Daddy?"

"Sure," David said, "Go ahead. Just make sure you hook the door after you check."

Pam watched Missy run toward the kitchen and then turned to her husband. David recognized the expression on her face. It was her look of irritation.

"I know you're concerned, David. So am I. But was it really so important to expose Missy to that? You didn't have to take her to the hospital. I would have gotten up."

"I needed her in case we could get Marty to sign. Missy is the only one who might have known what she was saying. And our daughter's not a baby, Pam. She was fine."

"Of course she was, in front of you! She wouldn't let you know if it disturbed her; you might be disappointed in her. Did Marty sign?"

"No."

"Then it wasn't as crucial as you thought, was it?"

"Pam—"

"All right . . . all right, let's not argue. It's done. Is Marty really that bad?" David nodded. "But she is going to make it, isn't she?"

David collapsed in a slouch on the couch. "Right now she's in a semi-coma, but at least all her vital signs have stabilized. The arm couldn't be reattached, though. And the doctors aren't sure about her being able to talk.

. . . They say maybe." David rubbed his face with his hand, and then looked up. I'm going to lay the thing out right now, Pam. When Marty begins to recover, when they release her from the hospital, I want to bring her here to recuperate. Now, before you say anything, I know you're not going to be crazy about it, but the plain fact is, we ran out on her last time, and I'm not going to do it again. She told me some things about her surgery the other day, and it was far worse than we imagined. She really could have used us, Pam, believe me. And you know what we were doing."

"You're second-guessing me, David. I don't know why you're so sure I'll object. As a matter of fact, I agree with you. I think we owe it to her. It won't totally erase the guilt, but at least it would help a little."

"There's something else you should consider, too."

Pam sat down opposite David. "I know—what's going to happen among the three of us after Marty is okay. But our first concern is to make sure she recovers. And as I told you, David, I'm not running from any of this anymore. I committed myself when I decided to come back yesterday."

"Actually," David said, "I think what you're saying makes this all easier to deal with, but to tell you the truth, I was thinking about Jinks."

Pam sighed. "Now look, David, let's not push it. I've already gone more than halfway. I'm sure there are places around here where he could be provided for better than we can possibly manage."

"I know how you feel about the chimp, Pam. But, first of all, we're certain now that he's not dangerous. I mean, he wouldn't have attacked Marty, for crying out loud. Furthermore, nothing means more to Marty than Jinks. And I think his being here would be better for her than anything any of us could do . . . and I'm including the doctors in that."

"Do you honestly think the people on the chimpanzee project will allow Jinks to stay with us?"

"If I explain why it's important? Yes, I think they will. It will also please Missy. You know she loves the animal."

"I also know what he does in front of her. You want that to continue?"

'I think caring for Jinks is a very important part of what we owe Marty. Isn't it?"

"All right, David. All right. . . . All right," Pam said, closing her eyes and nodding. "But not in the house. I will not have that animal in the house. That's the only way I'll agree to it."

"Fine," David said, "The important thing is that Marty knows he's here. And she'll be able to see him whenever she wants."

Pam spoke without opening her eyes. "Well, now that we have all that settled, all Marty has to do is start to recover."

As the days passed Marty's wounds began to heal, but she did not recover. She remained totally unresponsive to the environment around her and did not so much as even attempt to sign again.

And, even though David fixed up the shed, and the chimp was under Missy's constant care, Jinks didn't do much better than Marty. He would sit in the shed and pull at his hair, weaving back and forth for hours at a time. Worse yet, he would sleep in his own urine, which David felt was a pretty clear indication of training regression.

However, David remained convinced that the key for both Marty and Jinks was to make it possible for them to see each other when the time came, so he did not inform the people from the primate institute of Jinks' condition when they called. They expressed their concern about Marty, and, after being assured by David that he would look after Marty during her convalescence, they told David someone would come by to bring Jinks back to them. David insisted, however, that the chimp stay with him and explained why. The arrangement was agreed to, at least for a trial period.

David was always aware that, since the killer obviously wasn't Marty or Jinks, there was, in fact, some unknown murderer still at large on Fire Island. He had not struck again; it occured to David that his guests had been perfect scapegoats, and he was probably waiting for another. He told the police as much during one of their several conversations. They agreed it was a possibility, and had to admit there were no concrete clues about Marty's attacker, but the investigation was continuing.

When Marty was well enough to be moved, she was brought to the Paddock home. David put her in the guestroom and hired a private nurse. Being both weak and nonresponsive, Marty could neither feed nor relieve herself without help. David decided not to bring Jinks into her presence for a while. He didn't think Marty would be aware of the chimp yet, and he didn't want to upset Pam prematurely by bringing Jinks into the house. In spite of what Pam had said, her mood had not been very cheerful since Marty's arrival.

After two weeks in the house, Marty continued to show absolutely no signs of improvement, and David was very tense. Every aspect of the situation was frustrating, including Missy's constant worry over Jinks. In spite of her efforts to improve things for him, the chimp had steadily deteriorated. David was beginning to regret his decision to keep the chimp with them.

Then Sam Kline came to visit.

At first David thought the doctor had just dropped by

to check on Marty. However, as they left her room, and headed into the kitchen for coffee, Sam's question was about something else.

"So what have the police come up with, David?" The doctor eased himself into a chair at the table. "Anything?"

David poured coffee into the mugs on the counter in front of him. "Zip. You want anything in this?"

"Black is fine. How about you? Any new ideas?"

"Not really," David said, setting the steaming cups on the table and dropping heavily into a chair. "It did occur to me that Marty might have stumbled onto something that she hadn't had a chance to tell me about. I know she was pushing people with questions that afternoon. Clyde told me. Who knows? Maybe she hit a nerve with someone. Just a thought."

Sam sipped his coffee before he spoke again. "How about that theory you spoke to me about? Have you given that any more thought?"

David frowned. "What's that mean?"

"Well, I saw something recently, David, that reminded me of the discussion we were having that afternoon before Marty was attacked. You know, about the split-brain surgery?"

"Now wait a minute, Sam."

"Let me finish. Obviously, it was Marty you were talking about. I figure she had to undergo this type of operation as a result of that accident you told me about. Am I right?"

David nodded. "Yes, but—"

"The point is this. Earlier this week I saw a case where the *corpus callosum* had been severed while I was visiting at Pilgrim State, a mental hospital out on the island. Coincidence, really. I got there early for a meeting so I went with Ellen Marshall, one of the staff doctors, on her rounds. The boy I'm talking about was one of her patients. I probably wouldn't have thought twice about it if you and I hadn't talked, but when she pointed him out, he caught my interest. The boy had been in Viet Nam, and had suffered a major head wound. And, the way Ellen explained it to me, the doctors decided to disconnect the *callosum* to help alleviate severe malfunctions within the nervous system. Now, isn't that similar to what happened to your friend?"

David leaned forward. "Basically. What was he like? Did you talk to him?"

"Yes, I did, David. That's why I'm here." Sam shifted in his chair and wrapped both his hands around his cup of coffee. "You could sense immediately that he was just a nice, quiet kid. You know, the kind of person you can't help liking. Freckles, shy smile, kind of sincere and innocent. Didn't seem to belong on the ward at all. I mean he seemed normal."

"But—"

"Well, of course, he had had trouble adjusting to his condition. Buttoning his shirt with his right hand while his left hand tried to unbutton it. That sort of thing."

David nodded. "Marty mentioned the same kinds of difficulties. What else?"

Sam looked directly at David and held his gaze. "'After a period of time, they released him on an outpatient basis. Two days after he was released, in a fit of rage brought on by some meaningless argument, he went after his sister with a pair of sissors. Almost killed her." David said nothing. "According to Dr. Marshall, our ability to control our emotions has a lot more to do with the interaction between the two hemispheres than was formerly believed. In this case, severing the connection between the two sides of the brain seems to have negated the involuntary control that helps keep our emotions in check."

"Okay," David said with a sigh, "that's one case. How about others? Is the same thing true?"

"Not enough data. Hard to say, according to her. That is the big question though, isn't it?"

"Sam, I don't see that this does much good. About the last thing Marty has to do right now is deal with her emotions. She doesn't even seem to have any, for crying out loud."

"I know that, David, but I'm not finished. I said the kid seemed normal, and he did. I even talked to him for a while, about his home in Brooklyn, his sister, whom he'd lived with before the war. Likeable and shy is the best way to characterize him. The way he scratches his head nervously as he asked me for a cigarette. It's funny, even at the brief mention of the war I could see his face cloud, grief tearing away at his shy innocence. I think it was the wholesomeness of his face that got me, David. That convinced me I'd better talk to you. There's no way I would have believed what happened if I hadn't seen it."

"Well, come on," David said, gesturing impatiently, "let's have it. What happened?"

Sam pushed his empty cup aside. "The kid went completely berserk not more than three minutes after I talked to him. I had moved on with Dr. Marshall, but there were some other non-patients in the ward—students, I guess. Anyway, I was kind of half watching them and this kid too when he went up to one of the female visitors, and I guess tried to bum a cigarette. Anyway, his right hand was scratching his head. But I noticed that his left hand was, in what seemed an unconscious movement, massaging his groin. That should have tipped me off, but it didn't, because mental wards tend to bring out that kind of unacceptable behavior. And it was as I stood there staring at him that it happened.

"The girl was fumbling in her purse, searching for cigarettes, so she missed the kid's movement. At first it was all his left hand because his right hand was still involved in the head scratching of his cigarette request. Frantically, almost savagely, David, this kid's left hand tore at the front of his trousers, pulling them open and down until his genitals were exposed. Then, in a swift blurred movement, just as she looked up, his left hand tore away the front of her blouse. She started screaming bloody murder, and I ran toward them as the kid's left hand grabbed the girl's shoulder and pushed her to her knees, forcing her exposed breasts against him. Then his right hand jerked into action. And, I swear, David, this is the God's truth. I saw it happen and it was incredible to watch.

"In a forceful sweeping motion, the boy's right hand swung around and grabbed his left wrist, wrenching it free from the girl. She fell backwards, sobbing, as his hands grappled with each other. I ran to where the girl had fallen and stooped to comfort her, but found I could not take my eyes from the kid. His hands were actually fighting with one another. The left hand pulled to free itself, and the right hand tightened its grip, pushing the other hand up and over his head. Then it sharply pulled his entire left lower arm and hand across the back of his neck and downward so that he found himself in a sort of self-contained half-Nelson. His left arm pulled against the restriction, and the kid, his legs becoming tangled in his pants, fell to the floor just as Ellen Marshall and several others reached him.

"Then there was complete confusion. The kid kept screaming, 'I'm sorry! I couldn't help it! I'm sorry!' over and over. Finally, some aides got him to his feet and started leading him away. And as they passed me, I saw his face at close range.

"The expression on that face was wrong somehow. It

had changed. Now it was slightly disjointed, like a picture where the faces of two different people are joined together. And, although the agony and hysteria were there, I also saw a greedy exhilaration. It seemed as though some sort of schizophrenic chasm was stretching across the kid's tortured face, David.''

"What was your friend's reaction to this whole thing?" David asked intently.

"Very matter of fact. I guess it had happened before. The hands fighting each other, I mean. She said that they were convinced that his operation had merely aggravated his personality problems, rather than caused them. There's no way of telling, of course. Could be true, and it could also be surgeons covering themselves.''

David rubbed his forehead and stood up. "You want some more coffee?"

Sam shook his head. "No thanks." David picked up the empty cups and took them to the counter. "Well, what do you think, David?"

"I think you're right, Sam," David said, turning back toward the table and leaning against the counter. "It sounds pretty incredible."

"You understand why I thought I better tell you, though, don't you?"

"Yes," David said. His voice had a tired and hollow ring.

Sam cleared his throat. "Look, David. You know her. I don't. And you came to me with the idea in the first place. I'm not making any judgements here. I'm just giving you information."

"What's your opinion?" David said. "Is it possible? Could Marty have attacked herself against her own will? I mean, that's a hell of a lot more extreme than two hands fighting with each other."

Sam nodded in agreement. "I know. Frankly, I just

don't think it's possible. But I figured you should know about this.''

"But why, if you're sure self-mutilation wasn't possible on her part?''

Sam stood up. "I wouldn't have believed what that kid did to himself if I hadn't seen it. So, even though from my medical viewpoint it is not possible that your friend attacked herself, the fact is I could still be wrong. And there's another reason. Let's face it, David. Dune Beach is quiet. Not a damn thing has happened there since the attack on Marty. Now there has to be an explanation for that.''

David looked through the doorway toward the guest room for a moment, and then turned back to face the doctor. "Sam, I don't have to tell you that having Marty in this house under these conditions is no picnic. I'm sure you can imagine how Pam feels about it. It's only because she's out shopping with Missy that the tension level has dropped a few notches around here. But, in spite of that, goddamn it, I'm going to keep that helpless woman right here until I'm absolutely sure there's nothing further I can do to help her. Because I was wrong, Sam. I know the kind of thinking that led you here to tell me this, because I've been through the same process. But I was wrong. And there's no doubt in my mind about that. I'm not saying I understand what has happened, but I know Marty is an undeserving victim in this. And my only concern now is to help her get well.''

Sam pursed his lips and nodded. "Good enough, David. It does tend to take me back to square one, though.''

David frowned. "Which is?''

"The animal theory.'' Sam gave David a nervous smile. "Where's the chimp?''

"Sorry, Sam,'' David said, shaking his head, "I'm

231

afraid I was right on that one too. Come on, I'll show you your killer chimp. Or rather what's left of him. That's another problem I've got to deal with pretty damn soon.''

David led Sam outside to the small metal shed in a far corner of the back yard. The door squeaked loudly as David opened it after flipping the lock, but the chimp, who was hovering against an interior shed wall, seemed oblivious to the sound and to the visitors. It took Sam's eyes a moment to adjust to darkness within the enclosure. However, when he finally could see Jinks clearly, he reacted with a soft whistle of disbelief.

The change in the chimpanzee was incredible. He seemed smaller and much older because of drastic weight loss. And his movements were slow and without definition. But the most disturbing thing about him was his hair. Patches of hair were missing all over his body, and where the hair should have been, bare pinkness showed. Some of the hairless areas were scabbed but others were open, festering sores.

"Not very pleasant, is it?" David said as they stepped back into the sunlight. He closed the door after them and flipped the lock. "He's been like that for the duration, Sam. All those bare patches were caused by his constant and unending grooming . . . he just wore away the hair. Just can't snap him out of it. Even Missy has no effect, although he will eat a little bit for her at times.''

Sam shook his head. "Well, he's not good, that's for sure.''

"I think it's grief, to tell you the truth. Over losing Marty . . . either that, or shock over seeing her attacked. He was with her, you know.''

"I know, and don't get angry, David, but that means he could also be suffering from severe guilt. If he was there, why didn't he try to stop it? And why wasn't he attacked?''

"You don't give up, do you, Sam?''

Sam raised his eyebrows. "Just trying to be objective. He's an animal. And one who has had his basic intelligence tampered with. Maybe he's the one with schizophrenic tendencies.''

"Sam, he wouldn't attack Marty. He just wouldn't do it.''

"You don't know for sure though, do you, David? Take my advice and keep him in that shed, all right?''

David opened the back door, and allowed the doctor to pass in front of him. "You've been talking to Clyde too much, Sam. But I'll give you another possibility that the two of you haven't considered.''

"What's that?''

"A setup,'' David said, ushering Sam into the living room, and to the front door. "Marty and Jinks could have been used. And the killer has not struck again because if he does, all the heat will be focused directly on him. There won't be any scapegoats.''

Sam thought for a moment and nodded. "Good point. Any suspicions?''

David shook his head. "None. And that's the bitch of it. Don't you see, Sam? Marty and Jinks know who it is, and it's locked up inside of them. I have to find a way to reach them. I have to get one of them to sign.''

Sam opened the front door. "Well, don't get your hopes up, David. As far as I could tell, there has been no change in Marty's condition at all since you brought her here. How long do you think you can keep this up, considering the way Pam feels about it?''

"I don't know,'' David said. "I'm pushing it now.''

It was during the evening meal a couple of days after Sam's visit that Pam's patience ran out. David was pouring milk into Missy's glass, and there was a tense silence as Pam, with disgust, watched the uniformed nurse feed Marty cream of chicken soup from a plastic bowl. Marty, dressed in a bathrobe, was slumped in her chair. And, as the nurse lifted the next spoonful of soup to Marty's lips, Marty's eyes rolled back in her sockets, the soup dribbling out of her mouth and running down her chin. Pam slammed her fork down and stood up.

"David, damn it! Enough!" she said angrily. "I'm sorry, I know what I said and I've tried to be understanding, but this is absurd! I cannot watch her drool all over the table anymore! And I won't have Missy subjected to this any longer, either!"

"What do you want me to do, Pam?" David said.

"I don't know, but for Christ's sake do something . . . for once in your life get a grip on the situation and do something."

David glared at his wife, took a deep breath and stood up. Then, ignoring Pam completely, he dismissed the nurse for the evening, and walked over to the phone and started to dial. Pam helped the bewildered nurse gather her things and was showing her to the door when David spoke to Missy.

"Missy," he said as he finished dialing, "go out to the shed and get Jinks."

"Oh no," Pam said, closing the door after the nurse, and turning quickly toward her husband. "Not on your life. I will not have that chimpanzee in here. Forget it, David."

"Why don't you just keep out of this?" David said, his voice raising in volume as he cupped his hand over the mouthpiece. "Huh? Why don't you just shut your goddamn mouth and keep out of it! Missy, I said to go out and get Jinks. Now do it!"

Missy gave her mother a worried look, then hurried out the back door. Pam said nothing, but stood staring at David.

"Bartley's," Clyde's familiar voice crackled

impersonally on the phone.

"Clyde," David said, forcing his mood to improve as he spoke. "This is David Paddock. How's everything in Dune Beach?"

Clyde's voice brightened. "Pretty good. How's things with you, Davy?"

David gave Pam a glance. "Only fair, Clyde. Has there been anymore sign of trouble there?"

"Not a rustle . . . but don't you worry about old Clyde. It'd take a hell of a lot more to drive me and the wife off this island."

David tried to sound casual. "What's the feeling there, Clyde . . . about the murders, I mean?"

"Well, the way I hear it, Nilscoff still thinks it's the monkey. Thinks you're too involved to admit it. Said you'll probably get ripped apart in your sleep some night and it'll serve you mothering right, I believe was the way Charlie said the mayor put it."

"What do you think, Clyde?" David said.

"Funny, Davy, but Sam and me was just talking about it last night at Homer's. I know you don't want to hear this, but we think it's the monkey too. The way we look at it, you have no idea what happened out on that patio. Now if it was the chimp all along, he already had the taste of blood, and could have just gone haywire when the fish were cleaned and all. You know what I mean. The attack could have been pure instinct. An impulse kind of thing. And Sam says the chimp could have just . . . withdrawn was the word Sam used, I believe."

"Well, maybe you're right. And maybe you're not. Personally, I can't forget the fact that because of Jinks, he and Marty were perfect decoys for the killer to shift the blame to. And I'm going to try to find out what happened. Want to help me?"

There was silence on the line for a moment.

"Depends," Clyde said. "What you got in mind?"

"I'm going to bring Marty and Jinks back out to the beach house, Clyde. They're both in some sort of shock that relates to the attack. We know that. But they're also the only ones who know what happened. If I bring them back, it might help somehow. Anyway, it's worth a try."

"Sort of return to the scene of the crime, is that it?"

"Something like that. I don't want to take the ferry because I now what kind of a commotion that would cause. So, if you'll agree, I'd like you to meet us at Robert Moses State Park and bring us in by way of the beach in your jeep later tonight. Will you meet us?"

"David, you sure you know what you're doing?"

"No," David said. "Look, Clyde, I know how you feel about Marty. But she was quite a woman at one time, and now she's like a vegetable. And, I can't explain it to you, but I've done her a great injustice. I owe her, Clyde. Will you help me?"

"Where shall I meet you?" Clyde said.

"At Robert Moses in parking lot A. At nine o'clock?"

"See you there, Davy."

"All right. I have a green Datsun. Thanks, Clyde."

"You must be nuts!" Pam said loudly as David put down the receiver.

"You wanted me to do something? Well, I'm doing it," David answered, returning to the table where Marty was still sitting. He placed his arm around Marty, lifting her gently, and, as he did so, Missy came through the kitchen door with Jinks. Missy nervously watched her mother as she cautiously brought Jinks into the room. The chimp seemed listless, but David could sense a change in Marty. He felt her limp body gather strength. There was also a change in her eyes. They were open and her pupils were centered, staring blankly at Missy and

Jinks.

"Marty," David said, "it's Jinks. Jinks is here. Can you see Jinks, Marty?" Marty's mouth opened and closed several times. It wasn't much, but it was something, and it encouraged David. He cursed at himself silently for not bringing Jinks in to Marty earlier. "Take Jinks out to the car, Missy. We'll be right there."

Pam stepped forward. "Absolutely not. You stay right where you are, young lady."

Missy hesitated, looking from Pam to David and back again. Then she took Jinks by the hand and led him out the front door. Pam started to step toward her daughter, but David's voice, hard and threatening, stopped her.

"Let her alone, Pam. I said to stay out of it, and, by God, I mean it."

Pam spun around. "David, you can't do this. It's crazy. You can't take Missy. You don't know what happened out there. Damn it, David! We've done our share. It's just not good enough. Send Marty to an institution, and let them handle her. Please stop."

David moved toward the front doorway, holding Marty's waist and supporting her as she walked. Pam stood in the open frame, blocking their way.

"I can't stop, Pam," David said. "Look, she's almost walking by herself. She's better. It happened the minute she saw Jinks. The doctors may have given up, but I haven't. Marty deserves better than this. She's always deserved better than she got. She has spent her life trying to do worthwhile things. She's not like us. She never tried to run from anything in her life. Christ, let's face it. I've never been dedicated to anything in my life . . . unless it was getting into your pants when Marty really needed me. I can't live with that now that she needs me again. Goddamn it, if I can't help her, she's probably lost. I'm following this through, Pam.

237

No matter what.''

"Oh, David. . . .'' Pam said desperately, and drew a deep, shuddering breath. "We'll just have to go on until you can think of some other way to help her. This trip to the island is madness.''

David stopped in front of his wife. "Taking her there will snap her out of it. I know it.''

"Do what you want, damn it!'' Pam yelled. "But you're not taking Missy.''

"Yes, I am. I need her if either of them starts signing. Don't worry, I'll be there and so will Clyde. Now get out of the way.''

Pam did not move. "No, David. Missy stays!''

"Pam, Goddamn you,'' David said through clenched teeth as he dragged Marty closer to the doorway, "I'm fed up. You want to know the truth? Do you? Huh? The truth is I'm sorry you changed your mind and came back to Fire Island. Marty and I shared something together that night that you and I have never had. I made a terrible mistake when I deserted Marty for you. Marty and I could have been happy together. I know that now. I know it, and it's probably too late. Now get the hell out of my way!''

There was a long silence as Pam's eyes filled with tears. Then, suddenly, Marty's left hand slowly rose and gently pushed at Pam's shoulder. Pam cringed and moved out of the doorway, pushing Marty's hand away. David looked at Marty's face. There were tears at the edge of her eyes and her mouth moved soundlessly. David took one last look at Pam, and then led Marty outside and into the car. Missy sat waiting with Jinks in the back seat. Then David shoved the Datsun into first gear, and headed for Robert Moses State park.

It was time. Joy spread through the senses as the beast-signs surfaced once again.

It was time to draw upon all the cunning that lurked within, to be stronger and more savage than ever before. This time, fear would not get in the way. This time, the actions would be clear, precise, and deadly.

David was forcing it all into the open. And she was with him. And so was the little girl. David wanted to find the answers. And he would. All the answers.

Again the senses screamed in joy. With care, with all the craft and strength that could be summoned, it just might be possible to kill them all. . . .

TWENTY

Parking Lot A was empty except for Clyde's jeep and David's car. The wind swirled the sand across the blacktop as they changed cars under the overhead lamplights.

It was cold as they headed through the underpass and out onto the beach. And, as the wheels ground through the sand, the wind whipped off the ocean in huge gusts, and whistled through the openings in the canvas sides of the jeep. David shivered and glanced into the back seat. Missy was huddled under a blanket between Marty and Jinks. The chimp was whimpering, and Marty's body swayed slightly. Her head was back and her eyes rolled upward, revealing only the whites. David gave his daughter's knees a reassuring pat, and she smiled back at him. Then the jeep jumped. Clyde was staring out the windshield, straining to follow the headlight beams disappearing into the darkness in front of them. David noticed the surf was breaking very close to the wheels.

"Sorry, Davy," Clyde said, not taking his eyes off the windshield. "Tide's coming in, and I have to ride close to the dunes. Might be rough. Hang on." The jeep jumped again, and as David leaned forward, grabbing at the dash, he noticed what looked like a long, narrow steel barrel protruding from underneath Clyde's seat.

"You have a gun with you, Clyde?" David said.

Clyde's head jerked an affirmative, and, reaching down, pulled the barrel further out until it rested on the gearshift box between them. "Shotgun," he said, giving David a quick glance. "I've taken to carrying it lately."

About an hour had passed by the time Clyde brought the jeep to a halt in front of the steps that led up to Holly Lane. Even before the jeep stopped, David noticed that the lights inside his house were on and that someone was standing on the outside deck. He looked questioningly at Clyde.

"Jerry Dile," Clyde said in answer to David's expression. "When I told him you and Missy were coming with your friend and the chimp and all, he insisted on opening up the house for you. Probably waiting to see if there's anything else he can do. He must like you, I'll tell you that. I've sure never known him to come out and help anyone before."

David nodded and stepped out onto the sand. He helped Jinks climb from the back seat, and was lifting Missy from the idling jeep when the realization came to him.

"Of course!" he said quickly, setting Missy on her feet, "Jerry Dile."

"What, Davy?" Clyde was leaning across the gear shift toward the open passenger door.

"Jerry's amplifier. Maybe Marty could talk with it. You think she could make it work, Clyde?"

Clyde sat back up. His hand rested lightly on the barrel of the shotgun beside him. "I don't know, Davy."

"Well, it's worth a try," David said, crawling into the back seat and then guiding Marty out. "I'll tell you that."

"Hard to tell how Jerry'll feel about it, though," Clyde said as David closed the jeep door. "I'm goin' on up here a ways to bring the jeep off the beach. I'll check

241

in on you later."

"Okay . . . thanks, Clyde," David called. He felt a certain sense of security leave him as he watched Clyde's jeep disappear down the beach.

Missy led Jinks as David shone his flashlight ahead of them and helped Marty climb the steps. They stopped on the platform. One look told David that the town had not recovered from the murders yet. The path was empty and the houses that lined it were dark. The only lights came from his own house and a streetlight on the corner at Midway. David nodded to Missy, and then, followed by his daughter and the chimp, he led Marty up the sidewalk and into his vacation house.

Jerry Dile was there in the living room, waiting for them. His heavy body seemed almost obscenely overweight in the stark light, and he was sweating profusely. His fat, thick fingers brought the amplifier to his neck, and the familiar crackling voice greeted them as David led Marty to the sofa.

"How is your friend, David? Is she in pain? Is she?"

"Hard to tell, Jerry," David said, easing Marty into a sitting position. "She's not very responsive. I hope bringing her back here will help solve that. I appreciate your opening the house up for us. It was nice of you to help."

Jerry said nothing, his eyes staring out from under thick lids at Marty. Being in the house seemed to have no effect on her. She sat motionless, her white eyes upward as David leaned her head back against the cushion. Smiling up at Jerry, Missy stood in the middle of the room. Jinks huddled beside her.

"It's cold, Daddy," Missy said, with a shiver. David crossed to her. Her teeth were chattering.

"I know, honey," David said, rubbing Missy's arms and kissing her forehead. "Are you okay?"

Missy nodded. "Ummhummm. Just cold."

David frowned and walked to the fireplace. He pulled back the screen, opened the flue, and picked up the hatchet lying next to the poker set. Then he lifted the lid of the old trunk which stood next to the fireplace and served as the wood chamber. The trunk was empty. David closed the lid, placing the hatchet down on top of it, and turned to his daughter.

"Missy, where's the wood?"

"We used it to build a fort on the beach. Don't you remember? You helped us. We put big sand castles around it and a trench."

David nodded and sighed deeply. He had to go after wood, and he couldn't take everybody with him. He looked around the room. Marty was sitting on the sofa; her eyes were now closed and she was not moving. Jinks was squatting on his haunches weaving slowly back and forth. David took the chimp by the hand.

"I'm going to take Jinks and get some wood, Jerry," David said. "Maybe you could stay here with Missy."

"You go ahead, David," Jerry said, nodding in agreement. "I'll stay . . . I made Marty leave my garden because I was angry, you see . . . but she shouldn't have to suffer . . . not like this. . . . And she was nice, nicer than most around here. . . . You go ahead."

"I'll be right back." David went to the door quickly, pulling Jinks after him. He did not see Marty's head turn after him, her eyes open and pleading.

"Want to see how I make rabbit ears, Jerry?" Missy said, moving to the fireplace. "You have to wrap them tight so the paper will burn long enough for the wood to catch."

Jerry's breathing was heavy as he came up behind Missy. She smiled, and took some newspaper from the magazine rack which she proceeded to roll into a tight cylinder. Then, she tied the cylinder of paper into a knot, and shaped the ends into long "rabbit ears."

"It's easy," she said, as Jerry smiled. "You can try one if you want to." Jerry's small sunken eyes gleamed as he stooped behind Missy. The hatchet was lying on top of the trunk next to them, and Jerry's gaze rested on the metal blade for a moment. Missy turned to Jerry as she rolled another sheet of paper. "Daddy thinks that Marty might be able to tell us what happened to her if we put your voice-box up to her neck. What do you think?"

Jerry squinted over at Marty, his face was serious and flushed. "Maybe she could, Missy," he said, his voice harsh, ". . . Maybe she could."

Behind them, Marty's body stiffened and sat bolt upright. Tears were flowing from her eyes, and her mouth was opening and closing soundlessly as her one good arm pushed her up from the sofa.

On the beach David had found some sticks of driftwood and stooped to pick them up. Then he heard Missy scream.

He dropped all the wood except for one piece and, ignoring Jinks beside him, turned and ran back towards Holly Lane. He took the steps three at a time, his muscles straining automatically. When he reached the front door, Missy screamed again, and David ripped the door open, the wood in his hand raised and ready. Then, as he rushed inside, he tripped over something and fell sprawling.

It was the dead body of Jerry Dile. The head was at a bizarre angle to the body on the floor, and what was left of the skull and pudgy face were matted in the thick blood that flowed from a gaping gash in the neck. Jerry's amplifier was lying next to his hand.

"Oh my God! No!" David gasped.

"Daddy! Help me! She's after me . . . *Daddy!*"

Missy's voice came from beyond the master bedroom. David ran. The sliding glass door was open, and the drapes that lined it were blowing into the room. The light spread its glow out onto the deck, and there David saw the grotesque figure of Marty Goodman stalking his daughter. The fireplace hatchet was in Marty's left hand, raised above her head. At the glass door David screamed.

"*Marty. . . . Don't. . . .*" The figure stopped and turned to David. It glared in his direction, and a loud, hissing sound came from its throat. When it paused, the figure's eyes rolled upward showing the whites. David gambled that its vision was blurred for a second, and shouted at his daughter. "Run to me, Missy. . . . *NOW!*"

Missy's little legs pumped and she came through the door's opening just before the hatchet sliced down after her. David pulled the glass door shut, flipping the lock. Missy was sobbing as her father grabbed her hand and pulled her with him.

"Into the living room. Hurry!" David cried. He could see Marty's figure pushing at the glass door, and they reached the bedroom doorway just as the hatchet shattered the glass and the figure came surging forward. David raised his arms against the slivers of flying glass, pulled Missy through the doorway, and slammed the door behind him. "Missy . . . out the front door. Run! Run to Clyde's."

As Missy ran around the body of Jerry Dile and toward the front door, she suddenly jerked to a halt, squealing in fear. Jinks blocked the doorway that led to the screened-in porch. His hair stood on end, and he weaved from side to side as low moans rose in his throat. Then the bedroom door opened.

The sound of the door brought David around just in time to see the hatchet coming at him. He spun, raising the wood against the blow. The club struck Marty's wrist, and the hatchet dropped from her hand and clattered on the floor. Without pausing, David pulled back the club, and brought it forward again, jamming it into Marty's stomach. Jinks' moan became a screeching wail as Marty doubled over. David grabbed Marty by the hair, and pulled her head up. She fell to her knees. He raised his club and was about to bring it smashing down on Marty's head when Missy screamed at him.

"No, Daddy. . . . Don't!"

Missy's voice stopped David's arm in midair. He looked at Marty's face. Her eyes rolled, and blood streamed from small cuts in her cheeks. Shards of glass from the patio door were still embedded in her flesh. Her dry, bitten lips silently formed David's name, and then in a harsh whisper they uttered the word "please." David stared at the lips; their shape changed again to mouth his name.

Suddenly, an idea seized him. He glanced around; Jerry Dile's vibrating amplifier was lying near him on the floor. David lowered his club, scooped up the round device, and pressed it against Marty's neck. Instantly, the hissing gasps escaping from Marty's throat became rasping sounds, the words coming in long, breathy monotones.

"Please, David . . . help me . . . pleassse . . . Help me . . . kill me. . . . Ohhh, God. . . . Pleassse, if you care at alll . . . killl meeee. . . ."

Tears streamed down Marty's face. David stared, horrified. Then, in one sweeping movement, Marty's left hand found the handle of the hatchet shot upward burying the steel blade in David's back.

David dropped the wooden club in shock, and staggered, groping desperately motions for the hatchet head in his back. Missy screamed. Then he fell to the floor, and Marty was on him, snarling, the fingers of her left hand on his throat.

"No!" Missy shrieked. "Marty! Leave him alone!" David, pulling at Marty's arm with his hands, saw Missy come up behind them. He gagged and struggled for breath while Marty's fingers curled into a vise-like clawed grip, tearing at the skin which covered his windpipe. Then Missy was kicking and biting Marty, grabbing at her in an attempt to pull the figure off of her father.

In a rage, Marty released David's throat and spun on Missy. Her hand closed on Missy's belt, and, as Missy screamed, Marty stood, lifting Missy into the air. Then there came a loud, savage, deafening cry. It was Jinks.

The chimpanzee in the doorway was at his full height, his huge chest expanded. He was rocking violently from foot to foot. His lips were curled back tightly exposing his yellow teeth. White flecks of foam were dripping from his mouth, and his fists were smashing over and over against the doorframe. Then he roared again, and charged.

A rasping cry came from Marty's throat, and she raised Missy over her head and hurled the little girl's body at the charging chimpanzee. The throw was off balance and Missy hit the wall behind Jinks; her body fell limply to the floor. David screamed his daughter's name as Jinks reached Marty. He tried to get up; he could not. She had turned to run, but the chimpanzee caught her arm, and spun her back around. David heard the arm crack. Then Jinks wrapped both of his great paws around Marty's throat, and, roaring loudly, pulled her upward until her feet left the floor. Higher and higher the ape raised Marty, shaking her violently.

The chimpanzee shook Marty harder and harder until finally she hung loosely in his hands like a rag doll. Then he jerked her body sideways, caught it, and lifted her sagging form horizontally above his head. A savage cry tore from his throat. He spun in a circle, his cry rising and falling. Suddenly, a shotgun blast cracked loudly. Jinks jerked to a halt. He stumbled backwards and, with a howl, the chimpanzee crumbled to the floor, his mistress's body dropping on top of him.

Clyde walked across the room and over to Jinks. Another blast filled the room with its sound.

"Clyde," David gasped. "Missy . . . check Missy." He tried to pull himself forward, but Clyde's voice stopped him.

"Stay there, Davy . . . I'll see to her."

"Is she alive?" David said as Clyde knelt down beside Missy.

"Yeah . . . . she's breathing. Hang on. I'll get Sam."

As Clyde crossed the room, he paused a moment over the body of Jerry Dile, and then hurried to the phone. David felt his body shaking, and he realized that he was crying. Then the pain enveloped him, and, as he slipped into unconsciousness, from somewhere far away, he heard Clyde's voice speaking into the phone.

". . . Get over here right away, Sam. I'll call the 'copter. Yeah, Missy and David are both hurt. Jerry's dead . . . and so's the lady. It's pretty bad. No, don't worry, it's dead . . . . I took care of that. Yeah . . . just like we thought. It was the monkey all along."

EPILOGUE

Late in October David returned to Fire Island. He pulled his jacket collar up against the cold breeze that whipped across the dock, and stepped off the ferry. Dune Beach had a deserted look to it as David walked toward Homer's. The vacation months were over. The sun worshippers had left the island to the few who were hardy enough to brave the cold winter that would clamp its grip on the narrow strip of land between the ocean and the bay.

When David came through Homer's front door, Clyde was there, just as he had promised on the telephone. And Sam Kline and Charlie Bende were there also, the three sitting at their usual table in the corner. Charlie was leaning back in his chair, relaxed, and Sam was bent toward Clyde, his aging eyes glistening. Clyde was probably telling him of some boyhood incident on Fire Island.

They all looked toward the door when David entered, smiled. David got his draught, set his glass down on the table and dropped into the one remaining chair.

"Good to see you, David," Sam said. "How's the wound?"

"Still pretty sore," David answered, placing his hand at his side and arching his back in an attempt to ease the ache. "Let's just say I'm not ready to sit in a chair the way Charlie does, yet."

Charlie remained slouched against the back of his chair, and his smile widened as he spoke quietly. "How about Missy? She doin' all right?"

David nodded. "Seems to be. The cast is still on, but she's home and in good spirits."

Clyde's head jerked in agreement. "She came out of it okay then, you think?"

David forced a smile. "I think so. She hasn't mentioned anything about it since she came out of the hospital. She did talk to me about Jinks as she started to recover. I didn't mention anything about the shotgun, of course. I simply told her that Jinks had saved her life, and that he was no longer alive. She didn't ask me any more questions after she discovered he was dead. Just kind of fell silent. We'll discuss it someday, when she's older."

"Sure you will," Charlie said. "For now she's tucked the incident away in her mind somewhere . . . that place of terrible memories."

David sighed. "It's a lot easier to do that when you're a child, though, isn't it, Charlie?"

Sam Kline cleared his throat. "Clyde tells us you're planning on staying here for the winter. That true, David?"

"Yes," David said, pausing to sip his beer. "Pam has filed for divorce and custody of Missy. And according to her lawyer, there's no question but what she'll win both hands down. Apparently he's going to argue I'm unfit to raise a child. He'll cite the danger I exposed Missy to that final night in the beach house as proof." David took another, longer drink from his glass. "And, since the hatchet wound prevented me from going back to work right away, I just said to hell with it and took a year's leave of absence. I figured this was a good place to spend some time. Clyde assured me there's plenty of work repairing cottages and painting them up for the coming season, and it'll give me a chance to think things over.''

Clyde snorted. "Shit, I'm just glad to have someone else to drink with, Davy. These two get boring as hell after the cold weather sets in.'' Everyone laughed. Then Sam spoke up, his face turning serious.

"What do you think it was with your friend, David?'' he said cautiously. "I mean, you don't have to talk about it if you don't want to, but I'm sure you've given the whole thing quite a bit of thought. You think you were right when we originally talked about it?''

"I honestly don't know, Sam," David said. "You're right. I've gone over and over it. Some aspects are clearer to me now, but I have no answers. It was Marty all along, of course. Her self-mutilation is what threw me off. But I've thought a lot about what you told me concerning the two hemispheres, and the only thing I can figure is that Marty's right hemisphere must have made a final grasp at total domination. I can't help but think that when Marty learned sign language she inadvertently taught that mute side a language which tipped the scales just enough. And, since it was independent because of the operation, her primitive and emotional side surfaced and made a grab for the controls. There may even have been other murders before she came here. She told me that she frequently had horrifying dreams, and there is a good possibility considering what happened here, that they were more than just dreams. Anyway, the police are checking through her past activities. As I see it, the mounting pressure here could have forced the violent side into the desperate act of severing the arm and ruining Marty's voice box . . . that gave it control because it made the left hemisphere unable to communicate in any way. Irrational, of course, but as you said, Sam, the mute side is not capable of

251

reasoning. The irony is that Marty's right side would have destroyed itself in its attempt at supremacy if you hadn't been there. Of course, this is all just conjecture. I don't really know or understand what happened. I can't even begin to guess what went on in Marty's brain. I only know there is absolutely no Goddamn justice to it all . . . because she was a very good person, in spite of what happened. As I said, I just don't know, really."

Sam pursed his lips and nodded. "Well, I tell you, Dave. The medical field is slowly coming to realize that almost anything is possible in the brain. One thing is for sure. Your theory is as good as any other."

David drained his glass, suppressing a belch. "Who knows, Sam? The more I think about it, the more I think maybe Clyde is the one who's right."

The handyman pulled his head toward David. "Me? I was dead wrong. I thought it was the monkey."

"No," David said, smiling and shaking his head, "I mean what you said on the beach that day to Marty. Maybe there are some secrets that we shouldn't know. There have been vengeful gods in Africa for a long, long time."

"Damn right," Clyde said, "it's like I said. Secrets watched over until the time is right."

David sighed. "Anyway . . . that's it. I'm going to work here and try to sort my life out. Right now, I've lost a lot. Marty. My marriage. Missy. . . . I'm still not too sure I can deal with not having her with me. But it's even more than that. I can't help feeling I've totally missed it in life, you know what I mean? It's just. . . . I don't know . . . hollow, I guess. The whole thing." David saw the concerned looks on the faces of the three who sat with him, and he cracked a tired smile. "Don't worry, I'll snap out of it. All I have to do is watch a few sunsets across the Great South Bay. Can't do me any harm, right, Charlie?"

"That's right, David," Charlie said. "You just have to be patient."

David exhaled heavily. "Patient till when?"

Charlie Bende leaned forward and folded his hands on the table. "Until the time is right, David. Until the time is right."

More Bestselling Science Fiction from Pinnacle/Tor

More bestselling science fiction from Pinnacle, America's #1 series publisher!

Best-Selling Sports Books
from Pinnacle